FARSEER

'WHAT DO YOU mean?' asked Janus Darke.

The two eldar smiled at him, and they were not reassuring smiles.

'You possess a great gift, Janus Darke,' said Auric. 'Although your people do not regard it as such.'

'I do not know what you mean,' Janus blustered.

'You are a psyker. Your mind is attuned to the forces of the warp. Unfortunately this also means the forces of the warp are attuned to you.'

Janus slumped down onto a cushion, too tired and too ill to protest. All of his life he had been warned about the evil nature of psykers, and now he had found out he was one.

A WARHAMMER 40,000 NOVEL

FARSEER

William King

For Michael Mooney,
Clear Ether, Grey Lensman.

A BLACK LIBRARY PUBLICATION

First published in Great Britain
in 2002 by The Black Library,
an imprint of Games Workshop Ltd.,
Willow Road, Lenton,
Nottingham, NG7 2WS, UK

10 9 8 7 6 5 4 3 2 1

Cover illustration by Paul Dainton

A CIP record for this book
is available from the British Library

ISBN 1 84154 244 X

Set in ITC Giovanni

Printed and bound in Great Britain by
Cox & Wyman Ltd, Cardiff Rd, Reading, Berkshire RG1 8EX, UK

See the Black Library on the Internet at
www.blacklibrary.co.uk

Find out more about Games Workshop
and the world of Warhammer 40,000 at
www.games-workshop.com

ONE
A DESPERATE MAN

'SOMEONE IS LOOKING for you, captain.'

Janus Darke looked up drunkenly from the sediment of his drink, a concoction of Cadian firewine and the last of the powdered golconda. There had been nothing too interesting at the bottom of his glass anyway, he decided. His bleary gaze took in his surroundings warily.

Unsurprisingly, the Palace of Pleasure did not look any different from the last time he had raised his head. Same kidney bean-shaped pit filled with drinking booths, drinkers and scantily clad bargirls. Same dim reddish glow-globes floating in their mock-Imperial chandeliers below the ceiling. Same poison snoopers hanging like metal-legged spiders above every table. The voice was somehow familiar... soon he might be able to put a face to it. Alternatively, he thought, he could just try and bring the face into focus. The little man was far from the prettiest sight Janus had laid eyes on. He was skinny, with thin, receding hair and a rat-like face that went well with his general demeanour.

'I know you. You're Weezel, you gretchin-spawned bastard informer,' he said. Feeling the trader's eyes on him Weezel began to dry-wash his hands, and coughed apologetically. Over Weezel's shoulder Janus could see Dugan glaring at him. He didn't like Weezel's sort and he particularly didn't like Janus, at least not since he had taken up with Justina. Janus suspected the hulking bouncer was sweet on his employer. Too bad, he thought. 'Who is looking for me, Weezel?'

Weezel coughed. Janus supposed he wanted money. It was his trade, after all, selling knowledge and people and things, a dodgy deal here, a friend handed over to the Arbites there. Janus wondered if it was worth handing over any ducats to find out who was supposed to be looking for him. It might be important. On the other hand it might just be a figment of Weezel's imagination. He was not above telling a few lies to support his habit. When the need for weirdroot was on a man, he did whatever was necessary.

'I said *who*, Weezel?'

'You're a friend of mine, captain, but one good turn deserves another. A man's got to eat–'

'I am no friend of yours, Weez. I know what happened to the last few who thought they were. I've no urge to end up in a slaver's hold, a skavvy's belly or an Inquisition cell.'

'I wouldn't do that to you, captain.'

'That's because you would be very dead very quickly if you tried.'

'It's not just that, captain – I like you.'

'If you like me so much why don't you tell me who is looking for me, and how you came by this knowledge? Or have you been smoking 'root again? Too much makes a man see things, so they say.'

Janus took a sip of what was left in his goblet. Money was in short supply and golconda was too expensive to be wasted now. The drug tingled on his tongue and immediately he began to feel a bit better. Golconda in wine stilled the voices for a little while, and kept him from seeing the other things. Weezel watched him sip the stuff and licked his lips.

'I wouldn't lie to you, captain, and I ain't been at the root for weeks... well, days anyway,' he corrected himself, seeing Janus's cynical smile. 'There's strangers looking for you. I saw them myself down in Blind Bob's. They were asking for a captain, and they described you pretty exact: tall man, white streak down the middle of his hair, long red trench coat. How many men answering that description they gonna find in Medusa Freeport, I ask you?'

Janus considered this for a moment. He did not like the sound of it at all. Too many people wanted him found at the moment, a fair few even wanted him dead, for him to feel comfortable with Weezel's information.

He raised a finger and signalled to the bargirl, then jerked a thumb at Weezel, letting her know she should bring him a drink. Janus watched the wiggle of the girl's hips as she strode away – the long diaphanous skirt did nothing to conceal them – then gave his attention back to Weezel.

'By the Emperor, she's a pretty one, right enough,' said the informer, licking his lips again with more emphasis.

'They all are,' said Janus. 'That's why Justina hires them. That's why sailors come to the Palace of Pleasure. But it's not why you're sitting here. You're sitting here to tell me about these strangers you claim to have seen, the ones who are looking for me.'

Weezel nodded and looked contrite. 'Big men they were and not sailors, I could tell. I've seen their type before. Moved wrong, not with the bounce of men who hit grav-wells irregular like. Well armed, well armoured and too confident by half for strangers at night in the darkest corners of the Warrens.'

'Mercenaries? Bounty hunters? Hired thugs?'

'Yes. Maybe.'

'Which?'

'Maybe all three. Not locals. One of them had Killean tattoos covering his whole face and head. Hands too, arms most like as well coz I could see two dragons disappearing up his sleeve. No Medusan would go in for those. Too proud of their fair skins to mark them.'

'Plenty of off-worlders in the Freeport, Weez. Lots of them live here.'

'I would know any hard-boy that looked like that, captain. Muscle like that is hard to miss.'

'Maybe you would at that. You said there was more than one.'

'Aye. Tall man, massive, garbed all in grey. Robes, boots, tunic, cloak. Only thing that wasn't black was his hand. All silver it was – prosthetic gauntlet of some sort, I guess. Expensive by the look of it, forge world stuff, maybe even Old Terran. He was a monster – bigger than Dugan by a half, and maybe there was something wrong with his mouth. He left the talking to the tattooed man.'

Janus liked the sound of this less and less. In a long career in the darker corners of the Imperium, he had made too many enemies. When his star had been in the ascendant it had not mattered. Nobody would touch a man with his reputation, particularly not a man with the backing of the Medusan syndics and one of the big Navigator Houses, but lately things had been different; he was not a force to be reckoned with any more. He had heard it said that not a few of the syndics wanted him dead. He had laughed those rumours off. The syndics after all were merchants, and they did not murder men when there was no profit in it. Not unless those men had cost the syndics a great deal of money, and were privy to all manner of disturbing knowledge, the more cynical part of his mind whispered.

Who were these men then? Heavies from the syndics sent to teach him that failure did not pay? Or were they from Fat Roj, trying to find out when he was going to pay off his gambling debts? He did not relish the prospect of explaining to the Fat Man that the last of his money was to be found floating in that goblet there. Roj had been known to pull men's fingers off with a pair of pincers for doing things like that. He didn't even get his muscle boys to do it, because he liked doing the bloody work himself.

How had things gotten so bad, so quickly, Janus asked himself? Not so long ago he had been at the top of the world, a rogue trader whose services were sought out by half the wealthy merchants of the sub-sector, an explorer who was known to always come back wealthy, whose backers always got at least a four or five hundred per cent return on their investment.

He already knew the answer: Typhon. That hellworld had changed everything. It had cost him more than half his crew and nearly his whole complement of mercenaries. It had damn near cost him his life and almost certainly cost him his soul. He should never have gone there, but he had been a different man then, filled with confidence, his ego bloated on a decade of success. I was an idiot, he thought. Greed and arrogance led me to places where no man is supposed to go. I thought I was different. How wrong I was.

He rubbed the amulet that dangled over his breast. Justina had sworn that it was a sovereign protection against evil when she had given it to him before his last voyage. Somehow he still found the feel of it reassuring, although so far it had proven less effective protection against the voices than the booze and the golconda. At least when he stunned himself with those he could sleep without the dreams.

Perhaps he should simply hand himself over to the Inquisition, as he was supposed to. When he had started hearing voices and seeing things he had known he should, but he had not. That would have been the end. 'Who were they asking about me, Weezel?'

Weezel looked down at the table. He seemed a little embarrassed. He began to draw small circles on the ceramite tabletop with his long bitten-nailed index finger. Slug trails of moisture from the wine Janus had spilled earlier followed his finger. 'Lots of people: Blind Bob, Murray the Skink, Old Elisa...'

Suddenly it occurred to Janus exactly how Weezel knew people were looking for him, and just how he could give such an accurate description. 'You?'

Weezel's face became a picture of outraged innocence, so outraged in fact that Janus knew at once he was lying. 'Me, captain? I told them nothin''.

'But they asked you?' He could tell that Weez was considering denying it, measuring his chances of being believed and coming to the correct conclusion.

'Aye.'

'And you didn't mention this place?'

'No, captain. Why would I do such a thing? You're an old friend of mine.'

'And they wouldn't be outside right now, waiting for you to finger me to them, or lead me out?'

'Emperor forbid, captain! May he and all his primarchs strike me down if I did such a thing.'

'Weezel – they wouldn't have to. I would do it before the Emperor could even lift himself out of his golden throne.'

'There's no need to be blasphemous, captain, nor take that high-handed tone either. I never led them nowhere. I never told them nothing.'

'That's a double negative, Weezel.'

'What do you mean by that, captain?'

'Never mind. I doubt grammar was ever your strong suit.'

'My grandma was as strong as an ox.'

'Where did these strangers go, after they left Blind Bob's?'

'Don't know, captain. I came straight here to warn you.'

'Any chance they followed you?'

'No man can follow me through the Warrens when I doesn't want to be followed.'

That was probably true, Janus thought. Weezel was as slippery a customer as they came. Too slippery by half.

The bargirl set a glass of doomberry juice in front of Weezel and looked at Janus. He flipped her a silver terce. 'That's for you. Put the drink on my tab.'

The girl smiled at him. She was indeed very pretty, Janus thought, then decided he'd better not show too much interest. Bad for him and bad for the girl if Justina found out. She was getting to be a surprisingly possessive woman, all things considered. Weezel slurped the drink down noisily and instantly became calmer and less fidgety. Doomberry was known, among other things, for its tranquillising effects. Janus had used it for a few months to drown out the voices, but eventually they had broken through, and he'd needed to take something stronger. And the dreams that stuff gave you...

'It will give you nightmares, Weezel,' he said.

'Couldn't be worse than my life,' said Weezel with a certain gloomy satisfaction. 'Not that I'm not grateful to you for the drink or anything, captain.'

'These strangers do anything else? Mention any names, carry anything unusual?'

'No – what you gonna do about these guys, captain? Round up your crew and give them a seeing to? Hop aboard the *Star of Venam* and shake the dust of this hellhole off yer boots? If you're looking for another crewman, count me in. I did my time on starships, captain. I wasn't always a dirtside rat like I am now.'

Was he serious, Janus wondered? Did he really imagine I would give a drughead like him a berth on the *Star*?

Why not, part of him answered cynically? You would have something in common. It was not something he wanted to consider too closely at this moment.

'Oh, I forgot,' said Weezel, not without malice in his tone. 'You can't, can you? Not since the syndics had your ship impounded since you couldn't pay for the refit and all.'

Janus suddenly felt like hitting the little man. That was the last thing he wanted to be reminded of. Too many people were looking for him right now, and he was stuck without a ship, without a crew...

It was always the way, wasn't it? Maybe he should just stick the muzzle of his bolt pistol in his mouth and pull the trigger. It would save everybody a lot of trouble, not the least him. It wasn't the first time he had considered this in the last few weeks – he had fallen further, faster, than any man ought to.

'Don't have a crew neither, so I hear,' slurred Weezel. The doomberry juice was obviously taking effect now, for he would never have dared to mention such things a few minutes earlier. 'I hear next to nobody made it back from your last voyage. Sailors say you're cursed. Something about a temple on a world near the Eye.'

Now Janus really was angry. He unholstered his bolt pistol and set it on the table in front of him. Weezel's face went white. A sudden silence passed over the bar and lots of strangers glanced uneasily in his direction. A few of them unclipped the flaps of their own holsters. Two of Justina's bouncers came up on their toes. One of them reached behind the bar for something.

'And I hear you are a fast runner, Weezel,' said Janus.

'What… what do you mean?'

'I am wondering if you are fast enough to be out the door there by the time I count to ten.'

'What did I say, captain?'

'Think you can outrun a bolter shell, Weez?'

'I didn't mean to offend you, captain. If I said something out of line, I am sorry. I only want to help out. After all, I came here to warn you about those strangers, didn't I?'

'*One.*'

'Captain, you've been drinking, and you look like you've been doing way too much 'conda, begging your pardon. You wouldn't shoot a man just for flapping his lips, would you? Think of the trouble you'd be in with the Arbites!'

'Maybe I don't have anything left to lose, Weezel, not having a ship and any crew any more. *Two.*'

'I didn't mean nothing by that, captain. I was just thinking aloud.'

'Thinking had nothing to do with it, Weezel. And by the way, you're running out of time. Reckon you can make it to the door on a seven count? *Three.*'

Weezel tipped the last of his drink down his throat and rose to his feet. 'Sorry, captain. See you around,' he said as he scuttled for the door.

'*Four*.' Weezel turned and tried to walk away with some dignity but his strides got longer and longer, and he was almost sprinting by the time he hit the door. Janus had reached nine, on a fairly slow count.

Once he was through it, and Janus had holstered his gun, everybody started to relax a little. A Hydraxian bosun made some nasty remark about Weezel and everybody at his table laughed. Shaven-headed Maggot, the biggest and meanest of the bouncers, put whatever he was holding back down behind the bar. It was only when Weezel had vanished that the reaction hit Janus and his hands started to shake.

That was madness, he thought. I really might have shot him. I might have killed him just because I did not like the tone of his voice. Stupid, stupid, stupid. Too much booze, too much golconda and too much time spent in dives like this trying to drown out the voices in his head, and blot out the things he saw. He was getting worse. Maybe he really should turn himself in to the Inquisition. If what the preachers said was right, it was only a matter of time before the daemons came and ate his soul. Maybe he should save that little bit of himself, before it was too late.

It came to him that he was finally confronting the thing he had been avoiding for so long: he was going mad, he was losing his soul. His personal daemons were closing in. It seemed that they always did, no matter how hard he tried to escape them.

Once it had all seemed so easy. His life had been good. He had looked forward to the prospect of one day being one of the richest and most powerful men in this part of the Imperium. Now he was reduced to terrorising pathetic rootheads because he couldn't stand seeing himself reflected in the mirror of their contempt. Maybe he should just go back to his chamber and end it all. It did not look as if he had anything left to lose any more.

Why bother, though? He could just sit around here a while longer and let somebody's tame killers show up and do it for him.

After what I just did, I am sure Weezel will run off and bring them right back, and I doubt if anybody around here will mind too much if they take me outside for a short walk to the graveyard.

He smiled sourly and took another sip of the drug-laced wine. He glanced around and saw that no one would meet his gaze, not even the bargirl he wanted to bring him another drink. It seemed that he had suddenly acquired all the social cachet of a skavvy with para-leprosy. How could things get any worse, he wondered?

It was at that exact moment that the strangers walked in through the door.

TWO
TWO STRANGERS

JANUS FOUGHT DOWN the urge to reach for his gun. These people did not look like the ones Weezel had described. There were two of them alright, but they were garbed in massive black cloaks, trimmed with white fur of some sort. Cowls covered their heads and cast their features into shadow. They were taller by far than most of the men present, and thin. Janus was reminded of the low gravity dwellers on Talus's Wheel – the thin, sickly ones too weak to move in anything like Earth-normal gee without an exoskeleton – but when the strangers moved he put that thought aside.

Not even the bulky cloaks could hide their grace. They did not so much walk as flow over to his table. Their movements had a liquid smoothness that was more cat than human, and put him in mind of a large predator. If a devilcat had taken on the shape of a man it might have moved like that. He was all but hypnotised by them as they flowed up to him. Suddenly they were just there, looming over him.

'Janus Darke,' said the taller of the two. It was not a question but a statement, so Janus nodded his head in acknowledgement. 'We would have business with you.'

The voice was beautiful but muffled, as if the speaker wore a helm and their words were being forced out through a rebreather grille. There was something not at all human about the intonation. Was he looking at some sort of mutant, Janus wondered?

'Go ahead,' said Janus, 'take a seat.'

'Private business,' said the second cowled figure. Its voice was clearer and higher, and Janus was suddenly convinced that it belonged to a woman. Or a female at least. He was not entirely sure the speaker was human.

'This is as private as it's going to get,' said Janus. 'I don't know you. I am not going anywhere with you.'

The female said something in an alien language which sounded more like singing than speech. The other made a curt chopping gesture with his hand. 'Athenys, it is polite to speak in a tongue that all present can understand. We want no misunderstandings here.'

'Very well, Auric, I shall wrench my throat with their barbarous words.'

'Don't trouble yourself on my account,' said Janus. 'You want to talk business, talk business. You want to jabber at each other in bird speech, feel free.'

'Perhaps I should teach this rude one some manners,' said the female. She spoke to Janus directly. 'The One Who Sees requires respect, human. So do I.'

'When you start behaving like you deserve respect, I will give you it,' said Janus.

'A fair response, Athenys, now please restrain yourself. Forgive my companion, captain, she has spent too long walking the path of the warrior. Confrontation is her chosen means of communication.'

'But not yours,' said Janus.

'Only when necessary.'

Janus gestured again but the strangers did not sit. Janus passed his hand over the centre of the table and a control panel rose into view. He reached out and touched a stud upon it. Suddenly the background noise was cut off.

'I have activated the privacy field. No one can hear us. If they are very clever they might be able to read my lips, but as long as you wear those cowls and keep your backs to the room no one but us will understand a word you say. Is this private enough for you?'

'It will do,' said the taller stranger.

'What do you want?'

'I want a ship and a captain.'

'You are in the wrong place. I have no ship and my charter has been revoked by the planetary governor, pending inquiries into my financial situation.'

'I will rephrase that. I require a specific ship and a specific captain. I require *you* and *your* ship.'

'That might be difficult.'

'I understand that money can always change things here.'

'With enough money, anything can be arranged.'

'I have enough of your money.'

Janus laughed, not quite sure whether he was dealing with somebody who was either very naïve or very clever. 'I am glad we are in the privacy field. It would not do to be saying such things too loudly in a place like this. There are some here who might start to think about ways of parting you from it.'

'Then I too am glad you were courteous enough to respect our privacy.'

'How much are you prepared to pay? I must warn you that there are some… administrative difficulties that must be overcome before my ship is allowed into free space again.'

'Whatever difficulties there are, I am sure they can be overcome.'

'Talk is cheap.'

The stranger shrugged, a peculiarly boneless gesture, and extended a black gauntleted hand. The fingers flickered open and Janus caught sight of something glittering there that almost took his breath away.

'Dreamstones,' he whispered. If those were real, they were worth a fortune. Perhaps enough to buy a new ship if he could not get the *Star* out from under embargo. 'May I see one?'

The stranger pushed one of the things into Janus's hand, in such a manner that it was hidden from sight. Janus felt a strange tingling when it touched his flesh. Ghostly fingers flickered up and down his spine. He seemed to hear the echoes of strange distant music in his head. Once, long ago in a far different place, he had touched a dreamstone. It had been the prize of his patron's famous collection, and it had felt just like this one. No doubt this was real, unless he was under some sort of a spell. There were collectors out there who would pay a rich man's ransom for this; sorcerers who would pay more. He started to slip it into his pocket, but the stranger gestured and without thinking, without any voluntary control over his own muscles, he returned it.

'I must come highly recommended.'

'You have the highest recommendation,' said the stranger. Janus could have sworn there was amusement in his voice.

'Who?'

'My own.'

Janus wondered whether to challenge the statement but decided against it. If this was a maniac, he was an extremely rich one, and he might as well listen to the man's proposition.

'What do you need a ship for?'

'To take me into the Eye of Terror. To Belial IV.'

Janus looked at the stranger. It was not every day you met a madman who sounded so lucid. 'You're insane,' he said.

'Be that as it may, it is where I want to go, and you will take me.'

'You think so?' Janus could think of no place in the universe he would rather avoid than the Eye of Terror. It was a place avoided by all the ships of the Imperium and any sane person, a massive turbulent cluster of lost star systems, cut off from the realms of humanity by awesome warp storms, inhabited by the most degenerate of all the worshippers of the Dark Gods of Chaos. A place mapped on all the old star charts with the legend: *Abandon hope all ye who enter here*. Before Typhon he might have considered the stranger's proposition. With the voices troubling him, and the visions haunting him, he would just as soon cut off his arm than go there.

'I know so,' said the stranger. 'I have seen it.'

'You're not doing anything more to convince me of your sanity.'

'Our destinies are intertwined, Janus Darke. Our life paths meet at this moment, as they were doomed to since the dawn of time. I will go to Belial and you will take me. Have no doubts on this score. You will take me there or the thing in your head will consume you and you will become a terror unto your fellow man.'

So compelling was the stranger's tone that Janus almost believed him; it was impossible not to. He sounded as certain as a man saying the sun was red, or that gravity pulled things down. Janus sat startled for a moment and then slowly a terrible truth rushed into his booze and drug addled mind. This stranger was privy to a secret he was prepared to kill to keep. He knew about the things in Janus's head.

'What did you just say?'

'I know what you are, Janus Darke, and I know how you came to be that way. There is nothing about you I do not know. Already we have had this conversation a thousand times. I have followed all the probability lines leading from it. I know that if you do not do what I wish then death, aye and worse than death, will come for you. The voices in your head will drown out your thoughts. The thing that waits behind the locked door in your mind will consume your soul. A hundred exits lead from this room into the future, Janus Darke. Ninety-nine of them lead to a place where your body is a shrivelled husk consumed by the daemons of Chaos. One of them charts a course to safety, and, believe me, I know which one.'

Janus felt himself teeter on the edge of sanity. This stranger in some strange way knew the truth about him. It was not possible. He had taken every precaution, had shielded himself from any who might detect him, or ran from those he could not. There was only one way that was possible.

'You're a psyker,' Janus spat. 'I could have the Inquisition on you in a moment.'

'I have heard you say this a hundred hundred times, and I have always given this same response: but you will not, will you, Janus Darke? For to do so would bring their attention to yourself, and like a cockroach scuttling from the light, that is something you wish to avoid.'

'I could do with less of the cockroach analogies,' muttered Janus. The stranger gestured towards the doorway.

'Go,' he said. 'Pass through that doorway, and you will meet the Inquisition sooner than you would wish. One future that lies down that road ends in a dungeon where men's bodies and spirits are broken on engines of agony. And compared to your other futures the Inquisition's cells would be a mercy.'

This is not happening, Janus told himself. This is a trick, a trap. There has to be some way out. What does this strange creature want, what does he have to gain by doing this? He shook his head and grinned mirthlessly. When he had woken up this morning, he had had an ominous feeling that this was going to be a bad day, but he had had no idea exactly how bad it would turn out to be.

Kill him, kill him now, whispered the voices in his head. *Kill them both! They are a danger to us*. Janus slugged back all of the remaining powdered golconda in one long draft. That evil insidious whispering was not what he wanted to hear. The worst part of it was that the voice was his own, strangely mutated, steeped in aeons of sin.

'Look at him, Auric,' said the female. 'He is close to the Abyss. Are you sure he is the one you have forseen? He can only lead us to evil. The Great Enemy almost has this one in their clutches already.'

Auric shook his head. 'This one does not belong to him. Not yet, anyway. There is that within him that will resist, at least for a while, although he does not know what he resists, or why.'

'Nonetheless, they will have him. The signs are clear.'

'Unless we help.'

'Talk as if I am not here, why don't you?' muttered Janus. The voices seemed to be receding as the drug took effect.

'If you come with us, there is a way you might be saved,' said Auric. 'If you help me, I will help you. I know the nature of that which consumes you and will show you a way to overcome it.'

'Would that involve scourging my body on the autorack, and my soul with confession?' Janus asked cynically. 'Is this some new method the Inquisition uses to get to people like me?'

'Now you speak like a fool, human,' said the female. 'You know we are not from your Inquisition. If we were, we would not be speaking. Warriors would be carrying you off into captivity.'

Janus looked at her. The cowl had slipped slightly. He could see something of the features of the lower half of her face. Her chin was narrow and sharp, the lips wide and full, the teeth small and sharp and very, very white. There was more than the suggestion of inhumanity about that narrow face. She could be eldar, he thought. So could the other one.

'Will you help us, human?' she asked. 'Or are we wasting our time?'

'What will you do if I say no? Find someone else to take you into the Eye?' From Auric's manner earlier, Janus knew this was unlikely. For whatever insane reasons he might have, the psyker seemed to have decided that Janus was the only man for the job, and in a way he could be right.

Janus was perhaps the only man in the Freeport who would consider taking a ship into that zone of death.

There probably was no one else who would. Had someone on the Council guessed his secret and put these two strangers onto him? Maybe no psychic powers were involved, only convincing play-acting and ominous words.

Janus considered his options. There was absolutely no way he was going into the Eye of Terror. Of all the potentially suicidal decisions he could make, that was the most suicidal. But these people knew too much about him, that was for sure, and that gave them leverage.

On the other hand they seemed no keener on facing the authorities than he was. He needed time to think, and time to get sober, and most of all he needed money. If he was going to get his ship and his crew back, and get off Medusa, he most assuredly needed lucre. There was one easy way of getting that; best work his way round to it now.

'I need to know more about you,' he said.

'We are strangers here, like yourself. We have business elsewhere. Our business is your business, though you do not know it yet. That is all I can tell you for the moment,' said Auric.

'Got secrets to keep, eh?'

'Like yourself, yes.'

'Will you help us?' asked the female. She certainly did have a one-track mind, Janus thought. What was it Auric had said earlier about her being frozen on a specific path? Her manner suggested that was the case.

'Yes, I will help you, but it will take time to make the arrangements, and I will need money…' He gestured to Auric, indicating that he wanted the jewels. The tall psyker bowed his head in acknowledgement. There was a flicker of light and a shiver of sensation as he dropped one of the stones into Janus's hand. Janus licked his lips.

'Are you sure that is wise, Auric? He does not seem entirely trustworthy,' said the female. Sensible woman, Janus thought. Maybe I will take the proceeds and hire myself some assassins and get the rest of the gems off you that way. The plan had a certain appeal. Or maybe he would pay off his gambling debts to Fat Roj. The stone was

certainly worth enough to get the Fat Man's hunters off his
back. But not the other things... There was not enough
money in the galaxy to get rid of them.

'He will do what he is paid to do, Athenys. Believe me. I
know this. He may not think so now, but he will.'

Janus did not like the way their conversation passed over
his head, even when they were being 'polite' and speaking
his language. It reminded him too much of the way people
talked about their pets. He was used to feeling superior to
those around him, not being made to feel inferior.

'Our business is done for now,' he said. 'Meet me at the
starport terminal in six hours and I will inform you of any
further arrangements.'

'See that you do meet us, human,' said the female. 'Or
you will have cause to regret this day.'

'I already regret it,' said Janus wryly, feeling the hard tingle of the stone in his hands and laughing inside. If he
could just get a fraction of its value, he would be out of
here, on his way to a place where these strangers would
never catch him.

He glanced up to see if they had managed to read any
expression on his face, but to his surprise, they were gone.
He thought he caught the faintest flash of a white trimmed
cloak vanishing through the doorway. Good riddance, he
thought, wondering what the safest way to dispose of this
loot would be. He grinned to himself: if anybody would
have an answer to that, it would be Justina.

Time to go see her. *Yes, yes, yes,* whispered the voices in
his head, but for once he managed to ignore them, knowing it was probably a mistake. He gestured for the nearest
bargirl. She wriggled her way across the room towards
him.

'Where's the boss?' he asked. She shrugged and ran a
hand along his forearm, then leaned forward and whispered in his ear. Her breath was hot against his skin.

'Up the stairs, handsome. I am sure she will be waiting
for you.'

THREE
THE HARBINGER OF SLAANESH

JUSTINA'S OFFICE LOOKED like the hub of the successful business enterprise it was. Portraits of famous courtesans covered the walls. A glittering chandelier hovered over a massive circular desk.

Only by the presence of a faintly thrilling narcotic scent did it differ from the chambers of some of the famous merchants Janus had known. And even then not much from some of them.

Justina sat at her desk. One of the new girls massaged her neck, another manicured her long fingernails. She looked up when he entered, the door having opened to his discreet coded knock. 'Janus,' she said. 'This is an unexpected pleasure. I thought you were busy drowning your sorrows downstairs.'

Her voice was low, thrilling and pleasantly suggestive. The accent was closer to that of the high nobility than a street urchin who had clawed her way up from the gutters of Medusa. As a man who had painfully learned the accents of the Imperial upper classes the hard way, Janus could spot and appreciate the effort that had gone into that. It was one more thing they had in common.

'Business came up,' he said. 'Private business,' he added, echoing the strangers. Justina clapped her hands and the two girls retreated from the chamber. The owner of the palace unsnapped a fan and waved the air in front of her face languidly. The motion blew the narcotic perfume into Janus's nostrils. Justina was very good at those sort of tricks. She was also very serious about money.

'I take it you refer to our two mysterious black-clad strangers,' she said. It was not really a question. Justina monitored everything that happened in the salons and bedchambers of her establishment via a network of televisor crystals. 'What did they want?'

'They wanted to hire my ship.'

'At least someone doesn't hold your last few voyages against you,' said Justina. She meant it as a joke but still it raised his hackles. He wondered how much of it had been artless. Not much, he guessed. With her everything contained a coded message; he was just not sure he had cracked the code yet.

'Where did they want to go?'

Janus felt a sudden reluctance to tell her, so he ignored the question and instead showed her the jewel. That got her attention. For a moment, something like shock, surprise and pure naked lust showed on her face, then her smooth visage returned so quickly he might have thought he had imagined the whole thing if he had not known her so well.

'Dreamstone,' she said, holding out her hand imperatively. Janus slipped the stone into her hand and then closed her fingers around it with his own. As always, he noticed how small her hands were. He could almost have held both of hers in his fist. She closed her eyes and took a long deep breath. 'Pure dreamstone,' she said.

'That was my surmise,' he said.

'Wherever it is they want to go, they are prepared to pay you well. I could dispose of this for... a considerable sum.'

'Such was my hope. How much?'

'Five thousand ducats. Possibly more.'

'Knowing you I will double that and double it again,' he said, his old mercantile reflexes taking over automatically. Negotiation was something he had mastered long ago.

'You know I would not cheat you,' she said coquettishly.

'Certainly,' he said. 'But I must make sure you are aware of the real worth of this treasure.'

It was a joke. No one would be better placed to appraise the worth of this stuff than she. She smiled appreciatively, but there was something sinister about her smile. 'I do not believe you can be truly aware of its value,' she said.

'What do you mean?'

She giggled. 'These are said to be used by... sorcerers for...' she paused and he could almost see her changing her mind about what she was going to say.

'...for certain arcane rituals.'

It was not the first time Justina had hinted about knowledge of the arcane. He sometimes wondered if she were trying to lead him on to ask about it. There were rumours about certain proscribed cults that she had alluded to. Most people would not even dare mention them. It was not something he wanted to think about.

'This may be the first of many.'

Now she did look a little shocked. Her eyes widened slightly. 'That is not likely. Dreamstones of this purity are very rare, and they come only from the eldar themselves.'

He told her of his suspicions concerning the strangers. She smiled more, showing small, sharp teeth that reminded him of a predatory animal at the moment, a mink or a devilcat. 'I am serious now, Janus,' she said. 'Upon my life I am. You must tell me all you know about these strangers, and tell me everything they said. Everything. I will not help you otherwise.'

This was a side of her Janus had never seen before. She sounded completely sincere and utterly serious. And unless he was a much poorer judge of character than he thought himself to be, she was masking a deeper excitement. He paused for a moment to consider his position. The merchant in him wanted to examine this from all angles, to see what he could find out before proceeding. He wanted to make sure he was giving nothing away, and see if there was any way to take advantage of what she had.

It never did to give in to threats in a negotiation. On the other hand, he did need her help desperately and she knew it. Or did he? Surely there would be others willing to take those dreamstones off his hands. Maybe not. Not with the syndics' ire focussed on him, and Fat Roj on his trail. He would need a front through which to sell, and she was just the person to act as one. She knew everybody and every shady thing in Medusa.

But there was no way he was going to tell her everything Auric had said. He was not going to tell her about the voices in his head or the dooms the stranger said lay in wait for him. Perhaps he could give her an edited version, leaving that out. Suddenly he wished he had not drunk all the golconda laced wine earlier. He knew it put him at a great disadvantage now. Should he tell her that Auric wanted to go to the Eye of Terror? Did he want to admit that he was certain that Auric and Athenys were eldar? His mind reeled. Somewhere in the back of his head voices gibbered. Something loosened his tongue.

'They are eldar,' he said. 'They want to go into the Eye. To Belial IV.'

She looked electrified now and a look passed over her face that reminded him of a raptor contemplating a feast. She leaned forward, unconsciously straining like a hound at leash smelling prey.

'That they are eldar would make sense. In the end all dreamstones come from the eldar. They grow them somehow, although no one knows how. But why did they choose you to take them?'

'I don't know. Perhaps because I am a famed explorer,' he added with a touch of asperity.

'Why not take their own ships? There are eldar ships, after all.'

'You tell me – you know more of these things than I do.'

'Yes, oh famous explorer, perhaps I do.' Her tone was acid.

'In any case, he seemed certain I would do as he wished.'

'Certain?'

'He said he had foreseen it.'

'Did he now? Were those his exact words?'

'More or less. I thought him a madman, so I was not paying close attention.'

'Really, Janus? You did not pay close attention to someone who was offering you a governor's ransom in dreamstones for making a voyage? That is very unlike you. The wine and the golconda must be affecting you more than I thought.'

'Will you help me dispose of the gem – without any of my creditors finding out?'

'I *am* one of your creditors.'

'Yourself excepted then.'

'Yes. And I will set about it right away. I must make inquiries now. I will talk to you later.'

It was a dismissal. Janus was not sure he liked the sudden decisive way she got up to go. He could sense some underlying motive, something far more than a desire to help him or simply make money. It was something connected with the eldar, but what could it be?

No matter. The die was cast. With the money the dreamstone represented he could pay off his debts, get his ship back and wipe the dust of this wicked world from his boots. But where would he go?

JUSTINA WAITED UNTIL the rogue trader had left before she allowed a smile of triumph to appear on her face. Could it really be possible that Janus Darke did not know the true value of what he had been given? She supposed so – after all, he had no idea of the true value of what he was becoming. He had taken the amulet without any hint of suspicion; little knowing that it forged a link between him and the great master that would soon be all but unbreakable. It had been a lucky day for her when she first encountered Janus, luckier still when she saw the potential within him, and had brought it to the attention of her superior in the worship of the cult.

She looked down at the dreamstone and felt the strange alien power within the thing. She did not try to draw on it. It would not let her. In fact it would harm her. The thing had been made to protect against people like her, against agents of the Lord of Forbidden Pleasures. If poor foolish Janus had known how to use it, it might even have protected him for a time. But then he did not.

And eldar too, she thought. What a night! The reward for those would be immense. More than anything else, her master desired the souls of eldar. She had much to report.

She studied her beauty in the full-length mirror and was pleased. She had come a long way from the back alleys of Medusa Warren on the strength of that and her indomitable will. All the way to chief priestess of the Cult of Pleasures on this world. She intended to go a lot further yet. She strode around the room making sure all the locks were in place. There was no way anyone could enter now. The doors were reinforced and a horde of ogryns armed with battering rams could not have battered their way through them.

She strode back to the mirror and felt the same thrill of fear and anticipation she always did when about to contact the master. She lit two tapers of hallucinogenic incense and breathed deeply, letting her mind relax, feeling the pulsing waves of pleasure pass through her body as she gathered her inner strength.

She closed her eyes and felt the tingle on her skin. She breathed in the sickly sweet perfume. She reached out with her left hand and made the sign of the horns as she passed her palm across the mirror and repeated the ancient words as she had been taught.

'Amat ti, amat Slaanesh. Amak klessa, amak Slaanesh. Amak Shaha Gaathon!' The ancient words from the language of daemons rolled off her tongue. As she spoke them she felt something twist inside her. She opened her eyes and saw that her reflection had started to shimmer and change.

As she watched, her reflection twisted and transformed itself into someone even more strikingly beautiful than herself but with a skin of purest alabaster, hair of brightest red. Small horns protruded from his forehead. Sharp fangs showed in a smile of ruby red. The eyes had no iris and no pupils, and glowed like lilac flames. A toga of sheer silk covered the vision's androgynously lovely form. As ever Justina felt the tug of attraction and loyalty and devotion. She had felt it ever since she had known her first caress from the master.

The chamber in the mirror was no longer her room. She could see dark red walls carved with all manner of erotic statuary which writhed with a slow stony life of its own. A naked girl and boy crouched at the vision's feet and looked up with adoring eyes before gazing out at Justina with jealous resentment. Beyond them, she could see a huge arched window, and through it the monstrously bizarre landscape of the daemon worlds. Huge chunks of the surface broke off from the surface, formed into great spheres and drifted up into the sky. Sometimes they became obscenely writhing suggestive shapes.

'What is it, slave?' asked the vision. 'What do you desire of me?'

'I have news, Great Harbinger of Slaanesh. I have news, Lord Shaha Gaathon,' said Justina, allowing some of her adoration to show in her voice. She was proud that she did not sound too worshipful.

'Speak then, for I have other business to attend to.' The daemon stroked the head of the youth. Justina could see that his nails were long and sharp – like bird's claws.

'Darke has been approached by the eldar,' said Justina, and was pleased by the smile that played across her master's face. 'They have given him a dreamstone.'

Sudden anger swirled across the daemon's features. 'They must not be allowed to interfere, slave. The eve of my return approaches and my vessel must be prepared. We must have that man. He will be a vessel of rare power.'

Justina nodded, although fear suddenly filled her. Shaha Gaathon could be inventive in his punishments, and some of them contained not the slightest hint of pleasure. 'Darke suspects nothing, master. He has given the dreamstone to me, to sell for money.'

Warm laughter echoed from within the mirror. 'How foolish mortals are,' he said. 'To give away the one thing that might protect him.'

'They promised him more, master.'

The laughter stopped as if cut off with a knife. 'Is it possible they have some inkling of our plans?' he asked. 'It would not be the first time their accursed seers have interfered in the Great Masque.'

'I do not know, master,' said Justina, her unease deepening.

'Of course, you do not, slave,' said Shaha Gaathon, in a tone so filled with affection that Justina knew that she would soon be rewarded. 'They are the most subtle and devious of mortals, and their seers more than most have some insight into their roles in the Masque. What are they offering him this bounty for?'

'They wish to be taken to Belial IV, great master.'

'What?' The daemon's voice was like thunder. Intense rage boiled in his expression. The mere mention of Belial IV had disturbed him greatly. Behind him lightning lashed the ever changing landscape visible through the window arch. 'Are you certain?'

'That is what Janus Darke said, great master.'

'They must be seeking to interfere in the Ascension. Why else would they go there, now, after all these millennia?'

Justina was not entirely certain she followed what the master was saying. She had no idea what the eldar could be up to.

'I must think upon this, Justina. Await my pleasure, meditating on the thousand sublime and intimate caresses as you do so.'

'As you desire. I await with pleasure, master,' said Justina and she composed herself to receive her daemonic master's instructions when they came.

FOUR
AMBUSH
ON THE BRIDGE

JANUS DARKE STEPPED out of the airlock and into the polluted streets, noticing as he did so two shadowy figures detach themselves from the mouth of the nearest alleyway and make to follow him. He lengthened his stride, placing one hand atop the butt of his bolt pistol and making sure that the knife he kept in the wrist sheath was loose enough to drop into his hand if he needed it. He wished he had brought a couple of bodyguards with him, but he had chosen, foolishly as it now seemed, to visit the palace on his own. He cursed himself and his drunken folly on the mad day he had thought he could recover his fortune on credit at Fat Roj's gaming tables.

It was dark. Flickering gaslights, effluent overspill of Medusa's factory hives, illuminated part of the street. Ahead of him- he could see the huge skyscraper cathedral of the Emperor, a massive temple to the faith of mankind's saviour that Janus did not really want to look at right now. Not that he much choice. By design it was the largest and most imposing structure visible, its triple spires talons on a great claw that ripped the underbelly of the smoggy clouds.

Dampness and industrial toxins gave the air a distinctive tang. All around loomed the huge multileveled buildings of the Freeport. Great stone bridges encrusted with gargoyles, barnacled with sculpted icons, linked them at all levels. Resting his hand on the balustrade for a moment, he could look down into the misty chasms below and see the lights of distant houses on the lower terraces. Across from him through the smog he could see the smudged yellow lights of another gigantic hive cone. It was like looking at a distant island rising vaguely from a mist-covered sea. He risked a glance back the way he had come, hoping for a glimpse of his mysterious pursuers, but the mist had swallowed them.

Raucous laughter sounded nearby. Looking around he could see a group of drunken youths, garbed in the latest fashion of the nobility, long leather coats with head obscuring cowls, massive wide sleeves, tight pantaloons and high boots. They were drunk. One of them walked along the stone barrier lining the bridge ignoring the hundred metre drop to one side, swaying and pausing to take bows as his companions egged him on.

More sober citizens in the rough spun tunics of industrial thralls watched them warily, their expressions half envious, half fascinated and more than a little full of hope that the young idiot might fall. None of my business, Janus told himself. He turned and strode off along the bridge.

Massive statues loomed over him every hundred metres. They depicted the Emperor, his primarchs, Imperial saints, governors of the hive world, holy men and heroes who had left their mark on the face of Medusa over the past ten thousand years. Looking up through a ragged rent in the clouds, Janus caught a glimpse of the stars. They were not the familiar constellations of his childhood, but the weirdly glowing clusters that marked the proximity of the Eye of Terror.

Given his past, it was inevitable that he could name many of them. They were, after all, the signposts that marked the paths between the stars. There was Gorgon, ill-famed red star of destruction, where an Imperial fleet piloted by Hogun Belisarius had vanished pursuing the retreating hosts of Chaos. There was Chimera, whose sun's rays were said to cause mutation in any who spent time on the surface of the nine worlds surrounding it. And there was Belial, most ill-famed of them all, said to be a haunted place covered in the ruins of a lost race, steeped in ancient evil. A place marked on the charts of the First Survey as Forbidden, under inderdict of the Ecclesiarchy.

What had those long-dead starsailors found there, Janus wondered? And why did Auric and his companion want so desperately to get there that they were prepared to pay a governor's ransom on the off-chance that he might take them? He shook his head, it was not his concern.

In his youth, perhaps, he would have jumped at the chance of doing what they had asked. Then his head had been filled with dreams, and he had loved nothing more than tales of the Great Crusade and the Age of Exploration, when the ships of the Navigator Houses had surveyed the systems that were to become part of the Imperium of Man. Then he had been obsessed by the idea of frontiers, and transcending limits, and seeing all of those out of the way places shunned in these later, more cautious times. He had hungered for those things almost as much as he had hungered to overcome his lowly background, almost as much as Simon Belisarius, his Navigator, had.

Perhaps that was a sign of the flaw that was in him too. Perhaps he should have spotted it at an earlier age. Perhaps he would have been able to avoid the path that had brought him to this place, to a world a thousand light years from home, and a future that promised only oblivion or something far worse. What was it Auric had said? *A hundred paths lead from this place and ninety-nine of them lead to destruction.* Something like that, and he supposed true enough in his case. It had not always been so; once every road had seemed a highway to fame and glory.

From the instant he had seized his moment and rallied the Imperial militia defending Crowe's Town from the orks, when their officers were all dead, a fortunate star had seemed to blaze down on him. In one moment of decision, he had gone from being a callow nineteen year old clerk in the office of Sansom & Sansom, Imperial traders, to being a hero. He had rallied first the militia and then the defenders of Crowe's Town, preserving the defence long enough for the Blood Angels to arrive and break the siege.

Even now a momentary sensation of triumph warmed him as he recalled those days of glory. At the time they had not seemed so glorious. He could remember the pinched, hungry faces of the defenders, counting their few remaining bolter shells, bullets and power packs. He could remember breaking up knife fights where men tried to kill each other over raw half gnawed carcasses of rats. He could remember the bellows of the great bull orks as the greenskins stormed the defences time after time.

Bullets had whizzed round his head. The old longsword that still hung in his cabin had been chipped and notched in hand-to-hand fighting. By the Emperor, those had been the days. He had held the defence together by force of will. He had encouraged the weary defenders with rousing speeches when morale was low. He had killed those who spoke of surrender out of hand, knowing that there could be no surrender to that bloodthirsty horde out there. He had discovered within himself a genius first for tactics, in the house-to-house skirmishing then for overall strategy as the older men, leaderless until then; had listened to his ideas; then for organisation and logistics as the virtual rule of the town had fallen into his hands. He had discovered an ability to anticipate the plans of his foes that was almost magical and, looking back now, he saw that perhaps this had foreshadowed what was to come. He pushed that thought swiftly aside.

It still seemed almost amazing to him that the soldiers had been prepared to listen to a boy who had no more experience than basic militia training, and what he had read in his small cot in the scribe's building of Sansom & Sansom in his few hours of leisure. But they had. The officers were dead. The rich merchants behaved like sheep. The corrupt governor had fled, later to be found dead in the burned out wreckage of his aircar in the steaming jungle, a chest containing all the revenues of the treasury still clutched in his skeletal fingers.

It had been then that he had realised that whatever it was it took to lead men – the look of eagles, the mantle of command, the voice of authority – he had it. And he had enjoyed having it. Once you experienced such a thing, you could never go back to obscurity, never relinquish your authority.

He had been fortunate that the senior partners at Sansom & Sansom had recognised his talent. They had been grateful to him for saving their go-downs and their property, and they had found it a great advantage to have the hero of the Siege of Crowe's Town in their employ. Promotion had come thick and fast, and with it wealth. He had enjoyed the money and what it could buy, but he had enjoyed command more.

It had not been too long before he had convinced the merchant princes to give him command of a trading ship and a force of mercenaries. They had underwritten his application for a rogue trader's charter and the cost of his first voyage, that long glorious sweep through the Draconic Arm, and he had repaid their investment ten times over in trade goods and monopoly treaties with the rulers of the worlds he had found. Ten new worlds he had brought into the Imperium of Man on that voyage, and every one of them had made him a pretty penny too.

His Navigator on that voyage as on all his subsequent voyages had been Simon Belisarius, that quiet, strange, driven man. He had impressed Belisarius enough that the young Navigator had become his business partner. Janus had made enough money from that one voyage to pay for his share in the purchase of the *Star of Venam*. Simon had raised the rest of the money from his House. Janus could still remember the interviews with the House representatives. If he concentrated he could almost smell the odd musky smell in the chamber, and those three wizened oldsters with scarves wrapped around their third pineal eye, the one they only opened to look upon the great void. They had been dour, cynical, crabbed old men and their interrogation had been long and thorough.

They must have been impressed enough by tales of the voyage and his previous battles for they had loaned Simon the money without demur. Perhaps it had not really been a loan, perhaps he had simply acquired a silent partner in House Belisarius. Even after all these years he was still unsure exactly of the relationship between his Navigator and his House. The politics of the Navis Nobilitae were complex beyond belief, as he supposed was only to be expected from a trading clan with its roots back in the legendary times before even the Imperium was founded.

Then had come the good years, the years in which everything he touched turned to gold. He had set about recruiting and equipping the best force of mercenaries money could buy and they had rewarded his investment a hundredfold. Darke's Company had become a legend in this part of the Segmentum Obscura – a force almost as feared and respected as the Space Marines, some said.

He had left his name on a string of unbroken victories right across the sector. He had helped put down the rebellion on Winterhome IX, staining the snows red with blood, and nearly losing a hand to frostbite. He had rescued the freighters of the grand fleet from an attack by Dorian corsairs, and then accepted a commission from the Imperium to wipe out the pirates who had attacked them. He had scoured that massive asteroid belt with measured ruthlessness, recruiting and taming the best of the reavers, forcing the others out through the airlocks without the benefit of a spacesuit.

He had undertaken another great voyage through the great blank areas on the edge of the star chart, discovering the migration route along which the ork hulks drifted into the sector and destroying three wrecks full of greenskins. He had planted the banner of the Imperium on Dykastra, and brought the long lost people of that benighted world back into the fold of civilisation. Honours had been heaped on him. Merchants had clamoured to fund his next voyage. Even the Inquisition had regarded him with a healthy measure of respect.

The money had flowed in, and flowed out again. He had built a palace here on Medusa and stocked it with the treasures of a hundred worlds. He had sampled all the pleasures Freeport had to offer, and thus met Justina and her coterie. His company had become a regiment. His single ship had grown into a fleet. By the time he was thirty he had become a merchant prince as great as any who held the reins in the millennia old house of Sansom & Sansom. Ships bearing his name had slid smoothly out from Medusa to all the worlds of the Segmentum Obscura. He had underwritten his voyages of exploration, picking likely men from his crews and sponsoring them as rogue traders. At one time he had controlled a fleet as great as the governor's, and a force of warriors who made up for what they lacked in numbers by sheer skill, ferocity and the quality of their equipment.

Perhaps, he thought, that was when it had all started to go wrong. Money and power always attracted envy and resentment. Looking back now, he could see that he had been too filled with pride, too armoured by his own arrogance, to see the signs of what was to come. Perhaps even then the taint had gnawed away at him from within, and the spores of madness had lodged in his brain.

He had made many enemies during his rise. Men he had mocked for their timidity when they would not sponsor his voyages. Men he had pushed aside in his endless quest for profit, grinding their businesses under his heel, secure in the knowledge that they would never be able to take vengeance on him. Men who had tried to betray him and who he had crushed for their folly. Oh, he had made enemies all right, but what man did not who rose from the gutters of Crowe's Town to a palace on the Avenue of the Emperor and a fortune counted in tens of millions of ducats?

He had thought himself secure, walled around by his fortress palace, guarded by eight hundred loyal soldiers who used his name as a battle cry, shielded by his alliance with one of the oldest and greatest of the Navigator Houses. He had dined with governors, the leaders of Space Marine Chapters and admirals of Imperial fleets. He had been consulted for the depths of his knowledge in obscure areas on the star charts. He had thought himself invulnerable as only a man of thirty-two, who has risen by his own efforts to the heights of power, could feel. He had been certain of his own genius, and his own shrewd judgement. He had remained certain as it all started to crumble.

He could not even say where and how it had all started to go wrong, and considering how much he spent on a network of spies, that was alarming. His enemies appeared to be well organised and well-funded. It seemed that he was not the only one with powerful allies back on distant Terra. One by one, the captains of his fleet had vanished. Rogue traders disappeared into the vast blank spots on the maps, never to return. Pirates took his merchant captains, striking with uncanny foreknowledge of all precautions he took to trap them.

It seemed that his luck had turned. A man who could do no wrong could now do no right. Now instead of turning to gold, everything he touched turned to dust. His golden reputation drained away, his aura of invincibility became tarnished. Allies and clients deserted him, starting with those toadies who had only followed his lead because he was the darling of the hour, but eventually encompassing those he had thought staunch at his side. Too late did he learn that the merchants of Medusa valued present success more than past triumphs. No matter how many ducats you had put in their coffers, it was never as important as the treasure they thought you might put there tomorrow.

As his wealth and his allies had deserted him, the vultures gathered. Creditors who once had been only too pleased to wait his pleasure for payment now demanded their money up front, bailiffs dunned him. Men who would never have dared speak out against him before began to decry his name in public. And then, he had at long last opened the forbidden book. He cursed himself for his folly and the fury drove him to lengthen his stride and try to forget.

He continued along the bridge, pausing to look into the windows of the shop houses built into its walls. His personal devil brought him to halt in an arch beneath the legs of the conquering hero Xanderius and made him glance into the windows of a bookseller. The book, he thought, it always came back to that accursed book.

Strange how he had paid it no attention for more than a decade. It had simply been part of a treasure cache he had found on an ork hulk and had been unable to dispose of. It was a logbook from an old starship, written in what appeared to be gibberish, until he had eventually pried open the cover and set himself to breaking the code. It had been desperation and the need for distraction that had made him do so as his empire crumbled, but once he had cracked it, triumph filled him, and he was certain that he had found a way to renew his fortunes.

The old book was a rutter, a journey log left by one of the ancient Navigators. It told of a long voyage through the dark places on the star charts, of the way to a world where an ancient temple contained one of the great grails all rogue traders sought, a Standard Template Construct, a legacy of the ancient dark age when men had first mastered the secrets of the universe, and built their galaxy spanning civilisation. These things were almost literally priceless; to any man who found one the Imperium offered a bounty which was enough to buy an entire planet. He could still remember the sense of astonished gratitude that had filled him. He had chosen to ignore the warnings.

He studied the musty leather bound tomes, their covers embossed in the scripts of a dozen different worlds. How many of those could he read? Five score or was it six? Not that it mattered greatly. Forced memory learning had given him that skill. His brain was stacked with vocabularies for languages that he might never use, but which nonetheless were there in case of need. In his youth he had paid a small fortune for the training. A servant of the Imperium might be able to spend his whole career speaking nothing but High and Vernacular Gothic, but Janus could communicate in the speech of every major starport he was ever likely to do business in.

And yet, when he first heard the liquid speech of those eldar strangers this evening he had been so drunk he had not even recognised it, and he should have been able to. He had heard it before: it was as different from human speech as the grunting of orks. He recalled traders he had encountered on the Far Worlds, representatives of some craftworld bargaining for statues, worthless junk or so it seemed to Janus, and yet which was of great significance to them.

Eldar, he thought, and shivered. Aliens. Xenogens. Creatures of the darkness to be shunned by all true followers of the Emperor of Man lest their deviance rub off and spread like a plague. Was it really possible that Auric and Athenys were eldar, or was this all simply another figment of his drug-tortured, hallucination blasted mind? Was he simply spinning something out that he wanted to believe? Yet he had held the dreamstone. That was real, wasn't it? It had certainly felt so.

The phaeton of one of the nobility drifted past, the coachman steering it carelessly as it drifted over the heads of the crowd. Its running lights sent probing beams out into the mist. Inside its passengers huddled in their cloaks of spun silver, safe from the poisons in the air. The coachman mounted in the open cockpit had no such pressurised protection. Instead a filter mask obscured his face and turned him into something resembling a giant humanoid insect.

Justina would know what to do with the gem. A strange woman, was the owner of the Palace of Pleasures, as cold and beautiful as the snows of Winterhome and possessed of an odd predatory intelligence. How she had come about her vast store of strange knowledge he did not know, although she had made some hints and he had made some guesses, all of which led in a direction that made further speculation uncomfortable.

Nonetheless, she would be able to dispose of the jewel for him at a good price. He was not entirely sure why she had picked him out of all the men who came to the palace to take a personal interest in, and he was not entirely sure he was glad of it, but he was certain that in this she would not cheat him. And with the money, he could settle old debts.

First things first though. It was time to start organising, and that would mean getting a crew back together – if anybody would trust him after the Typhon business. It was time to find his old crew before they left Medusa for good, signed on with some other captain, or just plain drifted down into the degeneration that afflicted so many on this frontier world.

Why was Medusa so corrupt, Janus wondered? It was a place where a man could get away with murder by slipping the Arbites a terce, where the nobility were said to be riddled by Chaos worship and the governor spent all day and all night in his harem smoking a hookah full of devilroot to give him potency for the coming pleasures. Justina hinted a man could gain entrance to all manner of exotic and proscribed cults with ease.

So why had he lived here so long? What had appealed to him? Once he had told himself it was simply the best place in this whole sector for a ruthless young merchant prince to do business; now he saw the shadow of other things. Perhaps the corruption here had called to the corruption within him.

It was a world, Janus was certain, that some time soon the Inquisition would come down on, and cut the very heart out of like a glutton scooping the innards out of a melon. It should have happened before now, and yet it had not.

Was it because they were so distant from the hub of Imperial government and so close to the Eye of Terror? Was there some sort of pestilential radiation emitted from that dreadful place that warped the minds of the locals? And what of the hints of bribery on a massive scale, a corruption that reached out from Medusa right into the vast web of the Imperial bureaucracy?

Long ago Janus had been to the Hall of Records on Terra, and knew how vast was the Imperium of Man. It would not take much effort to lose the records pertaining to Medusa, and the dockets that contained the reports of Imperial spies. Such things could be done for a price. Simon had hinted that House Belisarius did it, but indeed so did all of the other great Houses and trading concerns of the Imperium. It was all part of doing business. Perhaps the governor of Medusa, or whoever was behind him, had similar connections. Or perhaps he paid one of the great Houses to do it for him... maybe even House Belisarius. It was not impossible.

Such speculation was getting him nowhere. He needed to find Stiel, Kham Bell or one of the others and spread the word that they were back in business again, that he would settle all scores and pay off all back wages. Assuming of course that Kham Bell did not rip him limb from limb or Ruark did not brain him with a power spanner. He was not sure that they would forgive him for the last trip. Maybe they would. He had been a good employer and there was a time when they would have followed him into hell. Which was pretty much where he had led them, come to think of it.

And it would be good to get the old crew back together again. One thing was sure, no Imperial captain would be hiring them out, not with tickets blacked the way theirs

were. The *Star of Venam* was not a ship to say you had
served on these days. Only a smuggler or something worse
would hire them, and he would say something for his
crew, they were fairly choosy about things like that. No, he
decided, chances were, if he paid them, they would forgive
and forget, and they would be back in business again.

Although Janus was not exactly sure what that business
was going to be. Once he got the *Star* out of impound,
what was he going to do? He could not go back to work for
Fat Roj or the syndics. He might need to start taking on
basic cargoes, and he doubted he could find any of those
profitable enough to cover his expenses, pay the crew and
feed his habit. Well, it was something he would worry
about when he got there. Right now, he just needed to take
things one step at a time until the way was clear. First
things first though, he needed to find his Navigator, and he
had a fairly good idea of how he was going to do that.

Just as the thought passed through his mind, he heard
the sudden scuff of boot on stone behind him. He turned
swiftly, hand to pistol hilt, and saw two large, threatening
men emerge from the mist behind him. With them was
Weezel, looking very angry.

'There's the bastard,' he said. 'Blow him away!'

FIVE
SEVEN GOLDEN ARGOSIES

SIMON BELISARIUS STUDIED the pharaoh board intently. It was a difficult position even by the standards of the complex three-dimensional game. He rubbed the small pencil line moustache on his upper lip, touched his long delicate fingers to the patch that covered his third eye, then brought them back along his cheek to his moustache again. None of this helped him find a solution to his predicament. It looked like Alysia Nomikos had him well and truly trapped.

Surely not. He allowed a small amused smile to appear on his lips, as if he had suddenly thought of a good move. It would never do to let her think she was getting the better of him. Navigators played pharaoh because mastering the complexities of its involved three-dimensional structure was supposed to be good practice for the treacherous task of guiding a ship through the immaterium. For many, admitting defeat at pharaoh was like admitting that someone was a better Navigator than they were. Not that Simon was so foolishly vain and petty; he just did not like losing.

'Give up, Simon,' said Alysia. 'There's no way out.'

She knew him too well, alas. They had played pharaoh every time they had met for the last six years. After a hundred games, he supposed his reactions must be a little predictable.

'My dear Alysia, surely you must know that there is always a way out. Did not your tutors teach this elementary truth? There is always a way out, through or under.' He was not entirely sure he believed this truism. He sometimes thought it was only an article of faith designed to give Navigators hope in untenable circumstances. The Emperor alone knew there were enough of those in a Navigator's life.

'We're both too old to believe that, Simon,' she said and laughed. She had a pleasant laugh and a pleasant smile. And she certainly looked good in her black dress uniform with the opened book emblem of House Nomikos on it. He liked her greatly. It was a pity their Houses were only hereditarily neutral, or he might have petitioned his father to arrange a marriage with her or one of her clan sisters. Not that his father would have listened. The wishes of children counted as nothing in such things. Only clan politics and the constant shift and tangle of alliances guided the calculations of the algebra of marriage. 'It's been ten years since I got my wings. Must be twice that for you.'

'I am offended,' he said. 'Surely I do not look so… ancient. I know my stay in this barbaric wilderness has aged me, but not by so much.'

She laughed again and took a sip of mineral water. They were both a long way from home. Three thousand, four hundred and thirty-two point five light years to be precise, along Via Obscura Alpha twelve gamma four one, if anybody was interested in the exact way-path. The knowledge had been drummed into him since he was ten years old. It surfaced in his mind unbidden.

He leaned back and stretched, running through the ancient hatha/kata ritual, concentrating on his breathing as he had learned to almost as soon as he could walk.

Calmness came quickly as it always did, and he glanced around the chamber hoping inspiration would strike him from this unlikely source.

Not for the first time, he was amazed and a little gladdened to be here. On the inner worlds, where each of the Houses of the Navis Nobilitae maintained their own Houses, he would never have met anybody like Alysia. He would not even be sharing a city, let alone a chamber with one of his clan's hereditary enemies like Konrad Akura over there. Here on this frontier world things were different, less formal. Places like this, the House of the Great Eye, could exist and old hostilities could be buried at least for the duration of the visit to the planet's surface. He liked it, and knew he should not. If he met Konrad in space, with a command deck beneath his feet and powered weapons on call, things might still get savage, but here in this comfortable clubhouse they could eat and drink together, swap jokes and the smaller secrets of their shared trade.

It reminded him of how things must have been in the old days, in the ancient times before the Emperor and the Ecclesiarchy had come along to formalise everything, to set everything in stone. The words of an ancient poem comparing the Houses to flies frozen in amber came to his mind and he dismissed them. He did not want to think of that now, nor of the consequence of his own small experiment in recreating the ancient days by breaking the interdict on Typhon. For the moment, the House of the Eye was a haven against his troubles, and would remain so until the inevitable time when word of his folly made it back to his clan. Then things would become very uncomfortable very fast, he was sure. Still, keep the problems of tomorrow until tomorrow, as his old tutor Karadoc had always said. There were plenty of things to worry him today.

Like Janus, for instance. His friend had become increasingly secretive and irrational recently. Granted he did not have the Navigator discipline to steady his mind, but even so he was taking things far worse than Simon would have expected. He had followed Janus Darke into and out of far worse situations than this one, and never seen the rogue trader so rattled. Normally Janus was the very image of cool, calculating ferocity. Since Typhon he had become something else.

What had he seen down there? Simon had wondered about that ever since they had come back, but none of the surviving Company would ever speak of it, and he had not felt like pressing them. Seeing the look of horror in their eyes had been enough. There were some things he would rather not know about anyway, and he suspected that anything found on the surfaces of the forbidden worlds off the edge of the Eye of Terror would come under that heading. What could possibly be horrible enough to shake the confidence of ancestrals as hard and ruthless as Janus Darke and Kham Bell?

As he watched he saw an ancestral servitor, an ancient-looking human in the stark black uniform of a house servant, limping towards his table.

'Are you going to do the decent thing and resign?' asked Alysia. She sounded coolly amused and a smile of incipient triumph showed on her face.

Perhaps he should resign, he thought, and suggest they try a different sport in one of the sleeping chambers on the floor above. They had done so plenty of times before. He had a strange feeling of foreboding about the message the servitor was bringing, and he was a good enough Navigator to know when to trust his instincts. But no, best to confront any danger now. 'Kill monsters while they're little,' was another favourite proverb of his tutor.

'And why should I do that when I am on the verge of a stunning victory?' asked Simon. Alysia's smile widened.

'You are like your ancestral friend, Janus Darke, in one way,' she said.

'What's that?' he asked casually, wondering what gossip was doing the rounds about his business partner within the tight-knit community of the House of the Eye.

'You both think you can bluff your way out of anything.'

'I bluff about nothing, my dear,' he said with mock portentousness, just as the ancestral stopped in front of the table and hovered politely waiting to be noticed.

'What is it, Jaques?' Simon asked after he had allowed the ritual and customary five heartbeats to pass.

'There are strangers at the door, sir. They request a meeting with you.'

'Did they state their business?'

'No sir, they merely said that it was important, and that you would see them, and that it involved an old contract that needed to be discussed. They said it was something to do with a matter of seven golden argosies.'

Simon's smile widened as he fought very hard to keep the shock from his face. The strangers had used a code phrase known only to the upper echelons of his House, one of the five ancient signals, a sign of the utmost significance that heralded profound danger. He was proud of the fact that he managed to stop any emotion showing on his face, and that his cool, light smile remained on his lips.

'Tell them I will be with them in a few minutes,' he said. 'I have a game of pharaoh to finish.'

'Very good, sir. I will show them to the Azure Chamber.'

SIMON WAS A little shocked when he entered the chamber and saw his two visitors. He had seen their type before and not even their bulky black cloaks could conceal what they were from his trained eye. Their posture, their height, the way they moved all screamed *eldar*. He strode across the room, past the massive table, and gazed out of the enormous armour-glass window. Below him he could see the spires of the hive city emerging from the clouds like islands rising from an ocean of mist. Huge flames of vented gas illuminated the clouds around the peaks, surrounding them with moats of infernal red. Simon checked the security amulet on his wrist. There was no sign of surveillance, which was only to be expected since this room was supposed to be secure. Still, under the circumstances, it was impossible to be too careful.

'Greetings, children of Ulthwé,' he said in formal courtly eldar. 'I find you far from home.'

If they were surprised he spoke their language, they gave no sign. They made a ritual gesture of greeting, moving their fingers through a complex dance that spelled out one of their glyphs on the air. He gave the answering sign, as he had been taught in his protocol classes so long ago, and sensed their cool amusement. He felt like a child who had unexpectedly performed some ritual correctly before adults. He squashed that feeling immediately. He was the son of one of the most ancient Navigator Houses of most ancient Terra. He was not going to let them make him feel at a disadvantage. Behind their heads, through the huge window, he could see the running lights of several flitters and the plasma contrail of a sub-orbital shuttle heading upwards into the dark between worlds.

'We invoke the Pact of Anwyn,' said the taller of the two eldar, the male. Simon shivered. No messing around here. None of the long intricate rituals he had been taught to expect from the eldar. Somehow, the bare lack of formality in their manner worried him more than the fact they had called on the ancient secret treaty of friendship between his House and the eldar Craftworld of Ulthwé. Automatically his mouth worked through the prescribed response.

'You have brought the sign.' From within the bulky sleeve of the stranger's robe a black-gloved hand appeared. The far-too-long-to-be-human fingers opened and something glittered there. Cautiously, Simon took the thing and inspected it. On the surface it was simply an old golden ducat, one of the trade coins issued by his clan, and used as currency wherever their ships travelled. He checked the date: 101.M31. It was correct. The coin had been issued in the year the Pact of Anwyn was made. Closer inspection revealed it was one of the seven coins that Jubal Belisarius had traded with the farseer in the ancient days, tokens that promised his House would repay the eldar for saving their honour and their wealth.

Simon's mind reeled. Could it really be true? He had always thought the tale was a myth although he had seen the five coins that had so far been redeemed in the Belisarius family shrine on distant Terra. He took a deep breath, knowing that an ancient obligation had been passed on to him. He must fulfil his part in the prophesy. He was obliged to do whatever was needed to to take this eldar and his companions wherever they wanted to go. The farseer's words inscribed in the Byblos Belisarius returned to him.

There will be times when the eldar will need allies to do things they cannot or which are forbidden to them. We have helped you in your hour of need. You must, when the time comes, help us.

Still, there were precautions to be observed, safeguards to be put in place. 'Who do you come from?'

'I bring word from Eldrad Ulthran, farseer of Ulthwé, whose line befriended your people when they most had need of it.'

Simon nodded. The exact words, in the exact order, in the exact form they were meant to be spoken. After the proscribed five heartbeats they were repeated in eldar.

'I am Simon Belisarius, Master Navigator of the Ancient House of Belisarius of Terra. I am at your service.' He spoke the words in eldar. 'I will guide you where you must go, shirking at nothing, seeing you safe to port, no matter what may come.'

'I am Auric Stormcloud, farseer, of the line of Manan of the World of Ulthwé. I accept the offer of your service. I acknowledge that in faithfully discharging the task I set you, you will have repaid one seventh of the debt of honour that exists between your House and mine.'

'So let it be,' said Simon.

'So let it be,' said the stranger. Now the formalities were over, Simon felt a little more relaxed although he was unsure what would happen next and felt more than a little in fear for his own life. Three of the Belisarius starships that had answered the farseer's call had failed to return. One had come back a battered hulk, its crew all mad, its Navigator deranged. One had been found drifting and empty in open space in the Armageddon system. Simon allowed himself to smile. He had always wanted to find adventure; now it seemed adventure had found him. It looked like he was going to have his name written in the Byblos wreathed in the posthumous glory of those who had fulfilled one of the House's most ancient oaths.

'This is Athenys, of the line of Manan, of the Craftworld Ulthwé.'

'The pleasure of the meeting is mine,' Simon replied in formal eldar. Athenys responded courteously.

'How can I be of service?' Simon asked.

'I wish to go to Belial IV.'

Simon invoked his implanted memories. Belial IV was a world within the Eye of Terror. A forbidden place on the charts, the sort of place that the Inquisition would execute you for visiting. In short, a place much like Typhon, but actually within the Eye of Terror itself. He considered the difficulties of getting there. Massive warp storms cut off the Eye for decades at a time, threading through them was a task that could easily prove fatal for even the greatest of Navigators. The trip to Typhon had tested Simon's skill almost to the limit. And that was not counting the threat of reavers, Chaos fleets and the bizarre conditions that prevailed within the Eye itself.

'Such a voyage is extraordinarily dangerous,' Simon said, it being one of a Navigator's many duties to make clients aware of such things. 'There is every chance we will not succeed.'

'More dangerous than even you can guess, Simon Belisarius. But dangerous or not, it is there I must go,' replied Auric. 'And I must go soon.'

'That may prove difficult. I must requisition a ship from my House. It may take several months to arrange…'

'You already possess a ship. The *Star of Venam*.'

'It does not entirely belong to me or my House. We are co-owners. There is another.' The ancient pact pledged Belisarius to use its entire means to fulfil the commission. It did not say anything about using other people's.

'Janus Darke will not disagree. He has already taken payment.' Simon thought about this for a moment. In spite of the ancient pact, they had gone to Janus first, not to him; that spoke of a great deal of understanding of the situation, and a great deal of subtlety. What else should he have expected – these were eldar after all. And if time was of the essence, they had done the right thing, for if they took the *Star of Venam*, it would be a lot quicker.

'There are problems other than Janus accepting,' he said. 'Legal problems. Our ship had been impounded pending the payment of certain debts.'

'Given sufficient funds these can and will be overcome.'

'Since you have invoked the pact, Belisarius will spend what is needed but it will take time to raise the money. I must contact our factors and they must raise drafts and–'

'That will not be necessary. We have the funds. All we require of you is your vessel and your service until our quest is done.'

'Very well. How soon can we get access to these funds? Do you have mercantile scrip, letters of credit drawn on an Imperial commercial banks, chests full of ducats?'

The hand vanished within the sleeve once more; it reappeared with a conjuror's flourish, this time containing a small sack made from some sort of leather. The eldar tossed the sack to Simon, who caught it out of the air easily. He pulled the drawstrings around its mouth to open it. Inside, he caught the fiery glitter of some sort of gemstone.

He poured them out onto his hand and felt the tingle as they touched his flesh. Dreamstones, enough to buy a small planet if they were real and unflawed. Somehow, he knew that they were. Their value to himself and his House was incredible. Dreamstones were one of the few things capable of protecting the mind against the depredations of Chaos. They helped absorb the baleful emissions of the immaterium, and prevented the dreadful nightmares which could afflict a Navigator after too much contact with the stuff of the other realm. Of course, not just Navigators used them, so did sorcerers, alchemists – even, it was said,

members of the Inquisition. Anyone who had cause to fear
the evil influence of the Great Darkness had use for them,
and they came from only one source: the Craftworld of
Ulthwé. He had never heard of so many coming onto the
market at one time. He would have to be careful of course,
because such a thing could cause a catastrophic drop in
prices. There must be a hundred small and perfect stones
here, enough to manipulate the markets of the Segmentum Obscura for years to come. It was an enormous fee.

Then again, the task he was being set was an enormous
and potentially fatal one. 'May I ask why you wish to go
into the Eye of Terror?'

'You may, Simon Belisarius. But in this place, at this
time, I will give you no answer. There is a time and place
for such a giving, and this is not it.'

'Very well.'

'But know you this – we must act swiftly and secretly or
death will claim us all.'

Simon shrugged. He had expected nothing less.

SIX
A PAIR OF PINCERS

JANUS DARKE RIPPED his bolter from its holster. Too late he heard the footsteps behind him. He started to whirl but something heavy smashed into his hand. Agony surged through his fingers and the bolt pistol fell from his grip. Anger at his own stupidity filled him. He had stepped out into the night, drunk and drugged, and full of self-pity. Enemies had taken advantage of this to work his undoing. Now he was going to pay the price.

Anger and adrenalin sobered his thoughts a little but his body still responded slowly and his timing was off. He looked up at the man facing him seeing a huge burly bruiser, of the type Fat Roj favoured employing. The man held a heavy sap in his hand, a leather truncheon filled with ball bearings. He drew it back for another blow. Old reflexes, long schooled on the practice mats, tried to take over. Janus brought his numbed arm up into a guard position and then punched, aiming his blow just below the centre of the man's chest. It connected solidly, for Janus was a very big man, all muscle, and the force of the blow had come from the hip. Wind wheezed out of the bruiser's lungs and he started to bend double. Janus brought up his knee to connect with the man's jaw. He felt a surge of pain as it connected. The kick hurt him, but not as much as it hurt his opponent who fell over backwards. Janus felt a brief spurt of savage satisfaction before he realised that he had drunkenly miscalculated and left himself off balance. His boot slipped on the slick cobblestones and he tumbled to the ground.

As he fell his groping fingers reached out and struck the butt of his pistol. Quickly he grabbed it and swung it to bear on Weezel and his opponents. 'Don't move,' he said, 'or you'll be breathing through a hole in your stomach.'

He was rewarded by a sick look on Weezel's face. The two bruisers with him seemed less impressed. 'Fat Roj wants his money,' said the smaller of the two. He was very broad and his tattoos were very impressive. 'He's tired of waiting. You owe him. It's time to pay. Shoot us and it'll only go worse for you. It will be the pincers for sure.'

Janus pulled himself upright, and risked a glance at the man he had put down. His heart beat very fast and he realised that he had been lucky, far luckier than he deserved to be under the circumstances. He looked at the men again. He was impressed by the way they kept their composure under the circumstances. Not everybody could have managed a speech such as the tattooed man had made in this sort of stand-off.

'Roj will get his money,' he said and was pleased that his voice was just as rational and lucid as the tattooed man's.

'When?'

Janus considered the question. He really might have the money to pay soon, if Justina did the work she was supposed to, but doubtless it would still take a couple of days to line up a buyer unless he wanted to sell the dreamstone at a huge discount.

'Three days.'

'You said that three days ago.'

A not unreasonable point, Janus conceded, but three days ago he did not have the dreamstone, and now he did. It made all the difference in the world, but how could he convince the tattooed man of that?

'Something's come up,' he said.

'Something is always coming up,' said the tattooed man. 'You gamblers are all the same. You think tonight you will earn it all back playing hookjack. Most of you believe it too. I don't.'

Janus showed him a fierce grin.

'No game for me tonight,' said Janus. 'This time I lucked out. I will have the money in three days. And in a way you're just like me.'

'In what way,' asked the tattooed man cautiously.

'You're gambling right now.'

'I don't see it that way.'

'Then look at it this way. You have two choices. You can believe me and you'll have the money in three days. Or you can start shooting and one of two things will happen. You'll kill me, and Roj will never get his money and you will never get your cut. Or I will kill you, and you'll still never see the money. What seems the most sensible option to you?'

'There's another option,' said the tattooed man.

'And what would that be?' Too late, Janus felt the rush of displaced air behind his head. Someone else had approached out of the mist. A mountain crashed into the back of his head. He fell forward into a pit of darkness.

'This,' he heard the tattooed man say, from across an abyss as wide as the gulf between stars.

JUSTINA CONSIDERED THE words of Shaha Gaathon. It had not taken too long for him to decide what Justina must do. The Harbinger of all Pleasures had told her she must find Darke at all costs, and protect him until the eve of his ascension. He had made it very clear that failure was not an option. Knowing the punishments her master was capable of meting out, Justina had no intention of disappointing him.

She studied the reports that various agents had brought her. It was just as well she had thought to infiltrate Fat Roj's operation. Things were not looking so good. Lukash Grimm had just seen Weezel and Fat Roj's henchman pick Janus Darke up, and that meant the trader was most likely in the gang lord's clutches even now. Why did this have to happen now? Darke was ripe for the plucking and he had fallen so far that few would notice if he disappeared. No one would even investigate, which had certainly not been the case when they had first met. Perhaps even the Inquisition would have taken an interest then. Now...

What options did she have, she wondered, pausing to study her reflection critically in the mirror? She had done business with the Fat Man on occasions, sometimes using his services to collect debts from recalcitrant clients, sometimes purchasing some particularly beautiful youth or maid the gang lord had turned up against all reason in the slums. In return, she had provided him with customers for his golconda, and introduced the wealthy, like Janus Darke, to his illicit gambling empire.

What a mistake that had proven to be, she now thought. Who would have guessed that the Trader could have fallen so far so quickly and accumulated such enormous debts in such a short time? Janus Darke certainly had a self destructive streak. Then again, she supposed, that was only to be expected. Given his unique powers and talents, and his subconscious knowledge of them, and the way society looked at those who possessed them, it was only natural that he would feel guilty and deserving of punishment. The fools of the Inquisition made sure their propaganda ran deep.

In spite of himself, Darke would need to be saved. Her master had a great purpose in mind for him, and though he had not shared it with Justina, she had some inkling of what it was. Sparing Darke from death would not be doing him any mercies if Justina's suspicions were true. No matter; his eventual fate would advance Justina within the Masque and in the long run, that was what mattered to her.

What would be the best thing to do? The direct approach might be the best. She could simply buy Fat Roj's anger off. She had more than enough money to do so, and Darke's bauble was ample security against that. Under the circumstances, he could hardly object to her spending his money to free him from the gang lord's tender mercies. Fat Roj was not gentle with those who owed him money, and who did not have powerful friends to protect them.

On the other hand, that might cause some questions to be asked in the wrong quarters. Some folk might wonder why she was paying off Darke's debts, and look too closely at her relationship with the rogue trader. She had not survived so long by drawing unnecessary attention to herself. Perhaps she should consider alternative paths.

Word could be sent to the covens she controlled. A force of men and women could be mustered. Rich young nobles and their bodyguards could descend on Roj and free Darke at gunpoint, leaving any inconvenient witnesses more than a little dead. It was certainly worth considering but it would have to be done carefully. The great crime syndicates did not take kindly to outsiders eliminating members of their organisation. Best make it look like a gang war then, she thought.

It occurred to her that all of this represented a great opportunity. If Darke disappeared now, everyone would assume that Roj had taken him and disposed of the body. And if Roj was eliminated, who would know any better? She decided it was time to summon the hidden covens and take them to battle.

'AWAKE, JANUS? GOOD,' said the deep, booming jovial voice. 'I am glad you decided to join me. I had thought you were avoiding me.'

Janus opened his eyes. He swallowed. His mouth felt dry. His head felt as if it was about to split open. A giant tugged at his arms. His chest felt as if it was about to be wrenched open. 'This is the worst hangover I have ever had,' said Janus.

The booming voice laughed. It was a hearty sound, the laugh of a man who enjoyed a good joke. It came from somewhere behind Janus. He tried to turn his head to see the speaker but could not twist his neck far enough. The movement caused him an inordinate amount of pain so he stopped and studied his surroundings instead.

'I like a man who can laugh in the face of his misfortunes Janus, old son. I really do. After all, you've got to have a laugh, haven't you?'

Janus's nostrils switched. He could smell blood and raw meat. He noticed for the first time how cold it was. Looking around he could see the split carcasses of cattle and moondeer hanging from hooks. Looking up, he could see his wrists were chained and one link of the chain was looped over a hook. He too dangled like a side of beef. He was in some sort of refrigerated storage area, and felt a surge of horror entirely disconnected from his pain when his memory of all those tales of Fat Roj returned.

A huge hand slapped Janus heartily and painfully on the back and sent him spinning. The motion rotated him to face Fat Roj. Janus wished it hadn't. There was nothing reassuring about the sight whatsoever. Roj was a huge man: tall and broad as an ogryn, with an enormous belly that wobbled as he laughed. A belt of suspensor globes helped support its weight. He had at least ten chins and his eyes disappeared into deep pools of fat. His cheeks were rosy and chubby as a baby's. His little blue eyes twinkled with mirth. In one massive paw, he held a pair of pincers. There was nothing about him now of the urbane well-dressed man who had encouraged the drunken Janus to gamble on credit, using his share of the *Star of Venam* as collateral.

Behind Roj stood Weezel, the tattooed man and a group of gnarled looking thugs. The tattooed man had a chainsword in one hand, obviously much used for cutting up beef, judging from the scraps of meat and splatters of blood on its blade. At least, Janus hoped it was beef.

'Hello, Roj,' he said and swallowed. 'Long time no see.'

'Well, I think we should make up for lost time,' said Roj. He clicked the pincers with one hand. He was wearing only leather trews and a butcher's apron, leaving his entire upper torso bare. It was not a pretty sight. Janus noticed enormous slabs of muscle moving beneath the fat. Roj was as strong as the Niponan sumo wrestler he resembled. He clicked the pincers again, like a dancer using castanets. Suddenly his smile faded and he glared at Janus evilly.

'Where is my money?' he said, reaching out to administer a back-handed slap on Janus's face. The blow was given casually, with no apparent effort, but the force of it almost knocked Janus out. He realised exactly how strong Fat Roj was. The impact sent him to spinning faster.

'You'll get it in three days,' said Janus, doing his best to ignore the taste of warm blood in his mouth.

'You said that last week,' said Roj administering another tap. There was a note of almost hysterical anger in his voice. Janus's head snapped to the side. Over Roj's shoulder, he could see the nervous looks on the faces of the gang lord's henchmen. When Roj was in a rage, even the hardiest souls walked quietly. 'Are you trying to make me look like a fool? Do you think I am a fool?'

'No, Roj, just a madman,' said Janus. Despite his fear and his pain he was starting to get angry himself. There was no need for this. And there had been a time when Roj would never have dared treat him this way. From somewhere far off, something seemed to feed him strength and anger. As if at a great distance, he could hear voices whispering. He was not sure what it was they said, but he thought it was *kill them, kill them all*. A sour smile crossed his lips, for now he knew the voices were the siren call of madness. He was in no position to harm a fly, let alone the gang lord and his henchmen.

Roj closed his fingers into a fist this time and his blow struck with the force of a thunderbolt. Stars danced before Janus's eyes and he passed out. When he recovered he found that he was swinging backwards and forwards on the end of the hook, like the pendulum of some strange clock. He must have only blacked out for a few seconds, he realised. Roj grinned amiably again, looking for all the world as if he was greeting an old friend. He held the pincers up so that Janus could see them.

'Interesting how fragile flesh is,' he said conversationally. 'Pliable, too. When you pull out a man's tongue, for instance, it stretches a long way before it snaps. Fingers are different, of course. You can hear the joint pop as you pull the bone from the socket. It's an odd sound, sometimes mixed with cracking if the bone breaks. Toes are the same, but there not as much fun for some reason. The nadgers are the hardest to get off clean. Sometimes the testicle pops under the pressure. Nasty, it is.'

He moved a bit closer, till Janus's body came to rest against his huge gut. Fat Roj's china-blue, mad eyes glared into his own, exactly at the same level. He clicked the pincers again. 'Some men can stand a lot of pain. Stay awake right through the whole process. Some pass out halfway through. Some of the weedier ones faint before you even start, and have to be woken with a stim-shot. Strangely enough women mostly endure the pain better than men. Makes you think, doesn't it? Makes you wonder why.'

Janus could feel Roj's hot breath on his face, smell the garlic and herbs of his last meal. Roj reached up and almost gently caught the tip of his nose with the pincers. Their cold clasp was painful. Roj twisted and Janus was forced to move his head to one side as his nose was tweaked. He wondered if the gang lord intended to tear his nose off. But Roj opened the pincers again and reached out for his ear this time. The pincers bit flesh painfully and then released. 'No fun,' said Roj. 'Except for the vain ones, the ones who think you're going to spoil their beauty, and you're not one of them are you, Janus? Are you?' The second question was almost a scream.

Janus turned his head to look away. A deep throbbing filled his head, beating inside his skull in time to his heart. The voices chanted in time to its rhythm: *kill them, kill them, kill them all!* He felt an odd dizziness come over him, a vertigo that had nothing to do with pain or nausea, a sensation of standing over the mouth of a great abyss, while the ground beneath his feet crumbled. He took a deep breath and wondered what was about to happen.

Roj grabbed Janus's chin with his blubbery fingers and turned his captive's head around to face him. Once again Janus looked deep into those pale psychotic eyes. 'People are thinking you don't respect me, Janus,' he said. 'People are thinking that you think you can get away with things. When people start to think that, they think they can get away with things too. Then we have to make an example of somebody. It seems only fair that we should make an example of you.'

Janus did not answer. Partly because he knew that Roj was lost in some fantastic otherworld of his own, partially because the siren song of the voices in his own head was getting louder and drowning out the gang lord's words.

'Big shot,' sneered Roj. 'Won't talk to us now. Too good for us. Used to have a palace on the hill and a seat at the governor's table. Where are your fine friends now, Janus Darke? Who is going to help you now? You will make a good example. People will know that no one is beyond my reach.'

Janus ignored him. Nothing he could say would convince Roj anyway. The big man enjoyed cruelty would not be denied his sport. Janus was determined not to give him the satisfaction of showing fear. He knew that was what Roj really wanted. He suspected that for some reason, the gang lord feared him and did not want to admit this even to himself.

He is right to fear you, whispered the voices. *Let us loose and we will teach him the meaning of terror. He will learn how sweet and terrible the game he thinks he is playing can really be.*

Janus tried to ignore the voices too, but it was getting more and more difficult. He was sober now. The booze and golconda were gone from his system. There was nothing to drown them out. Indeed he felt in danger of having them drown out his own thoughts. They were loud as the roaring of a storm-tossed ocean, and more distinctive too. Each voice had its own character, sometimes insinuating, sometimes demanding, sometimes commanding, sometimes pleading. Janus wondered whether he would go mad before Roj could kill him or whether something worse was about to happen.

The gang lord reached up and unlocked the shackles. The chain jingled as one end ran free and dropped Janus to the hard, cold floor. He noticed how his breath misted. How could Roj stand there in only that apron? Maybe his blubber protected him. The thought made him laugh.

'Laugh all you like, Janus. Things won't seem so funny in a minute.'

Janus felt his wrist become immobilised by the enormous clamp of Roj's left hand. He was hefted onto his feet as effortlessly as a child. The tattooed man and his large companion slid forward and held him upright. The pincers came to grips, crushingly with the tip of his little finger.

'This won't take more than a moment,' said Roj, grinning, and began to twist and pull. At first the pressure was almost gentle. Janus's little finger eased forward in the socket. Then Roj began to twist and the pain began. A needle of ice and fire ran up the tendon on the back of his hand. The finger started to feel stretched. Enormous pressure was brought to bear. The skin of his hand was pulled taut. Bones creaked. This is not happening, the part of him which was still sane and aware thought, but all the time he knew it was.

The pressure increased. Something cracked and agony seared the length of his hand. His palm felt wet. He could not see it, but he imagined the flesh breaking and the white of bone and red of blood showing through. He clenched his teeth shut, determined not to scream. The beating in his head increased until he felt like a daemonic drummer was using his skull as an instrument. The voices thundered within his mind. In spite of his pain, he felt a deep, monstrous rage begin to build, an anger so powerful it might destroy the world, so corrosive it might eat through steel. Somewhere inside him something had started to feed on the anger and the pain and to take strength and pleasure from it.

Janus was fighting a war on two fronts, with the pain in his hand and the thing in his head. He knew that if he gave way to either his fate was sealed. He was imprisoning the thing within him now by pure force of will, and if once it got loose…

Roj gave a grunt of pure pleasure. A ripping, tearing sound mingled with the breaking of bones, and the sound of something popping from its socket. Agony lanced through Janus like an electric current. Roj grinned and held the pincers up in front of his face. At first Janus's dazed mind thought he was showing him a sausage or a gobbet of animal flesh, then he noticed the nail on the end of it, and the realisation slowly filled him that he was looking at his own finger. The drops of red stuff cascading down the front of Roj's apron were his own blood. Deep within him a wall began to crumble. The voices sounded louder. He knew that he could resist no longer, that he was at the end of his strength. He bared his teeth in a snarl and spat a gob of bloody spittle at Roj's face. The gang lord cuffed him angrily with the hard metal of the pincers. Blood from his own severed finger stained Janus's face.

'Now, what next I wonder?' said Roj, in a voice full of creamy satisfaction. Janus knew the gang lord's desire to cause pain had the upper hand now and he was not going to stop until Janus was dead. A desire for vengeance as much a desire to preserve his own life filled him. Hatred blazed in his eyes. Something in his mind shrieked a warning. He knew he must resist this urge at all costs even though he no longer wanted to.

'I am giving you one last chance to let me go, Roj,' he mumbled through bruised lips. 'Otherwise, you're going to die.'

'What makes you think you are in any position to threaten me, little man?' boomed the gangster heartily. 'Why should I give up on my fun?'

'Don't say you weren't warned,' said Janus, and let go of his grip on the thing within him. The chorus of voices swelled triumphantly. The thing within his mind grew until it filled his head and drowned out all his thoughts. His pain receded, flames danced around his skull. He saw a look of something like horror appear on Roj's face, and felt his own lips twist into a triumphant smile as the thing that was now wearing them tested its control. Blackness swept in from the edge of infinity, bringing with it a cold that burned more than fire, and a pain more pleasurable than ecstasy.

Janus felt as if something dark indeed was about to manifest itself in the meat-packing plant. Something old as the universe and evil as sin chuckled in the back of his head.

Then the screaming started in earnest.

SEVEN
DECISIONS MADE

SIMON BELISARIUS STRODE confidently into the Rat's Head
Beer Cellar. In his heart of hearts, he wished he felt as confident as he looked, but there was no helping it, he was a
little afraid. Still, it never did to show fear in front of the
ancestrals.

The Rat's Head was a place where mercenaries and other
less salubrious sorts chose to drink when they were down
on their luck. If you wanted a throat slit or a pack of butch-
ers to ride shotgun on your next cargo this was the place to
come. To tell the truth, it was more Janus's sort of place
than his. In the years of their partnership, the rogue trader
had always dealt with this aspect of things. He was much
more at home among these sorts than Simon could ever be.

At this exact moment, Simon wished more than ever that
he had a command deck beneath his feet, and a ship heading out into the Long Dark. He was all too aware of the
number of very hard men studying the cut of his cloak and
the look of his weapons. With consummate showman-
ship, he flicked his weighted grey cloak open to reveal the

emblem of Belisarius, a great eye flanked by two rampant wolves. Most of the onlookers went back to their drinks. Only the very foolish or the very desperate would risk the wrath of House Belisarius, or the bad luck that came from killing a Navigator.

And they were right to, thought Simon, since that bad luck usually took the form of a quick death. If the Imperial authorities didn't get a man for wasting one of the Imperium's most precious resources, then a knife across the throat or a bolter shell through the brain would come from the very deadly and very scary men the House would send to avenge him.

Despite all of this, Simon was reassured to see that Kham Bell and Stiel were at their usual table at the back of the bar. If he were dead, he would not get any satisfaction from his House's revenge. With the two mercenaries there, not even the hungriest and most desperate of rogues would trouble him for long.

Scattered about the place were the rest of the survivors of Darke's Company. They looked like they had been drinking heavily. He hoped they hadn't been drinking so heavily as to give anything away where an agent of the authorities might hear. No matter how many oaths a man swore, or how loyal he was, or how afraid of his commanders, once the daemons of alcohol got hold of a man's tongue, it would inevitably start to wag. It was a good thing, Simon thought, they would be pulling out in a few days; the sooner the better really.

But what then, what about the next time they hit port? We should never have gone to Typhon. We should never have broken the Interdict. It was only a matter of time before word got out and the Inquisition started showing an interest.

Cross that bridge when you come to it, Simon told himself. Not that it will matter anyway, he thought sourly. The chances are we won't be coming back from this voyage.

Simon strode across the bar and lowered himself into a chair directly facing Kham Bell. On the surface, the old

sergeant looked much the same as ever. He was medium
height and very broad. A well-trimmed grey beard framed
a deceptively open and honest face. Despite years of being
roughened by alien suns and winds, his cheeks were still
rosy. He looked more like a prosperous yeoman than a
mercenary warrior whose name was feared across the sector. It was only the eyes that showed any signs of their
Typhon excursion. There was a fear in them that had not
been there before, and would probably never leave.

'Good evening, Simon,' Kham said. His voice was deep
and resonant, and still held the twang of Crowe's World.
He had been one of the first to follow Janus, Simon
remembered, and it had been the making of him. The
broadsword that seemed almost an extension of his body
when drawn was hooked over the back of the chair. A
heavy bolt pistol was strapped to his thigh.

'Good evening, Kham; good evening Stiel.' Stiel nodded
politely as he greeted Simon in his light, flat voice. Simon
felt a faint trickle of fear when he contemplated the man.
Not that there was anything frightening about Stiel's
appearance: he was tall, slender and good-looking in a
dark way. His long hair gave him a faintly effete appearance. Stiel was dressed conservatively in a light green tunic
and high leather boots. There was nothing remotely threatening in his manner either. No one would guess what he
was from his appearance, which given his chosen profes-
sion was good. It was just that Simon knew many of the
things he had done.

Most of the crew and the mercenaries thought Stiel was
the *Star of Venam*'s senior clerk. Simon doubted that even
if he encountered one of the fabled Imperial assassins he
would ever meet a more ruthless, dedicated and ferocious
killer. Man, woman or child, heretic or fanatic believer, if
ordered to slay it, Stiel would, and never for a moment
would the expression on his pleasant features change. If
Stiel felt any different about things since Typhon there was
no sign of it in his face. He was the only one of the three
who had passed into the temple's inner sanctum who

showed no signs of being haunted. Simon guessed that with the amount of guilt that must steep Stiel's conscience, nothing held any terror for him any more.

The cutthroat carried no visible weapons, but Simon knew this meant nothing. Doubtless there were one or two poisoned daggers concealed in his wrist sheaths. The ring he wore would have a small needle capable of injecting Daxian mongoose venom, one of the seven most lethal poisons in the Imperial alchemical roster. The chain of the pendant he wore round his neck could be converted to a garrotte at a moment's notice. Simon knew Stiel had once sawed off a man's head with it.

If push came to a shove, Stiel could kill with his bare hands or any weapon known to man. He was also an expert sniper.

Apart from his attractiveness, Stiel looked like a non-entity and spoke like a merchant's clerk. He could pass almost anywhere without comment. Simon knew nothing of his past and had never known where Janus had found him. He knew that of all the people in the universe, Stiel obeyed only the rogue trader, for reasons Simon could only guess.

'Anything new?'

'Prosperity flows,' said Simon with an ironic smile, and slid one of the dreamstones across the table under the concealment of his hand until it dropped off the table edge into Kham Bell's outstretched paw. The sergeant let out a low whistle and passed the gem discreetly to Stiel. The killer looked down and his eyes crinkled. For him, it was the equivalent of a broad grin and a hearty cheer.

'Looks real,' he said.

'It is real,' said Kham Bell. 'Haven't seen its like since I took one off those bastards who killed my sister.'

'Which ones were those?' Stiel asked politely. He was the only man who could have got away with asking the mercenary that question. Pretty much any man Bell killed and plundered bore a startling resemblance to the men he claimed had killed his family. Even a few orks did.

'Winterhome,' said Kham Bell, in a tone that would have warned off anybody except Stiel. The killer just nodded. Simon could have sworn he wore a faint air of amusement. It sometimes seemed that his main pleasure in life, aside from killing people, was tormenting Kham Bell.

Interesting as watching a fight between two such hardened brawlers would be, Simon decided that he had better things to do.

'We have a commission.' That got both their attentions. 'And we have enough money to reclaim the *Star* and pay off the crew.'

'For whom?'

'I cannot discuss that here.' Both men nodded. The beer hall was not the most secure of places.

'Where are we going?' Bell could not resist asking.

'I cannot tell you that either.' Fairness prompted the Navigator to add, 'I can say that it will be dangerous.'

'That would make a change,' said Kham Bell.

'There is a very good chance that none of us will be returning.'

'It's the same every time we voyage,' said Stiel.

'This time it is different.'

'How different?'

'It may be more dangerous than anything we have ever done before.'

'I was with the captain on Crowe's World,' said Bell. 'What could be more dangerous than that?'

'Where Janus Darke goes, I go,' said Stiel.

'Why are you not with him now?'

'We are in port, and we left him in the Palace of Pleasure. What harm can come to a man like him there? If he needs us, he knows how to get in touch.' Stiel added, touching the comm-net bead on his earring.

'I tried reaching him earlier,' said Simon. 'No luck.'

'He's probably with that high class tart of his,' said Kham Bell. 'Doesn't want to be interrupted.'

'Have you activated his locator?' Stiel asked, more seriously.

'You think something might have happened to him?' Simon countered.

Simon shook his head. 'Janus can look after himself. You need to start getting the men together while I assemble a crew. We're shipping out as soon as we can get provisioned. Tell the men it's volunteers only, double hazard rates.'

'That bad?' said Kham Bell.

'That bad,' said Simon Belisarius.

'Better get the lads together then,' said Kham Bell.

'Get them to the port,' said Simon. 'We blast as soon as Janus checks in.'

JANUS DARKE LOOKED around the refrigerated chamber and dry-heaved. He would have thrown up, but everything he had eaten earlier was already a messy puddle on the floor in front of him. In his time, he had been on some bloody fields but he had never seen anything like this.

The thing that had once been Fat Roj lay on the ground in front of him. Most of his blood was sprayed over the walls. His entrails had erupted from his stomach and lay like coiled ropes about him. Janus could see the purple of internal organs, most likely the liver or spleen. His heart lay on the floor where Janus had dropped it when he emerged from his trance. The blood still covered his hands.

What have I done, Janus wondered? Horror and remorse filled him. He could not remember anything at all after Fat Roj had torn off the little finger of his left hand. He looked down at it and could not quite believe his eyes. The flesh was smooth. Instead of a bloody gaping hole where his finger had been, there was a smooth expanse of white flesh. He felt no pain. All he felt was tired and a little numb.

Janus looked around. Something flapped on the end of a meat hook. It looked like a carpet or a tapestry except that it was the wrong colour and dripped blood. Inspecting it closer, he made out some coloured patterns, then realised that they were tattoos. He was looking at the skin of Roj's chief henchman. A taxidermist could not have removed it so cleanly. That pinkish blood-dripping thing on the floor would be the man himself then. The body looked up at the ceiling, his blackened tongue protruding, his eyes, the only human thing about him now, wearing an expression of utter horror.

Weariness overwhelmed Janus. He slumped down on his knees and glanced around. Bodies lay sprawled here, there and everywhere. Limbs dangled from hooks. There was blood all over the place. It looked like a daemon had run amok with a chainsword but Janus knew it had been no daemon. It had been him.

He considered his options. What should he do? The right thing would be to give himself up to the Inquisition. There was no way he could kid himself now. He was possessed of evil mystical powers. The light of the Emperor no longer shone on him. His soul was forfeit. There was no telling what he might do if he allowed himself to run free. If what he had done here was an example, there was no end to the harm he might wreak.

Part of him argued that these men had deserved it. They had stood by and either watched him be tortured or had helped torture him. The Emperor alone knew how many deaths Fat Roj had been responsible for. But what if next time it was not a gang of murderous thugs? What if next time it was a group of children? There was no telling where this could lead, and he could not say he had not been warned. Everybody in the Imperium knew what happened to unbound psykers. They had it drummed into their heads from the first day they were old enough to attend temple school.

Something else nagged at Janus. He studied the bodies, then counted them, and checked against his memory. There were only seven corpses. Where was Weezel? The little man's body should surely be noticeable among the ones he had killed. After all, he had been much smaller than any of the others, an informer not a bruiser.

How could you tell if he was here, Janus asked himself? It looked like somebody had punched a hole into the bodies' abdominal cavities, pushed in a grenade and stood back to watch the explosion. Even so, he felt certain that he would have recognised Weezel's body. None of the severed limbs fitted Weezel's either. They were all too big. He guessed his subconscious was nagging at him, trying to tell him something. The informer had escaped.

This was not good news. Even if Weezel did not report this to the Inquisition, which was likely considering the circumstances that had brought Janus here, and the part the informers had played in them, he would still inform the Syndicate. They would not stand still for one of their own, and a high-ranking boss like Fat Roj at that, being killed in this way. They were like the Navigator Houses; they would never stop hounding him until he was dead. It would not matter where he went now, or how he tried to hide; there would be a price on his head. It was only a matter of time before the bounty hunters showed up. And they were quite capable of finding some way of letting the Inquisition know what had happened here too.

Slowly the enormity of what he had done here seeped into his mind. Unarmed, he had killed more than half a dozen heavily armed and very tough men. It was a feat he could only have managed by calling upon the powers of darkness, by receiving aid from the accursed powers of Chaos. It came to him that he was one of those things he had been warned about since his earliest childhood, one of those to be constantly guarded against, to be reported to the authorities as soon as they were discovered. He was a psyker.

What am I going to do, he asked himself? All the wealth the dreamstone represented meant nothing now. Once Weezel spoke into the wrong ears, no amount of money could save him. His former position would be no protection. His charter would be revoked, his remaining property impounded. He would have no rights under law.

He realised that he had made a mistake. He doubted if even Stiel could be counted on after what had happened here. He needed to get a move on, to get out before the assassin arrived, or bounty hunters or the Inquisition showed up.

Fortunately, there was no shortage of weapons. He picked up his own blade and pistol, and helped himself to the guns of two of Fat Roj's henchmen. He took several bandoliers of ammunition and a knife. Shivering he pulled himself to his feet and headed towards the doors. The blood, now a frozen puddle of red ice, crunched beneath his feet.

WEEZEL RACED THROUGH the night-shrouded streets. Every shadow menaced him. Every pool of gaslight was a momentary refuge from the horror that dogged his heels. Every moment he half expected a heavy hand to descend on his shoulders or to feel a blast of agony that would tell him Darke had caught up with him.

His skin crawled at the memory of what the trader had done. Had he not witnessed the scene with his own eyes he would have scarcely believed it. One of Roj's men had been turned inside out, his internal organs erupting through his flesh, his ribs emerging like ivory spears from his skin. Fat Roj's own intestines had burst forth from his huge gut and strangled him. The others had run to aid their boss, unaware that they were running to their doom.

Weezel, his instinct for self-preservation honed by decades of survival in the Warrens, had taken a different tack. While they had run towards the insanely laughing thing that moments before had been Janus Darke, he had rushed out of the door and slammed it closed behind him. Not that he had expected to stop the monster for more than a few moments, but instinct had made him want to put something solid between himself and the combat.

Now his lungs burned and his chest felt like it was on fire. Molten lead flowed through his limbs. Weariness threatened to overwhelm him. He knew that he could not run another step, and yet he somehow forced himself to stumble on. Just one more, he told himself. Lift your foot. And again. His soiled britches stuck to his legs. The chill of the refrigerated chamber seemed to have sunk into his bones.

Reeling with fatigue, his foot slipped in a puddle of slimy ordure and he plunged headfirst onto the pavement. All around people looked at him, wondering whether he was drunk. A few of the more likely looking lads were already starting to move in his direction, seeing him as easy prey. He forced himself to sit upright and fumbled in his jacket pocket for his hook-knife. Seeing that menacing gesture the boys backed off.

Slowly, it dawned on Weezel that he was still alive and that he was surrounded by people. Darke had not found him. And the chances were he would not be able to find him among the press of bodies. For a moment, tears appeared in Weezel's eyes, and he dragged himself to his feet. The first thing to do was find a refuge, a bolthole where Darke would never find him.

The next thing to do was decide who would pay him the highest fee for the very interesting information he now knew about the high and mighty rogue trader Janus Darke.

EIGHT
ON THE RUN

Simon Belisarius sighed wearily and strode over to the enormous observation window of the departure lounge. Down below, he could see the ramp that led up to the shuttle bay, where one of the *Star of Venam*'s landing craft now lay. Loading drones, forklifters and customs officials raced around like worker ants in a hive. To Simon, who had spent a large part of his adult life around docksides, it was a reassuring sight. And as doubtless the Emperor knew, he was greatly in need of reassurance.

He cast his mind back over the preparations needed. As far as he could tell everything was in order. He had dispatched the eldar's golden argosy back to House Belisarius via bonded courier, along with a detailed description of events so far. If nothing else, he would go down in history as a man who had redeemed part of his House's debt to the eldar.

He had visited the bankers at Commercial House and deposited three quarters of the dreamstones with them, as security against a draft worth more than the value of a hive city. The stones and his position as a Navigator were all the security those merchant princes required. He had cleared off the rogue trader's debts to the chandlers, provisioners and countless others. Having received their money they now clamoured for more business. The shipwrights who had refitted the *Star of Venam* had signed releases, meaning that they were clear to lift from Medusa. More provisions were already being shipped aboard under Stiel's supervision.

He looked down into the departure bay and saw that Kham Bell and his boys had rousted the crew out from under their assorted rocks. Simon smiled as he saw familiar figures hove into view and head up the departure ramps.

There were a few unfamiliar faces too. Some of the old crew would have shipped out with other craft or were lurking in some hellhole too remote for even Bell's bruisers, or were perhaps lying face down in a pool of blood with a knife in their back and their pay-packets in the purses of some dockside crims. A sailor's life could be a cruel one, as Simon well knew. No doubt a lot of those new men had signed on when they heard of the bonuses being offered for this trip.

A start of guilt passed through him. He did not expect to return from this voyage, and he had no idea to what fate he was taking these men. He had done all he could to let them know the risks involved without giving away any information about the eldar's mission.

Sometimes, he thought, being a Navigator was not easy. When he had been raised to the position, he had sworn an oath to bring his ship safely to port, or die in the attempt. While breath was in his body, and the spark of life in his soul, he would not shirk from that task.

A black-garbed figure had entered the departure bay. He saw one of Bell's security men move to intercept it, and then take it to the sergeant. He saw words being exchanged and Bell looking up at the window, then all three headed up in his direction.

He felt a little uneasy. Kham Bell was bringing the eldar up here, to him. He breathed deeply and tensed and relaxed his muscles in preparation. He was unsure of his ground, which was unusual for him. He was the scion of a House that predated the Imperium, and had held its wealth and position through ten thousand years of deadly intrigue, yet there was something about the eldar that made him feel like an unsophisticated barbarian. He allowed himself a small smile, wondering if that was a deliberate ploy on the part of the aliens or whether it was simply just their way. Maybe it had nothing to do with them, Simon thought, with a small flash of insight. Maybe I am merely projecting my own doubts onto them, seeing myself reflected back in the mirror of their faces.

After all, they were xenogens – who knew what went on in their minds? Behind the mask of those beautiful and human-seeming faces might lie a mind as alien as that of a tyranid. Merely because something wore the form of a human did not make it human. Simon reviewed what he knew of the eldar, hoping to find something to give him an edge in his dealings. Given ten millennia of intermittent contact between his House and the aliens, it was little enough.

The eldar were by reputation fearful foes. Swift, savage and ferocious they appeared for no reason, killed without mercy, and disappeared back who knew where. Their weapons and vehicles spoke of a science at least as advanced as mankind's, possibly far more so. No examination of eldar artefacts had provided any clue as to how they worked or what powered them. They appeared to operate on entirely different principles from the machines of men. Simon had heard it speculated that the underpinnings of their science were psychic or even daemonic, for the two were after all very close. Other philosophers claimed that their machineries were so advanced as to be beyond human comprehension, or the products of a way of looking at things that was beyond human understanding. Simon had himself seen enough eldar artefacts to understand how such a theory had come about. They were alien, and looked more like elaborate works of art than devices intended for mundane use. Their vehicles and weapons resembled sculptures more than technological artefacts.

There was no doubting that they worked though, and exceedingly well. Whenever eldar forces appeared on the battlefield, they usually contrived to more than hold their own against human forces. Simon supposed that was understandable given that they appeared to pick and choose their battlefields to suit themselves.

He had heard tales of torture and humans being taken as sacrifices to the Dark Gods, and saw no reason to doubt them. Not for the first time, he wondered what it was that this menacing and mysterious people could have done for his ancestors to so place them in debt. He resigned himself to the fact that he might never find out. The records from that period were sealed, and it was all so long ago that only the most tenuous and legendary tales even hinted at possible explanations. Nonetheless, the contract had been held to with all the tenacity of House Belisarius which showed that whatever its cause, the debt was real enough, and now it had fallen on him to repay part of it.

There was a mystery here that niggled at Simon. Why did the eldar need this ship? And why were there only two of them? He knew enough about the xenogens to be certain that Auric was a being of great rank among the old race. And he knew that the eldar had their own powerful ships. What need could they possibly have of a human one, unless Auric was doing something that was forbidden by his people, or was trying to keep his destination secret? But why would he do that?

And then there was the mystery of those eldar ships themselves. That they existed was beyond a shadow of a doubt. Eldar raiders had struck many an Imperial convoy. Simon had fought against them himself in his time. And eldar battle fleets had intervened in many struggles against Chaos and orks, as well as against the Imperial fleet. But not one had ever been sighted in the immaterium. Ork craft, Chaos craft and many types of human and xenogen craft had been logged by the Navigators who had sensed their presence, but never, not once in more than ten millennia, had an eldar ship been sighted.

Of course, statistically speaking it was possible that this was a result of chance. The odds against it were astronomical, given the number of Navigators and number of passages made, but it was still a possibility that had to be allowed for.

Had it been the only unusual thing it might have been worth noting, but there were other anomalies. Not once in all the times an eldar ship had been encountered in true space had one ever been seen to enter the immaterium. Eldar ships had been seen to leave solar systems, but they simply vanished. There had been no gathering of powers, no opening of ways, no transition of the ship into the immaterium. During their departure no Navigator had ever spotted the disturbance on the surface of true space that would have told him a ship had just been there. No Navigator had ever succeeded in following an eldar vessel to its port by following the ripples of a probability wake. There simply never were any. It was as if the vessels just vanished.

Of course, there were theories to account for this. It was possible that the eldar had invented some sort of cloaking device that prevented their ships from being spotted. Or perhaps their farseers, who were powerful psykers, could simply hide their trails or cloud the minds of those who followed. Simon found this idea hard to credit. He knew how potent the psychic shields that protected a starcraft were, and he doubted that they could be broached without the ship itself being destroyed. And, anyway, why would the eldar be so subtle?

One theory suggested they had something to hide, that they wanted no one to find their mysterious home worlds. Simon found this plausible. If the Imperium ever located the places they would be vulnerable to huge strikes by the overwhelming power of the Imperial fleet. So far nothing like an eldar home world had been found by humanity, only a few remote planets, lightly populated by relatively backward eldar, who bore little resemblance to the proud people Simon had encountered.

Another theory was that the eldar home worlds lay far beyond the boundaries of the Imperium and that the eldar encountered were simply the harbingers of some awesome and awful force to come. It was a possibility Simon did not discount. The galaxy was vast, and despite the size of the Imperium, huge swathes of the map were unexplored.

The door slid open, and Kham Bell and one of the eldar entered the luxuriously appointed lounge. It was Auric.

'He says he is one of our passengers.' Doubt and mistrust showed in the sergeant's every word and gesture. He liked xenogens even less than he liked most strangers, and he liked most strangers not at all.

'He has chartered the ship,' stated Janus.

'An eldar!' Astonishment turned Bell's words into a parade-ground roar.

Even used as he was to the sergeant's manner, it took all of Simon's self-control to keep from being startled. The eldar gave no sign of discomposure whatsoever. 'Does the captain know?'

'Apparently.'

'Apparently?'

'So our friend here says. When Janus arrives we will soon see if it is true.'

Kham Bell glared at them as he headed for the door. 'I'll be watching you. Some of your kind killed my family.'

Simon shook his head. Kham Bell made that claim to everybody he disliked. Maybe he even believed it. You could never be sure with him.

'A very strange man,' said Auric, as the mercenary disappeared.

'A very good soldier,' said Simon.

'Are you ready to depart?' asked Auric.

'We await only Captain Darke's arrival, and the last of our supplies.'

'Janus Darke will be with you soon,' said Auric with a strange certainty in his voice. 'And he will come with enemies snapping at his heels. You had better be prepared for instant departure.'

Simon considered asking more, but he was sure the eldar would be evasive. 'Then you'd best get aboard the shuttle. Where is Athenys?'

'She has some unfinished business. She will be here soon.'

JANUS DARKE LOPED out onto the darkened street. So far, so good, he told himself. No one seemed to have raised the alarm yet. No Arbites had appeared to check out the disturbance. No inquisitors had come for him... yet. It was only a matter of time now, he knew. He pulled his stolen cloak tight around himself. None of the crowd in the street paid him the slightest attention. That was good.

The chill night mist swirled clammily about him. The smell of sulphur and rotting food assaulted his nostrils. He staggered like a man drunk. Enormous fatigue lay on him like the weight of the world. Whatever he had done back there had drained him of strength, tired him more than a fifty kilometre march on half rations. He felt as weak as a man recovering from breakbone fever.

He strode along through the press of bodies, hoping to get his bearings. He was on a high roadway looping around the outside edge of a hive spire. Off in the distance he could see the running lights of a shuttle as it blasted off into orbit, its fiery contrail a line of light scratched on the darkness of the sky. Spaceport was that way then, he thought. Good. That means I must still be on Hark Spire.

He considered his options. He could wait for his enemies to come and find him, or he could call a phaeton and make his own way back to the port. Or he could find a place to hide, maybe make his way down into the distant labyrinths of the Underhive where even the Arbites feared to tread. That was not a prospect he relished. It was where the lowest of the low, the most lost of the lost, took refuge. Soon he should call on Justina and find out what she had done with the dreamstone. It was worth a small fortune and fairly soon he would need all the money he could get.

If worst came to the worst, he could try to contact the smugglers and get them to take him off-planet. It was a long shot. The smugglers were mostly in bed with the crime syndicates, but there were still one or two independents who would take him if the price was right. Even as the thought crossed his mind, he realised he had come to a decision. For better or worse, he was not going to give himself up to the Inquisition. They were going to have to come and get him.

In the long run that would almost certainly mean death or flight to those places where the Imperium's writ did not run, but he was prepared to face up to that. Soon, he thought, once the word is out, every man's hand will be against me. The sentence of the Inquisition would make him an apostate, and any man who aided him or gave him succour would be considered just as much a spawn of darkness as he, and liable to the same fate.

He thought about his friends and comrades – Simon Belisarius, Kham Bell and Stiel among them. Perhaps they would aid him, perhaps not. He would be doing them no favours by accepting any aid. Perhaps it would be better for him to simply disappear from the ken of man. If that was the case he was certainly going to need the money. He needed to see Justina again. She had his money, and she had the contacts to help him out.

Perhaps he might even begin to tease out some of the hints she had dropped – although part of him shuddered with fear at the very thought.

'THAT'S HIM, MISTRESS,' said Eruk. 'Shall we take him now?'

Justina looked out of the window of the parked phaeton, and saw that it was indeed Janus Darke, moving through the crowd outside the entrance of Fat Roj's meat packing business. Her informants had been right. She was glad there had been no need to use the amulet she had given him to trace the rogue trader's location – you could never tell when an Inquisition psyker might detect such a thing.

'Shall we take him now?' repeated Eruk. There was a petulant whining note in his tone of voice. The young noble sounded too eager. He had always been a little too quick to inflict pain, Justina reflected. Like many of his friends, he took too much pleasure in it, and she had carried the bruises as proof. She allowed herself a faint ironic smile. What was she thinking? How could a devotee of Slaanesh even think that there was such a thing as anybody taking too much pleasure in something?

'Wait!' she said, before the youth and his foolish and rather attractively muscular compatriots could rush forward and grab the tottering merchant prince. 'There is something strange going on.'

And indeed there was. Janus Darke reeled like a man drunk but he showed no obvious signs of wear and tear that Justina could see. It was not like Fat Roj just to let a victim go unmarked. One of her major worries on the phaeton bringing them here was that they would arrive too late. Fat Roj enjoyed his work and sometimes became overzealous to the point of fatality. How had Janus Darke escaped from his clutches?

Had he cut a deal with the gang lord? Janus could be a persuasive enough talker when he wanted to be, but it would take more than words to dissuade Roj from taking his pound of flesh. She was certain that Janus had no money, save a few terces in his purse. She held the dreamstone that was all the wealth he had in the world at the moment. No, it had not been that. Had he somehow fought his way clear? Impossible, she decided. Well, she would find out soon enough when her scouts returned from casing the meat-packing plant.

There were other worrying things going on. Her agents, normally so efficient, had lost sight of one of the two eldar.

The other was at the starport with Simon Belisarius. That was another troubling report. The Navigator had apparently paid off all of their outstanding debts, leaving the *Star of Venam* clear to boost. All the signs seemed to indicate that the trader was ready to lift, taking the eldar with him. That was not something she could allow. Shaha Gaathon had been most insistent that Darke be found and prepared for the great ritual. It seemed like he was just about ready to play his role. He could not be allowed to go roaming around the galaxy in the company of xenogens.

She considered her options. She could simply approach Janus in the phaeton, and lure him inside. That seemed easy enough, but how would she explain it? Did it matter? He would be suspicious, but not of her. She could simply say that she had sold the dreamstone and had street people looking for him. Why should he doubt her? No need for force at all, now that he was clear of Fat Roj.

Just at that moment Cutter strode up. The tall bodyguard's face was pallid beneath her makeup. She looked as upset as Justina had ever seen her. 'What is it?' she asked.

'I found Fat Roj and his men.'

'And?'

'You'd best see for yourself, mistress,'

Justina nodded and indicated for Eruk and his men to follow Darke. 'Make sure he doesn't get away. On no account must he reach the spaceport,' she said. 'And on no account must he be hurt.'

Eruk nodded and looked disappointed. Justina gave him a warning look to emphasise her command and then strode down the ramp way to the cold place where horror waited.

NINE
ASSASSINATIONS

Janus slumped down into the carved chair of human bone and glanced around. On three sides of him were the open fronts of shophouses, displaying their wares to any strangers who might pass.

Scattered in the open plaza between the shophouses were a sprinkling of tables and stalls selling food and beer. The fourth side of the area ended in a barrier wall that marked the edge of this external level of Hark Spire. Away in the distance he could see flames dancing along the side of another hive.

A small woman, thickly robed against the cold, emerged from her stall to take his order. Thinking it best to conserve his money, he ordered ten skewers of wall-rat and some pungee bread. He was hungry as sin, as well as tired beyond belief, but at least the voices in his head had stopped. He did not believe this would last for long, but he was glad of the respite. Despite the fatigue his mind felt clearer than it had in days. The woman noted down his order on a pad, then turned and bellowed instructions to the cook at his grill. She gave him a pleasant enough smile before retreating.

He glanced around. Considering it was the middle of the night, there were a fair few people out. Commerce never sleeps, Janus thought, remembering the old proverb, although I desperately need to.

He saw that he was attracting a few looks from the other tables. Most of the men were drinking honey beer and scarfing down food. Some looked like ne'er-do-wells, bullyboys, gamblers, muscle for the protection rackets of the syndicates. Others looked like small traders on their break or possibly dayshift workers from the facs, trying to get the necessaries of life before getting to work at dawn. It was the usual mix for such a time. He knew it well enough from the night markets of Crowe's Town when he was a boy. Things had certainly come full circle now, he thought. Back where you started.

A few of the bullyboys glanced his way to see if he was a mark worth taking. One look at his tattered clothing and array of weapons convinced them otherwise. He must look like a licensed bounty hunter, or some other high-grade muscle, he thought. He pulled his hood down across his face, hoping none of them could get a close look in the dim light of the flickering glow-globes. When word of what he had done to Fat Roj got out, many folk would be on his trail.

A nightbiter landed on his hand and began to suck blood. He could not feel the sting yet, and would not until minutes after the insect had flown away. He knew it was draining his blood, though, by the way its translucent wings slowly took on a reddish tinge.

The stallholder returned and placed disposable paper plates of food in front of him, along with cutlery made from recycled bone. He scooped a warm spoonful towards his mouth and then froze as he noticed the arriving new-comers.

At first he took them for slumming nobles. They had the look: their clothes were old but too stylish by far for this neighbourhood, and their flesh had that sleek, well-tended look that only the rich of Medusa wore. Their weapons were all new and well maintained. Some of the men moved with the hard competence of professionals. Body-guards was the instant assumption Janus made, hired muscle to protect their masters. He kept eating, head down to avoid notice. If the drunken sons and daughters of the local nobility chose to frequent a hellhole like this, it was none of his business.

Then he noticed a shadow had fallen on him. He looked up and saw a brawny young man standing in front of him. A faint whiff of very expensive cologne reached Janus's nostrils, confirming the youth's status as one of the local nobs. He wondered why the man had chosen to come over here? There were plenty of empty tables available for him and his friends. Without asking, the youth slid down onto one of the chairs next to the table.

'Take a seat,' said Janus, around a mouthful of food. 'It's free.'

'You're coming with me, Janus Darke,' said the youth pleasantly. Janus stopped chewing for a moment and pondered the noble's words. How had he known his name? What did he want? Janus wondered for a moment whether the boy might be looking for a fight. Not a few of the spoiled sons and daughters of the nobility liked to come down and bully the industrial thralls. This would not explain how he knew Janus's name, though.

'You've mistaken me for someone else,' said Janus and gave the boy a second look. A half-face mask, fashionable among some of the more artistic cliques, covered the bridge of his nose and his eyes. Clear plastic inserts pro-tected his sight from the muck in Medusa's air. The boy's hair was long and rippled in the tainted breeze. There was something about him that Janus really did not like. Though he could not quite put a finger on why, he trusted his instincts enough to heed their warning.

The youth reached out and strong fingers stopped the spoon en route to Janus's mouth. 'I don't think so.'

Janus shrugged off the youth's grip and resumed eating. 'It's flattering to be mistaken for a merchant prince,' said Janus, 'but if I were Darke, would I really be eating here?'

'We followed you from Fat Roj's,' said the youth. 'We know who you are.'

There was a cruel glint in the boy's eye now. He seemed to be enjoying this. Obviously Janus's discomfiture pleased him, and he enjoyed wielding whatever small power he had.

'Fat who?' Janus asked. He was trying to work out who could have sent this fop. He did not have the look of a Syndicate enforcer, nor did his friends. He was not one of the deadly quiet men the Inquisition would have sent. Where else could he be from?

'There are two ways we can do this,' said the youth. 'You can come with me quiet and friendly like, or I can have Anjor and his friends carry you out.'

'The Arbites might object to that,' said Janus mildly, knowing that there was no way he wanted to fall into the hands of the judiciary.

'By the time the judges get here, we'll be long gone,' said the youth.

Time for the direct approach, Janus thought. 'Who are you? Who sent you? What do you want?'

The boy considered this, and Janus thought for a moment he was going to refuse to answer. Reluctantly, he answered. 'I am Eruk. I am a friend of a friend. And I want to take you to see her.'

'And who would this friend be?'

'Justina.'

'Fair enough,' said Janus and kept eating to give him time to gather his thoughts. Why would Justina have sent this young blade to get him? And was he really from her? If not, why was he lying? Janus could see no point to it. Currents swirled around him here, and he felt momentarily out of his depth. Too much was going on that he did not understand.

'Get up,' said Eruk. Janus really did not like his tone, but he could see that now he was going to need all of the allies he could get. He pushed one more morsel of food into his mouth and lurched to his feet. By the Emperor, he was tired.

A hand sign passed between Eruk and the others and they began to withdraw out of the square. As they did so, Janus could see the stallholder looking at him nervously. Did she think Janus was being kidnapped? Janus shook his head slightly to let her know not to do anything foolish. He was not so sure that he was not doing something foolish himself.

'Where are you taking me?' Janus asked. Ahead of him he could see three phaetons. The aircars bobbed just above the ground, their drivers waiting patiently in the external seats for their noble charges to return.

'To a place where you will be safe,' said Eruk. The smirking youth could not resist adding, 'where you will learn the ways of the Lord of Pleasure.'

What did he mean by that, Janus wondered? He studied the vehicles ahead. The drivers were waiting a little too patiently; they seemed to be asleep in their seats. He glanced back, more than a dozen of the youths and their bodyguards followed. He got the impression that there might be even more people hanging back. Once more his instincts screamed that this was a trap, and he fought down the urge to run. Not that there was anywhere for him to go now, surrounded as he was by this mass of young bloods.

Eruk led him towards the leading phaeton, guiding him with a surprisingly strong grip. His bodyguards flanked him on either side. The rest were making for their own coaches. They seemed somehow disappointed, as if they had expected more excitement and had been let down. Janus glanced at the driver again, noticing that the man really was asleep. No, more than that. There was something wrong here. The angle of the man's neck was strange and his face looked very purple under his cowl. Suddenly

Janus realised that his neck had been broken. His hand reached for the butt of his pistol. As he did so a familiar figure loomed into view, a woman in a long black cloak, trimmed with white fur, moving with an eerie alien grace.

Without pausing, she aimed one of the long barrelled eldar pistols at Eruk and pulled the trigger. The youth's face disintegrated in a spray of blood. Janus sensed rather than saw the hail of razor-sharp projectiles whirl past him. Athenys continued to fire and the chest of the bodyguard beside Janus exploded outwards in long shredded strips of flesh.

'If you value your soul, Janus Darke,' said the eldar woman, 'get inside this vehicle and close the door.'

Something in her voice commanded Janus to obey. Resent her tone though he might, his instincts agreed with her. He aimed an elbow at the solar plexus of the surviving bodyguard and felt the man double up, then dived forward into the padded interior of the phaeton. Moments later he felt himself pushed back into the plush seat by a surge of acceleration. Bolter shells hurtled impotently off the sides of the vehicle. One of them impacted on the window. It cracked but did not break. Armourglass, he realised, and the whole body of the phaeton was reinforced too. Truly a noble's vehicle.

As he watched the spire receded below him, expanding in his vision as they moved skywards. He could see the dwindling figures of the young bloods firing at him, then as they realised he was getting away, they clambered into their own vehicles.

A few seconds later they realised that their coachmen were dead. One or two leapt into the external cockpits and the vehicles lurched into the air in pursuit. Once again Janus felt as if events were moving too fast for him. Why had Athenys showed up, and where was she taking him now? Why had she killed those youths? Did she not realise what was likely to happen when they caught up with them?

Like two enormous insects the phaetons buzzed after them, their running lights brilliant in the darkness. Bolter shells pinged off their own vehicle's sides. Janus could see that some of the youths and their bodyguards leaned out the windows and shot upwards at him. Sparks sprang up where they impacted. Armoured or no, Janus thought, the aircar could not take much more of this.

The phaeton veered evasively and they swept round the side of the hive. Below him Janus had a splendid view of the balcony gardens of the rich, roofed over with translucent crystal, illuminated by great jets of gas vented from the side of the hive. Seconds later, the other two phaetons swept into view. Janus was thrown forward as his own vehicle decelerated and then climbed. What was that eldar bitch up to? This was not a simple evasive action. A moment later he had his answer.

The first of the pursuing phaetons exploded. A blast erupted underneath it, and it leapt upwards for a second, propelled skywards on a cloud of superheated plasma. A couple of the figures inside it toppled out through the open door and fell to their doom. A moment later their vehicle plunged forward and followed them to destruction.

Within a heartbeat the second phaeton exploded. This time the blast came from within the passenger compartment. Janus could see the hellish flames within. For a few seconds it looked like the bodywork of the aircar might resist the force of the blast but then it ballooned outward and burst into a million pieces of shrapnel. Chunks of the chassis fell to earth like meteorites.

Slowly it percolated into Janus's mind what had happened. Explosive charges, he thought, detonated by remote control by a comm-signal, and I bet if I looked in Athenys's fist right now, I would find the detonator there. Even through the fog of tiredness and gathering sickness, he was impressed. The eldar woman had destroyed a force of more than a dozen nobles and their servants single-handed and with a precision that Stiel might have envied. What was she, he wondered – some sort of professional assassin?

He guessed he would find out soon enough and wondered how long it would take the Arbites to get on her trail. The aircar banked and he could see that they were sweeping towards the spaceport. I might have guessed, he thought. She and her companion seemed pretty determined to get me into their service. I wonder why?

He dismissed the thought. It had been a long night full of death, and he would begin to find answers soon enough. Right now, he had other things to worry about. A daemon lurked inside his head, and this alien madwoman was carrying it and him directly towards his friends and his ship, the very thing he had sought to avoid. He was not sure whether to laugh or to cry.

He huddled back in the seat and wondered how long it would be until dawn.

JUSTINA STARED INTO the mirror and watched the clouds of chaotic images swirl and coalesce. She swallowed uncomfortably. It was not pleasant to report word of her failure to her master, and she knew she was going to have to pay a heavy price for it, one way or another.

Kym, the only survivor of that fool Eruk's attempt to abduct Janus Darke had told her what had happened. Sifting through her excuses and evasions, Justina had worked out that somehow the eldar woman had either directly or indirectly killed all of the nobles or their retainers and abducted Darke. Kym had only survived by sheer incompetence, failing to board the aircars before they took off and exploded.

Her agents at the spaceport reported that two people very like Darke and the eldar woman had been sighted at the spaceport, taking a high orbit shuttle along with Darke's crew.

Another tantalising report had reached her ears too: the informer Weezel had begun to put about a tale of how Darke had invoked daemonic powers and used sorcery to kill Fat Roj. Given what Justina herself had seen in the meat plant, that tale was uncomfortably close to the truth.

The place had reeked of psychic power and the bodies looked as if they had been shredded by some demented daemon. The only question now was whether to have Weezel scooped up by her people or silenced for good before his tale attracted the attention of the authorities. The former would probably be for the best, she thought. He might possess other useful information that interrogation would reveal and, if keeping him alive was a mistake, it was one that could soon be rectified.

She had pieced together the events of the evening to the best of her ability, and try as she might she could not see what she could have done differently. Of course, her master almost certainly would not see it that way. At least she had managed to infiltrate her agents into Darke's crew, which meant that all was not yet lost, and there was always the talisman provided of course, they did not simply throw it away.

Even as that thought struck her, Shaha Gaathon's presence chamber leapt into sharper focus and her master's visage leered out at her. Blood dribbled from the corners of his mouth and splashed his cheeks in irregular patterns. Justina did not even want to begin to imagine what the great one had been up to, although the possibilities were interesting to contemplate. The Dark Feast was one of the rites of pleasure she had never taken part in, even though she was a woman who believed in plumbing the depths of every human experience.

'Speak, slave, and I will answer,' said Shaha Gaathon.

'As you desire, master.' Swiftly Justina told her tale, leaving out nothing, knowing how well Shaha Gaathon sensed evasion, and how subtly he punished it. At the conclusion of her speech, she saw that her fears were amply justified. Shaha Gaathon was angry.

'What do you suggest we do now, slave?' he asked.

'I have agents on board the *Star of Venam* who possess the means to contact us.'

'Best hope they do not try, little mortal, for doubtless the eldar possess the means to detect such a thing.'

'These are my best people, great one. They are cautious and discreet.'

'They will need to be, for the eldar are subtle and swift to slay our kind.'

Justina suppressed a shrug. Even if such were the case, there was nothing much she could do about it. She had done everything she could. A reflective look passed over Shaha Gaathon's disturbingly beautiful features. Justina noted the interesting patterns of blood that now dappled his cheeks. Did the crimson belong to the Great One or someone else, she wondered with a stab of something like jealousy?

Shaha Gaathon looked up, his eyes glowing with baleful red fire. 'The matter is out of your hands now, slave. I must find other tools to ensure that Darke is present for the ritual. Now all that remains is the matter of punishment for your failure. Don't worry, I shall make sure it is interesting.'

Justina shivered in anticipation.

TEN
OUTWARD BOUND

JANUS DARKE STOOD on the observation deck of the shuttle and watched the *Star of Venam* hove into view. Despite his weakness, despite the concerned gazes of his troops, and the predatory alien watchfulness of the eldar, he felt pride swell in his heart. The *Star* was an awesome sight against the velvet blackness of space. A massive engine of commerce or destruction at her commander's whim, a mobile fortress, a vehicle capable of making the great leap between worlds, in short everything an Imperial starship should be.

His eyes drank in the great crenellated turrets with their massive bristling weapons and the projectile tubes in her bows. He looked hungrily at the enormous superstructure where his own cabin and the ship's command deck lay. As he did so, he became aware that someone else looked on the mighty vessel with eyes as avid as his own.

'The repairs have gone well,' said Simon Belisarius, pride and contentment evident in every word. Janus nodded his head in agreement. The twisted plate and broken armour of their last voyage had been cleared away and replaced. The ship was spaceworthy again. Janus wondered where Simon had found the money to pay off the debt and reclaim their vessel from the shipwrights. A glance at the eldar told him the most likely source. It seemed that he had not been the only partner they had chosen to contact and, right at this moment, looking at his ship he was glad.

He was glad that he would not have to hide in a stinking slum on Medusa waiting for the hunters to come. He was glad that he had somehow, for a while, evaded the clutches of the Inquisition. He was glad that he was free of Fat Roj and his killers. The gladness lasted only a moment: he had merely delayed a reckoning he knew, not settled a score. And there was too much going on that he did not understand.

The men Athenys had killed, and who had claimed to come from Justina, were just one example. He had no idea what that was about, but he sensed deep and sinister undercurrents, and from the few words he had exchanged with the eldar woman, he knew that she agreed.

Indeed, the xenogens seemed to know more about what was going on than he did, and had apparently orchestrated much to their own ends in his absence. He wondered how they had got Simon to agree to their chosen destination. There was much he was going to have to talk about with his business partner once they were aboard ship and underway.

And that could not happen too soon. With every passing moment, he felt a weight lift from his shoulders. Soon they would be plotting a course out-system and every speck of distance between himself and the world below was fine by him. He could not wait to put a long starjump between himself and Medusa, and the events that had occurred there.

But what then? The eldar still wanted to go to their dark goal, and he was not sure that he could deny them. Even if they were privy to his darkest secret, they had saved his life. Something within him whispered caution. If the xenogens had saved him, it was surely for their own reasons and might mean no good at all. Indeed, it seemed all too possible that they might be preserving him for a darker fate.

Even sick and weak as he felt, he knew that soon he was going to have to solve the mystery they represented, and find out what it was they truly wanted. His instincts told him that doing so was essential for preserving both his life and his sanity, and he had lived too long by his instincts to deny them now.

The shuttle began to decelerate and rotate inwards as it made its final approach to the great starship's docking bay. In a matter of moments, it was swallowed like a minnow gulped down by a whale shark.

THE COMMAND DECK of the *Star of Venam* was huge. A massive armoured crystal window gave a view of the long hull of the ship stretching ahead of them. All around officers and starsailors went about their duties. Janus lounged back into the command chair and glanced over at Simon.

'We've cleared with starport, customs and the Inquisition,' said the Navigator. 'All hatches are sealed. We're ready to slip moorings.'

'Go to it, Navigator,' said Janus. 'The helm is yours.'

Simon turned and spoke into one of the vox-tubes. The ship rocked gently as the umbilicals connecting it to the starport loosened. There was a faint sense of acceleration as the lateral jets pushed them clear. Momentarily Janus felt weightless before the ship's own gravity kicked in. Janus studied the small screen that had deployed from the arm of his command chair. It showed a sensor map of surrounding space. They were a lighter dot against the green. The massive bolt of pulsing light was Medusa Starport. Other small dots of paler green were Imperial ships.

Tired and drained as he felt, Janus kept his position. It was a captain's duty to be on the command deck when his ship slipped moorings, and he was not going to be remiss. Besides, this was a moment he had always loved, and had done ever since he first set foot on a starship. Setting off always felt like an adventure, there was no telling what you would see or do, no telling if you would even survive the journey, warp travel being so dangerous. And still there was something about it to make the heart beat faster and lift the spirits no matter how gloomy you felt.

Janus felt a thin smile play on his lips as he looked up and surveyed the hub of his domain. Tech-adepts stood before banks of command altars, chanting the praises of machine spirits as they communed with their engines. Chief Tech-Adept Ruark strode among them, swinging his censer and lifting his voice whenever the chant faltered.

Simon Belisarius stood on the raised and sanctified circular dais that only a Navigator was allowed to occupy. Glittering copper cables flowed from the intricate machinery of the ancients to the interface circlet on his forehead. He stood with his hands clutching the gargoyled brass guardrail taking the feeds from the datacores directly into his mind, and sorting it in ways that only a Navigator could understand. The helmsman stood beside the two enormous metallic wheels, one directly in front of him, and one set off to the side. Two more copper datafeeds ran directly into the sockets on his forehead. He made small adjustments to the ship's course as Simon gave commands.

Janus glanced back over his shoulder and gazed out of the rear observation window of the command deck. Already the enormous, weapon bristling structure of the starport was slipping away behind them. He watched it dwindle from an enormous spoked and spinning wheel to just one more light glittering among the backdrop of stars.

Below it the great shining face of Medusa dominated the sky, all greenish toxic clouds and dark brown polluted sludge seas. As the ship gained speed it too began to shrink and more and more of it came into view. Well, thought the rogue trader, we're on our way.

As soon as Simon reeled off the coordinates of the transition point and Janus was certain it was safe to turn over command of the ship to the helmsman, he said, 'Navigator Belisarius. I wish to speak with you in my cabin.'

'Aye, captain. Mr Banes, the helm is yours.'

Simon Belisarius disengaged himself from the command chair. He looked directly at the rogue trader.

'A word, Janus,' he said, his tone of voice very cold. 'In private.'

'WELL?' SAID SIMON Belisarius interrogatively.

'Very well,' replied Janus Darke evasively. The Navigator smiled cynically and stroked his small moustache.

'That is not what I meant, and you know it,' said Simon.

Janus looked around his small cabin for reassurance. It was as much a home as he had ever had since he left Crowe's World all those years ago. If truth be told, he had probably spent more time here than in the huge mansion he had once owned on Medusa. He was glad that he had left most of his favourite possessions here. There were some things he would have hated to have left behind.

On the wall was an ork battle banner, all garish colours and primitive symbols. Beneath it, fixed to the bulkhead, were a crossed chainsword and bolter that he had taken from the dead hands of a warboss. They had the heavy, primitive yet utilitarian look of all ork technology. Janus got up from the chair and poured himself some dreamwine.

'Are you sure you want that?' asked Simon. 'You look like hell.'

'I thought you were a Navigator, not an apothecary,' said Janus sourly.

'I am also your business partner,' said Simon. 'What is going on, Janus?'

Janus was not sure he would ever be ready to tell the Navigator, even if Simon was the closest thing to a friend he had ever had. 'Good question,' he countered. 'You tell me.'

'I don't suppose your friend the Lady Athenys shared any secrets with you before she brought you back – like where we are going, for instance?'

'They haven't told you?' Janus asked astonished.

'Belial IV,' said Simon. His voice showed he fully understood the import of that particular destination.

'If you don't like it, why did you agree to come? I take it you have agreed?'

Simon looked as if he was considering something. He fell silent for a moment and stared deeply into his glass as if he might divine some dark secret there.

Janus helped himself to more wine and swigged it back before pouring another glass and sinking back into his chair.

'They offered me a huge amount of money.'

'It would have to be bloody huge to convince you to go into the Eye of Terror.'

Simon's glass fell from his nerveless fingers. The wine formed a dark puddle on the white fur rug, the pelt of a stormbear from Winterhome.

Janus looked at him in astonishment. 'What else have they told you?' he asked.

'They told me nothing.'

'And yet you still agreed to carry them. Come on, Navigator, I was not born yesterday. They must have done something to make you agree to this trip. You swore you'd never break another interdict after Typhon.'

'It's not that simple, Janus.'

'It never is, is it?'

'I have obligations to my House.'

'And you don't have any to me?'

'You're the one keeping secrets here!'

Guilt made Janus answer more angrily than he would have liked. He was tired and ill and he still felt drained by the events of the past twenty-four hours. Not even being in his own cabin and the reassuring feel of the *Star's* decks beneath his feet could rid him of the fatigue. 'What do you mean by that?'

'Come on, Janus, what is there that you are not telling me?'

'Nothing.'

'Really. You vanish mysteriously in Medusa, and show up looking like you've carved your way across a battlefield with an eldar princess in tow–'

'Is that what she is?'

'You order us off-planet as if the hounds of hell are on our tail, and now you're being as evasive as a dockside trader trying to sell a litter of vamphound whelps? What is going on?'

'More than meets the eye, obviously,' said Janus, trying to defuse the situation with humour.

'Don't try and wriggle out of it. Tell me what you know about these eldar, and where they want us to go.'

'Belial IV. The Eye of Terror. You already know that!'

'But why?'

'Are you going to refuse to take us there, Navigator? The place is under Imperial interdict, after all. If you won't do it, jump us close enough and I'll take the *Star* in. If it's only a short range hop, I can plot the course myself.'

Simon's shock kept him from speaking for a moment, then his words came out mechanically. 'You could never do it. The Eye is not like any other place. It is surrounded by warp storms, time rips, chronal vortices and undertows. The warp streams are turbulent, and there are all manner of cross-currents. Only the Cadian Gate is navigable with anything like regularity, and that infrequently. I am a full-bonded Navigator of a most ancient bloodline, and I doubt my own ability to find a safe channel through. There is no way an ancestral could do so.'

Janus could tell Simon was serious. He really did not have much faith in his own ability to find a way into the Eye, and none whatsoever in somebody who lacked his training. 'So you won't do it? You're going to tell our passengers it's impossible.'

Simon slowly shook his head. 'I must do it.'

'Must?'

'There is a debt between my House and the eldar that I must repay. That is all I can tell you. Do not press me further on this.'

Janus shrugged. 'To tell the truth, I was rather hoping you would refuse. I no more want to see the inside of the Eye of Terror than you do.'

Simon smiled wryly. 'You are still captain here, Janus. I am the Navigator. Until we begin our approach run to the immaterium, you are in command. If you do not wish to do this, do not. I will find another ship and take the eldar that way.'

Janus let out a low whistle. 'You are serious. That must be quite a debt you people owe the eldar.'

'I am not at liberty to speak more of it, Janus. Do not ask me to. And do not try to trap me with words either. I will simply leave.'

Thinking of his own secrets, Janus said, 'It's your debt. If you wish I will forget the matter.'

'Thank you. But do not forget the matter. Remain wary and alert. This will be a very dangerous trip if you choose to make it.'

'I will make it.'

'Again I find myself asking – why?' Janus considered his response for a long moment. Why did he want to make this trip? In part because the eldar had hinted that they could help him, in part because he owed them a debt of honour, in part because really he had nowhere else to go. If someone had wanted to devise a trap to push him into doing the eldar's will, they could not have designed it better. Was it possible the xenogens were so devious? He dismissed the thought at once but still the words came almost unbidden from his lips.

'Because I suspect our guests would not let me do otherwise.'

'I still would like to know what it is they want,' said Simon Belisarius.

'Then let us go and ask them,' said Janus, heading towards the door.

'You do it,' said Simon. 'I must plot our course.'

'What?' Janus could not believe that the Navigator was shirking from confronting the eldar, though he was glad of it. He did not want Simon finding out about the voices. Perhaps Simon sensed this. Navigators were very good about such things.

'I am in no position to question them,' said Simon. 'It would violate the terms of our agreement.'

'But you're going to encourage me do it,' said Janus. 'You are a cunning bastard.'

'Not as cunning as they are. Have no doubts on that score.'

JANUS TAPPED ON the door of the cabin assigned to the eldar. It was one of the largest of the guest suites, normally reserved only for the most important visitors. No matter how much the crew disliked having xenogens on board, it seemed like Stiel had decided they were personages of importance. Of course, he had given them chambers that were monitored by many discrete security devices. Doubtless, he wanted to eavesdrop on whatever they said. Janus would not be surprised to learn that Stiel spoke eldar. The man was full of surprises. If he did not, then Simon certainly did.

'Enter, human,' said Athenys's voice. The door slid open and Janus strode inside.

Already the eldar had started to make the suite their own. Strange silken banners hung from the walls, covered in intricate woven patterns that somehow hurt the eye. The chairs had been removed to be replaced by cushions. A large rug had been unrolled on the centre of the floor. Auric sat there cross-legged, dragging on a hookah. Athenys reclined on a cushion, her attention effortlessly taking in the whole room. Both of them wore loose fitting robes of black trimmed with white. A circlet of strange gems hung from Auric's neck. Athenys wore a weapon harness that looked as elegant as a courtesan's dress jewellery. The weapons might have been ornaments as much as implements of destruction.

'Greetings, Captain Darke,' said Aurik. 'May Isha grant you many blessings.'

'What is going on?' asked Janus abruptly. He still felt tired and ill, and whatever strange weed the eldar was smoking was making his nostrils burn and his skin tingle. Athenys looked at him as if she were a cat and he a particularly bedraggled rat. He was suddenly glad that he had washed and changed into new clothes before visiting their chamber. These feline xenogens were far too good at making him feel uncomfortable.

'If you could make your question more specific, Janus Darke, I will endeavour to answer it.'

Janus glanced back to make sure the door was closed and suddenly felt stupid. He was not about to ask about what he really wanted to know in this chamber with all of its listening devices.

'If you are worried about being overheard,' said Athenys, 'don't be. This chamber is secure.'

'You sound very certain.'

'I am very certain of that. Your primitive technology is hardly sophisticated enough to baffle our sensors.'

Janus filed this information away for future use. It was something worth knowing. He still did not feel like speaking, though. He wanted something more than the eldar's word that they would not be overheard. Trust Stiel though he did, there were some things he was not willing to risk his crew finding out. Aurik's next statement made all of his objections useless however.

'I can tell you wish to talk about the thing that is consuming your soul, captain. I do not blame you. The hour is late and things grow very dark indeed.'

ELEVEN
THE MARK OF THE ELDAR

'WHAT DO YOU mean?' asked Janus Darke.

The two eldar smiled at him, and they were not reassuring smiles. This was the first chance Janus had ever had to look at their unconcealed faces close up. Their heads were longer and thinner than a human's, their features far finer and more delicate. Their chins were chiselled and strong, their ears lobeless and pointed. Their eyes were large and almond shaped with long lashes. The pupils reminded him unnervingly of a cat's. For all their unsettling beauty there was something inhuman and threatening about those faces.

'You possess a great gift, Janus Darke,' said Auric. 'Although your people do not regard it as such.'

'I do not know what you mean,' Janus blustered.

'You are a psyker. Your mind is attuned to the forces of the warp. Unfortunately this also means the forces of the warp are attuned to you.'

Janus slumped down onto a cushion, too tired and too ill to protest. All of his life he had been warned about the evil nature of psykers, and now he had found out he was one. 'What has all this got to do with you?'

'Our fates are intertwined. So much has become clear as the probability lines settle.'

'Try and be a bit less vague,' said Janus irritably. Auric shrugged, a boneless gesture that was surprisingly human. Janus realised that was one of the things that was so unsettling about the eldar. One moment they were as strange and incomprehensible as tyranids, the next they reminded him of people he had once known.

'You are asking me to explain concepts so complex that you could spend a lifetime trying to master them and still fail.'

'I will settle for a brief précis, the sort that you might give a child.'

'Eldar children are rare and some who are older than you would still count as children.'

'You say I am a psyker. Start with that.'

'What you call psykers are people blessed or cursed with the gift to tap one of the root forces of the universe.'

'So you say – the Inquisition says they are possessed by daemons.'

'Does not your Inquisition employ psykers?'

'They are shielded by the Emperor, and by their faith.'

'And you lack that faith or are accursed by your Emperor?' countered Auric.

'I am not privy to all of the secrets of the Inquisition. I would imagine that there is some training involved as well.'

'Indeed there must be. For to successfully wield such forces without making yourself vulnerable to the manipulation of those who wait beyond takes decades, perhaps centuries of training.'

'Few humans have centuries to do anything, let alone train.'

'Alas, this is so, and it is one of the curses of your people, to be gifted with such power and yet never to have the time to fully master it. It is one of the reasons your race spends so much time blundering in the dark and causing so much harm to yourselves and to others.'

Janus had no comeback to this so he ventured a question. 'Are you a psyker?'

'I am. And as you can see I am not possessed by daemons.'

'I have only your word for that.' Janus sensed Athenys tense, as if she were preparing to attack. Auric calmed her with a flat chopping gesture of his hand.

'It is not possible for an eldar to be possessed by daemons, and live. We are protected from this fate in a hundred ways.'

'Such as?'

'You are asking me to reveal much, Janus Darke.'

'You are asking me to take a great deal on trust. Too much.'

'For one thing all of us have much stronger souls than you humans. All of us to a certain degree share what you call psyker powers. And all of us are trained from a very young age to resist the blandishments of Chaos.'

'Are you offering to train me in your ways?'

Auric laughed and shook his head. His smile was wide and surprisingly pleasant. 'No. It would take more years than you have left for you to begin to understand why that must be so.'

'You have a gift for being patronising, Auric.'

'That may well be so, but please believe me I do not mean to be so. There is very little common ground between our people, far less than our superficial physical resemblances would suggest. I very much doubt that I could begin to understand the means by which you tap into the power. It took me years of meditation just to be able to light a candle. It took decades before I had enough power to slay a man and yet, in a few months, you have acquired a strength it would take our warlocks decades to reach.'

'He has been doing this with none of the sane and sensible safeguards our warlocks would use. It's hardly surprising,' said Athenys, her voice cold and harsh. 'The warp calls to those whom it would swallow.'

'Nonetheless Janus Darke has come far, quickly, and has yet to be swallowed.'

Janus thought back to what he had done to Fat Roj and his boys in the meat-packing factory and was not sure of that. He hid his guilt with aggression.

'Am I supposed to be flattered?'

'Perhaps you should be. This may well be the first time a seer of my people has ever tried to explain any of this to one of your folk. I feel you are being needlessly aggressive considering I am trying to help you.'

'If this is an unprecedented event why are you doing this? Why now, and why with me?'

Auric took a long draw on the mouthpiece of his hookah and exhaled smoke. It was the first time he had even slowed before answering a question, and Janus sensed that he was considering his words carefully. Given the lightning speed at which the eldar seemed to think, he suspected this meant the self-proclaimed seer was being very careful indeed. After a long minute of silence, he looked up.

'Now we come to the nub of it. I am speaking to you because in all my visions of the future you are there. Our fates are intertwined, and in ways that are not entirely uncertain. I only know that it is so.'

He paused for a moment and closed his eyes. His features went slack for a moment, and a faint glow appeared behind the thin, clear skin of his eyelids. 'Moreover, you are a nexus of probability, Janus Darke. A focus for forces far greater than you can imagine. A bringer of dooms to my people and others.'

Janus heard Athenys gasp. 'Is this a true seeing?' she asked.

Auric did not reply at once. He remained silent for many heartbeats and his eyes snapped open. 'Forgive me,' he said. 'My gift sometimes comes upon me unawares.'

'A product of all those decades of training, no doubt,' said Janus ironically.

'We are more alike than you can guess, Janus Darke. I too know what it is like to have wild and uncontrollable gifts. My masters spent nearly a century trying to bring them fully under my dominion and they did not entirely succeed. Sometimes my gift still surfaces whether I will it or not.'

'It is your gift to see the future?' Janus considered this. If it were so, the services of a being such as this would be worth a fortune – if he could be persuaded to use them for profit, and if people could be convinced his powers were not daemonic.

'It is not that simple, Janus Darke. There are many futures fighting to be born, waiting to be shaped. There are many paths forward from the present. I am one of those who have the gift of seeing a few of those. I am a farseer.'

Janus looked at him and smiled savagely. 'And I am the Emperor of the Imperium.'

Auric cocked his head to one side quizzically and waited for Janus to expand on his point. Janus was not slow to do so. 'I know little of your people, but I have studied many histories, records of conflicts and battles mainly. I know that farseers are rarely seen, and when they do appear it is to take command of armies at the greatest and most savage of battles.'

'Such are the least of a farseer's duties,' said Auric mildly.

'If you are a farseer, where is your army? Where is your bodyguard of warlocks? Where are your ships? Why do you need my help?'

'Regardless of what you believe, Janus Darke, I am a farseer. The title goes to one who possesses the ability. Armies, companies of bodyguards, robes, riches – these are only trappings. What makes a farseer is possession of the gift and the power to use it, and the training to understand what he does. You do not know whereof you speak, and your words are empty things. Listen and gain wisdom.'

Something in the eldar's tone compelled obedience. Janus found himself straining to hear what the xenogen had to say, and filled with resentment that he was doing so. Was there some power at work here, some sinister alien sorcery that held his will enthralled? He resolved that if this was the case to fight it, and yet his resolution came to nothing, and he held his tongue and waited.

'You are in great danger, mortal, and you present a great danger to others, not the least my people, for you are a man the Great Enemy would give much to have under his dominion.'

'The Great Enemy?' asked Janus with some scorn, trying to hide the fact that the farseer's words had impressed him.

'The Dark Lord of Unspeakable Pleasures,' said Auric.

'The Lady of Forbidden Knowledge,' said Athenys.

'One whose name it is not well to utter, lest he hear,' said Auric.

'Her power is great, her malice unending,' said Athenys.

The Lord of Pleasures, thought Janus. There was something familiar about that phrase. Where had he heard it before? Something nagged at the back of his mind.

'You are talking of one the daemon-gods of Chaos,' said Janus.

'So you humans call them, yes. Although their true nature is beyond your understanding.'

'Like so much you want to tell me, it seems,' said Janus dryly. Anger sparked in him. He was suddenly tired of these aliens with their superior manners and their endless hints. They seemed incapable of saying anything in a straightforward manner, and he suspected that their evasiveness concealed manipulation.

'Spell it out for me, as you would for a simple child,' he said. 'Tell me about Slaanesh!'

The quiet that suddenly filled the room was chilling. Both of the eldar looked like he had slapped them in the face or insulted their mother in the crudest way possible. They had frozen to stillness and seemed to be waiting, as if expecting something terrible to happen.

'That is not a name that you should speak aloud,' said Auric very quietly. 'Or even think in your innermost thoughts until you have learned to shield them.'

Of course, having been told this, Janus found himself unable to think of anything else. *Slaanesh. Slaanesh. Slaanesh.* The refrain ran though his head like some old song dimly remembered just brought to mind. It was not that he wanted to think about it, he was incapable of avoiding doing so. As if in response, he felt something stir deep within his soul.

Like most well travelled men, Janus knew a little about the four great powers of Chaos. Little was known for certain save hints, conjecture and rumour. There were said to be unspeakable cults who worshipped the Dark Gods on many worlds. On Medusa he had heard rumours of the name of Slaanesh in connection with certain secret societies bound over to the pursuit of excess and pleasure. They were said to meet in solitude and secrecy and give themselves up to hedonistic orgies of debauchery, sin and carnality.

He had thought little about them, for he was of the view that what people chose to do in their spare time was up to them as long as it did not interfere with his pursuit of profit and adventure. Indeed, such people had been the source of considerable profit to him, for he had brought home to Medusa many exotic liqueurs, foods, spices and narcotics, and they had provided him with a ready market. It had been through just such an avenue that he had met Justina.

Justina! Now he had it. Eruk had claimed to come from her, and he had mentioned the Lord of Pleasures. Thinking back, he recollected other hints Justina had dropped about such things. He recalled once she had suggested he attend one of her special conclaves, but he had been too involved in some ongoing deal to do so. Was it possible that Justina was a follower of the Dark Gods, that she had attempted to draw him into their web? And was it possible that they had wanted him because they knew what he was?

He pushed the thoughts aside. All of these things were possible, but he was making too many assumptions based on too little information.

'And how may I shield my thoughts? Sadly it is a skill I have neglected to master.'

'You have the dreamstone we gave you?'

Janus shook his head.

'You gave it to a woman, a lover of pleasure.'

'You mean Justina.'

'Her name means nothing to me, but her soul is steeped in evil.'

'Perhaps.'

'We are not here to fence with words, Janus Darke. We are here to see that you do not fail your people or mine.'

'You are the ones who seem to do little else but fence with words.'

Surprisingly, Auric smiled. 'That may be how it seems to you. Such is the manner of our people. We are circumspect and take a long time to get to the point. We lack the bluntness of you short-lived folk.'

'I accept your apology,' said Janus, ignoring Athenys's snort. 'And I will accept any help you can give me.'

Auric rose to his feet. It was a swift, sinuous motion, almost eye-blurring in its quickness. Without seeming to move at all, he was suddenly standing over Janus. Something glittered in his hand. Janus just had time to flinch before something cool was pressed to his forehead. There was a burning sensation and stinging pain. It felt as if a red-hot coal had been pressed to his skin. He tried to pull his head back but found his head locked in place by one of the farseer's coolly delicate hands.

'The discomfort will pass in a moment,' said the eldar.

'Easy for you to say,' muttered Janus. 'You're not the one with his head on fire.'

The eldar muttered something that Janus at first took to be a reply, but then realised was not. The seer was singing something in the lovely liquid tongue of his people, and as he did so the pain in Janus's forehead increased. It felt like the hot coal was eating right through his flesh into his brain. As it did so, flickers of stinging shocking sensation passed through his skull, making him grind his teeth and close his eyes. He was determined not to howl in pain. He was not going to give these xenogen scum the satisfaction, no matter how they tortured him.

As the pain increased, Janus felt himself grow dizzy. Pictures began to form in his mind's eye, pictures of masked eldar faces, and a spacecraft the size of a small continent limned against the gloom of space. He saw long sleek ships flash back and forth in the void, and towering war machines being born in its heart.

He caught flashes of other tales, other songs and other visions. For a moment, he felt himself on the brink of an understanding of things that were beyond his ability to imagine, and then the sensation departed leaving him feeling more tired and drained than ever.

'It is done,' said Auric, and stepped back. The pain had vanished.

Gingerly Janus reached a hand to his forehead, not knowing whether he expected his fingers to encounter melted flesh or a charred hole. Instead they touched something cool and smooth and unyielding, gem-like in its consistency.

'What is it?' he asked. Athenys handed him a small round mirror and he studied his features. Something glowed and pulsed in the middle of his forehead. Its colours shifted from shimmering green to deep blue, to angry red and back. 'What have you done to me?'

'We have given you a dreamstone.'

'You could just have attached it to a pendant,' said Janus sourly.

'Normally that would be our way, but in your case it seemed wisest that it never leave close proximity to you. For maximum effectiveness it should be in contact with naked flesh. We have ensured that is always the case.'

Janus let out a long breath and strove for calm. It was obvious that at very least Auric's claim to be a psyker was true. How else could he have fused this hardened stone to his flesh? The eldar continued to speak, seemingly unaware of the turmoil he had caused.

'We sometimes use this ritual with the very young among us, those likely to throw away a pendant or amulet, or swallow it, or use it as a toy. I apologise for treating you so, but under the circumstances it seemed like the easiest way. Your safety rather than your honour is our paramount concern.'

The eldar's words hardly penetrated Janus's consciousness; he was too busy considering the implications of what they had done. They had marked him with their alien magic, as surely as if they had tattooed the mark of Khorne on his brow. Any inquisitor he ever met would immediately be interested in the unhealthiest way. He was branded in a manner that would be difficult to hide unless he took to wearing a helmet the whole time.

'What is it? What will it do?'

'It is a talisman created in the heart of our world. It is grown from something similar to wraithbone. It is used to shield against the influence of Chaos. It guards the mind while you sleep and are more vulnerable to the subconscious lure of the Great Enemy. It provides protection against mind-altering effects. It should prevent you from becoming a vessel for any thing of the warp that sees you as a potential host, at least for a time.'

'It is a thing of great power then?'

'You should consider yourself greatly honoured. Granting possession of dreamstones is the prerogative of our seers and warlocks. Normally they are granted only to those in whom they show great interest. You have been marked in a way that will let our people know that you are special to us. Should anything happen to Athenys or myself, others of the Old Race will act to shield you, should you encounter them.'

'It's well that they will, for my own folk are likely to tie me to the autorack or purify my body with fire and the scourge when they see it.'

'I suspected as much but it seems the lesser risk at the moment.'

'I would prefer to make such decisions for myself.'

'Alas, you are not qualified to assess the risks involved.'

'That is because you have spent a great deal of time not telling me them.'

'I am not entirely sure of all of them myself. I can speak only in terms of probabilities and paths I have seen. It is not yet certain which path you will take. The future is untrodden as yet, and your way is unclear.'

'You've taken a lot on yourself for someone who sees only the vaguest of things.'

'I am a farseer, Janus Darke. It is my burden to do such things, for in doing so there is a chance I will shield my people from great doom. A doom that it may be your fate to be bearer of.'

A sudden thought struck Janus. It was not one that he liked to voice but the words seemed to emerge from his lips of their own accord. 'Then why not simply kill me and have done with it?'

'Do not think I have not considered it, Janus Darke, but I have my reasons for not doing so – yet.'

'And what might they be?'

'While you live, I live. While I live, you live. Neither of us will survive this journey without the other.'

'Well, praise be to the Emperor in all his mercy. My life is spared for a little while longer.'

Athenys laughed. It was a savage sound with no mirth in it. 'Do not be so certain that it will always be so. Your death may yet be the only option left open to us.'

She rose to leave.

TWELVE
THE PERILS OF THE WARP

SIMON BELISARIUS CAREFULLY unrolled the ancient parchment, smoothed the cracking vellum flat on the tabletop and placed a paperweight at each corner. Charts and starmaps already covered the desk and table of his large cabin. Like all Navigators he was in possession of hard copies of all the necessary astro-cartography. After all, you could never tell when the ancient machine spirits might become temperamental and turn against you, or when a datacore might fail.

Simon had been trained to bring his ship home even if every navigational system on it failed, and the charts were normally just one extra way of ensuring this. But this map was special. It was his pride and joy, albeit a very dangerous one.

The musty smell of the thing told how old it was. It had probably been copied and recopied since the founding of the Imperium, and probably in secret too, for this was one of those documents the Inquisition would burn a man for possessing.

Simon had always liked being party to forbidden secrets, providing they were not too forbidden, and he had always been fascinated by the relics of ancient days. And this map was something special – a chart of warp currents through the Cadian Gate running into the Eye of Terror. He might not even have recognised it for what it was when he came across it in the antiquarians had he not spent every spare moment in the libraries of Belisarius when he was younger.

He gave a wry shake of his head thinking about the pleasure he had got from that. He had not possessed much spare time for rummaging about during his childhood and youth. From the age of three years old he had spent a minimum of twelve waking hours in training. First it had been exercises to discipline his body and mind – seven years of it. Next came seven years of higher learning – history, astronomy, various advanced mental disciplines and martial arts, all designed to strengthen his mind, his soul and his body for the rigours of his career. Then came the final seven years of studying the actual discipline of warp navigation, the ones that many did not even survive, let alone pass through. He did not want to think about those.

Instead he breathed deep of the stale scent of the scroll, and used the mnemonic recall techniques he had learned as a youth. Immediately he was back in the great library of Belisarius. He could picture the great painted ceiling one hundred metres overhead, the fresco showing the Emperor granting his charter to Mikael Belisarius, while his primarchs grinned down and all his defeated enemies gnashed their teeth in the background. In his mind's eye, Simon could visualise the massive cabinets of books, piled on top of each other so high that the ancient ancestral librarians needed ladders ten times their own height to reach the top volumes. He could almost touch the endless rows of leather-bound librams, and stick his fingers into the countless alcoves containing scrolls and star charts and aide memoires. He could remember the nooks and crannies, each with their tables of carved wood inlaid with leviathan ivory, where he had done his reading by the soft buttery light of a hovering glow-globe until the chimes of the monstrous clock tower in the west wing of the palace had told him it was time for sleep.

Once one of the librarians had told him that there were over a billion volumes in the library, a copy of almost every book released since the foundation of the Imperium and of millions of tomes printed or copied in the Dark Age that had preceded it. He had been told there were books in tongues no longer spoken, written in the glyphs of extinct races. He had been told that a copy of the logbook of every Navigator of House Belisarius that had ever been recovered was there too, along with all of those rutters captured or acquired by stealth from other Houses. He was not sure now that there really had been a billion books, but even if the librarian had been wrong there had been too many to catalogue or index. So much knowledge, he thought, gathered since the dawn of human civilisation. Who knows what secrets we might find there, if only we knew where to look?

Such remembrance and speculation were getting him nowhere he realised and ended the exercise, bringing himself firmly back to the present. He needed to get to work. He studied the chart laid out before him. To anybody but another Navigator it would simply have looked like an abstract geometric swirl of lines, curves, circles and arcs all linking a myriad of coloured dots and marked with hieroglyphs and runes.

To the trained eye, it was a complex mnemonic pattern that showed the principle flow lines of the immaterium in and around the Cadian Gate. Its near twin, a chart displaying the local area, lay on the other table. On both, hazards and vortices were marked, and the various colours of line and surrounding inked backgrounds gave some clues as to the flow and texture of the immaterium.

Judging by the small scribe mark in the corner the information was several centuries out of date, but that did not matter too much. Currents and channels would have shifted but a little over that period unless marred by the most violent of warp storms. These things changed, but slowly, over millennia. Forces at play in the immaterium might temporarily obscure the channels but their essence would remain. If he could find an opening, he could use these routes.

He checked the chart of the Medusa system. It showed the fabric of space-time there had its flaws, as had every system. There were always points where it was easier to enter the immaterium and, more relevantly to his current problems, there were always approach vectors that made it easier to jump in certain directions.

Like any other great starship the *Star of Venam* was capable of punching a hole in the fabric of space-time and entering the warp from any place outside the deep gravity well of a planet. But such a brute force method required enormous amounts of energy and placed colossal strain on the ship's generators and power cores, and given how far they had to go, and how dangerous the journey was likely to be, Simon wanted to take no chances. Every small fraction of a decimal point he shifted the odds of success in their favour, the greater the probability of a safe return would be.

The Cadian Gate was the most difficult passage in the history of Navigation, a route fraught with peril and horror, the main pathway that the fleets of Chaos used to enter the Imperium. Like most people, under normal circumstances, Simon considered the sheer difficulty of the way a blessing, for it shielded the realms of mankind from their deadliest enemies better than a hundred battle fleets. Now the problem was reversed he did not find it quite such an attractive feature.

I wonder if the Chaos worshippers have Navigators, he wondered briefly? There was no record of it, but that did not mean it was not so. In a lifetime of travelling the galaxy Simon had come across many strange things, and seen that many of the most cherished beliefs of his people were not necessarily always true under every circumstance.

There were Navigator Houses that had been expunged from the Imperial records but not from those of the Navis Nobilitae. Some of them had disappeared during the time of the Horus Heresy. It was possible they had gone over to the other side. These were dangerous thoughts, perilously close to heresy, so he dismissed them and returned to the task at hand.

He studied the chart of Medusa again, looking for the points where a jump off into the Eye of Terror would be easiest. That would take them closest to the entrance to the Cadian Vector, the great current of timeflow that swept in and out of the Cadian Gate, through gaps in the warp storms. If they timed things just right, if the current swept them in the proper direction, and if Simon managed the insertion of the vessel into the immaterium at exactly the correct time and place then timed their exit to perfection, there would be a chance of getting through. He did not want to think about the dangers of the return journey. The first priority was to get them to where the eldar wanted to go.

He checked his rutters for more information about Medusa. Inscribed in the complex rune-mathematical notation of his House, they contained what he had divined of the currents between the systems, the vector and intensity of the Astronomican at approved temporal intervals and the hazards to be avoided. If they survived the trip he would make similar notations about Belial. A second voyage was usually easier than a first because you had some idea of the hazards that lay in wait. Of course, this information would also be damning evidence of heresy as far as the Inquisition was concerned. He forced himself back from that line of thought to contemplate the relatively safe jump from Medusa.

Simon laughed softly. He was dangerously close to what Karadoc had once called one of the Seven Great Errors of Navigation. He could almost hear the old man's dry, rustling voice whispering: never, ever assume that a voyage will be safe, boy. You can be approaching an entrance point you have used a thousand times, and a warp storm might arise. Or a temporal vortex might spring up. Or the daemons of the warp, for their own unguessable reasons, might suddenly decide that your ship looks like a tasty morsel. There's no way to tell what might happen, even on the most routine of trips. You must be constantly alert and aware. To be otherwise is to court destruction, for you and your ship.

But then I am already doing that, thought Simon, wondering what his old tutor would have thought of this mad trip. He would have told me not to question my oaths and to see my ship safely home, he answered himself.

In his mind he pictured the chart of the Medusa system and its exit points, and one last time began the unimaginably complex calculations needed to throw the ship through the immaterium between them.

He was torn between two routes. His current choice took point alpha null twelve, and rotated the ship thirty degrees to the galactic plane twelve pulses of the Astronomican after insertion, so that they should catch the main current. Alternatively, insertion at omega delta five with a twenty-nine point two rotation would achieve the same thing but with a possible great decrease in time of transit. The system chart showed turbulence at the entry point there though, and a permanent vortex that you could fall into if you were not careful. Still, the turbulence could be used to give the ship more velocity if caught just right.

It was the sort of showy manoeuvre that would have appealed to Simon under normal circumstances but right now he decided that it would be better to err on the side of caution. He would avoid temptation and stick with his original plan.

He touched one of the control runes on his view screen and called up the ship's present course. Perfect. The ship would reach the jump point within twelve hours on its present course. The time saved by using an easier breakthrough point would more than make up for the extra time spent in real space. There seemed little to do but rest now, for he would have little enough time to do so once they entered the immaterium.

Another shiver of excitement passed through him. Despite the number of jumps he had made, they never ceased to thrill him. Soon he would have a command deck beneath his feet and his pineal eye would gaze out on the warp. The life of his ship and everybody in it would rest in his own hands. He would be the sole master of his destiny. It would be down to his skill whether the ship made it to port or foundered with all hands. Perhaps only warriors on a battlefield could feel a similar excitement, as they faced the turbulence of war. There was no feeling to quite compare with it, and the prospect filled him with excitement even as it also filled him with dread.

A KNOCK ON the door of his chamber roused Simon from a doze. Absent mindedly he checked his chronometer. It was not yet time for the helmsman to rouse him. There were still several hours to go before they reached the insertion point. What could be going on?

Like all good Navigators, he had a basic feel for any ship he was on. He sensed nothing different around him. The vibration of the floor had not altered, nor had the basic sounds of the vessel. The air moved at the same rate through the ducts. No alarm bells were sounding. No warning lights flashed. This could hardly be an emergency. What could it be?

He pulled on his tunic and boots and stalked over to the door. As always, from force of habit, he had set the doorseal so that it could not be opened from outside. 'Who is it?'

'I wish to speak with you, human,' said a faintly familiar voice. Even through the duralloy Simon could tell it was an alien. He slammed the door-release rune with his palm. It whooshed open to reveal the female eldar.

'Yes,' said Simon. 'What do you want?'

'I wish to talk to you about the voyage we are about to make. There may be trouble.'

'So you're expecting enemies to show up?'

'Perhaps.'

'Would you care to tell me who?'

'Auric tells me that there is a vanishingly small possibility that other eldar might try to intercept us.'

'He's not showing his usual certainty there then.'

'Auric is certain of nothing. He deals in probabilities, nothing more.'

'You're putting me to a lot of trouble and risking a lot of men's lives on his probabilities.'

'Yes. Auric judges it worth the risk. I concur.'

'Who might try and intercept us?'

'Corsairs.'

'Eldar pirates?'

'There are no eldar pirates.'

'I have fought many vessels who did a good impersonation of it then.'

'Those were not true eldar. They were our decadent kin.'

Simon had heard that the eldar might be divided into two or more factions but this was the first time the information had ever come directly from one of them. He made a mental note for the sake of his log. 'Their boarding parties looked like eldar to me.'

'They share our blood, but nothing more. They fell into darkness long ago.'

'Tell me more.'

'That is not the reason I came here.'

'What do you want?'

'Tell me about the procedures you use to make a warp jump.'

'Surely you must have made one before?'

'Imagine I have not.'

'You must have made one to get to Medusa. It is not exactly an eldar home world.'

'We did not.'

'You're telling me that there is a secret colony of eldar there that the Imperium knows nothing about?' Simon let his disbelief show in his voice. Did this alien madwoman seriously expect him to believe she had not used a ship to reach Medusa?

'I am telling you nothing. You will tell me about the warp jump.'

'I will tell you everything I am bound by oath not to reveal.'

'That will be sufficient.'

'I will tell you providing you tell me why you want to know.'

'It is not something of which I wish to speak.'

'Tell me anyway.'

'Or what?'

'Or I will reconsider my decision to tell you about our trip. I am bound by my House's promise to take you where you want to go. It says nothing about talking to you on the way.'

At first Simon thought the eldar woman was angry, her eyes widened and a strange mewling sound like a cat might make came from her mouth. After a few seconds he realised she was laughing.

'Very well. It seems I must share something with you. I wish to know because I have never made such a jump before and it makes me nervous.'

It suddenly struck Simon that the prospect of the jump made her more than nervous. If she had been a human, he realised, he would have thought her terrified. Why?

Why not? Many people were. Ships got lost in space and time and never returned. Many and varied were the perils of the warp, and the Navigator Houses did not share all of them with their potential clients. Their secrecy did nothing to dispel those fears. And if truth be told, the fears were more than justified. Simon knew what was out there, and there were times when it terrified even him. The risk was more than just to a man's body when he passed through the immaterium. There was a very real risk to the soul also.

'You are very quiet,' said the eldar woman.

'I am considering where to begin.'

'More likely considering what you think you can get away with telling me.'

'I would never have guessed you such a good judge of character. Would that I were such a good judge of yours.'

Athenys laughed again. This time she even smiled. Simon might have warmed to her a little but he was suspicious of her now. He suspected some subtle manipulation or probing. She seemed to be able to read this from his face, for her smile vanished as if a switch had been thrown. 'I suspect that you are a better judge than you might imagine.'

Simon shrugged. 'Think of our ship as a vessel which sails on two seas. It passes through normal space, where we are currently, and it can enter the immaterium.'

'The immaterium?'

'The warp, the empyrean, whatever you want to call it. It is a dimension outside our reality, a place more or less of pure energy, where space and time as we understand them no longer exist.'

'Such things are known to us.'

'Then you understand that being able to enter this place has its uses. By passing outside our own space we can ride the currents of the warp and re-enter our own space light years distant.'

'Yes. Such things were known in the infancy of my people.'

Simon felt a flicker of annoyance. The eldar seemed so distant and superior. Still, just the way she spoke was giving him valuable insights. He decided to push on, and note down what she said in his rutter. After all, it would not hurt for humanity to understand this ancient race a little better. At least he hoped not.

'Then you understand why my people make use of it. Why do yours not?'

'There are dangers...'

'Yes. There are always dangers. The warp is a place where normal senses do not work, the sight of which can drive men mad. Finding a path through it is not easy.'

'The sight of it has not driven you mad?'

'That is because my people are different from the normal run of humanity. Over millennia we have adapted to the warp. My pineal eye can gaze upon the immaterium and comprehend it. My brain has been altered so that I can make sense of what I see.'

'Has been altered?'

Simon flinched. With unerring accuracy she had put her finger on one of the sore spots of the Navis Nobilitae. 'Perhaps we evolved to be what we are. Perhaps in the dim, distant past we were changed to enable us to perform our functions, in the same way it is said, that the Emperor altered the primarchs.'

Simon knew that what he was saying was very close to what the Inquisition would call heresy. Nonetheless, it was common enough talk in the sealed Houses of the Navigators.

'I thought your Houses predated the appearance of the Emperor and his primarchs. So at least my people say.'

'Perhaps – the origins of our guilds are lost in the mists of time. We only know that in the early days, men used many means to navigate the warp. Drugs, psychic powers, machines, all were tried with varying degrees of success.'

'And varying degrees of failure.' Once more that mocking smile appeared on her lips.

'Such is implicit in having any degree of success less than perfection.'

'And your people represent the best attempts of mankind to master the dangers of the warp.' The level of mockery had deepened. Do they really feel such contempt for us, Simon wondered? Are we really just brutish barbarians to them?

'We have been successful in our task for more than ten thousand years.'

'That you have performed such a function so long is not to be denied. But how many of your ships have been lost? How many never return? How many are taken by those who wait beyond?'

Another reason for her attitude suddenly became clear to Simon. She was terrified and covering it with this display of subtle aggression. He sensed an opening, decided to probe.

'If you know of a better way, why then do you not take it?'

'There is no other way, let alone a better way.'

'Why not? If your starships are so much superior to ours why not have one of them take you?'

'It is not that simple. Our starships cannot go to some of the places where yours can.'

'That sounds unlikely. Surely such a superior race could build void screens and warp shields just as good as ours, if not better. Surely a people so ancient must have mastered the secrets of astrogation better than our poor intellects ever could.'

'There is no need to sneer. We travelled between the stars while your people were still swinging from trees.'

'Then it seems improbable to me that such an advanced race could need our help for anything,' said Simon, making his tone as cold as he could. 'Unless of course you are criminals and your people will not help you.'

'It is not that. We do not use the warp as you call it because there are things in the warp that hunger for us. Our word for what you call the warp is *sha'eil*. Translated literally it means place of daemons – hell.'

Simon closed his mouth with a snap. He was not surprised that she knew this but it still felt wrong to him that anybody outside the Navis Nobilitae and the select few of the upper echelons of the Imperium should understand that. There were entities that lurked in the warp, malign entities, daemons for want of a better name, and they had caused the destruction of many a ship.

'They hunger for everybody,' he said.

She shook her head very slowly and then glanced at him directly. Her expression told him that he had missed something or did not understand something nearly as well as he thought he did.

'They hunger for us in particular.'

'You and Auric in particular, or the eldar people?'

'Both. You see there is something about us that attracts them, which drives them insane with lust to devour us. That is why we are taking a terrible risk travelling with you.'

'Then you are putting all of us at terrible risk. The entities of the warp can swallow an entire starship at a gulp. And there are worse things – if they should break through our screens...'

Simon shivered. He was all too familiar with the tales of ghost ships, whose crews had fallen prey to a daemon of the warp, who were stalked through their ships by the possessed corpses of their friends and killed in the most unspeakable ways until only a few gibbering, insane survivors were left to die shrieking when their craft emerged from the immaterium.

He knew that no matter how potent the shields of his vessel, and how thick its armoured hull, there was always the chance of a breach, and, if that should happen, a dreadful death. Anything that increased the number of attempts to penetrate the hull, and therefore increased the chance of disaster, was to be avoided. Suddenly, he thought of all those ships that had responded to the ancient golden argosies that had never returned. Was it possible he was close to divining the reason?

'What you are telling me is not good,' he said eventually.

'We want you to be aware of what might happen. Auric would do his best to shield you, but there is always the chance that his attempts might backfire.'

'You can thank Auric for me. Tell him I will do my best to save you from the daemons that might come for you.'

She rose to go in one smooth sinuous movement. When she turned in the doorway and gave him a sinister smile, he knew that she had saved the worst for last.

'It is not just for us they will come,' she said. 'It is for your friend, Janus Darke.'

THIRTEEN
CONCERNING DAEMON PRINCES

ANGRILY, JANUS DARKE smashed his palm into the override on the door and strode into the eldar's suite. Rage filled him, but even so he had enough self-control left to wait until the door slid shut before he started to bellow. He hoped he would find Athenys, but she was not there, so he took his anger out on the eldar who was present.

'Just what the hell do you think you are up to?'

Auric looked up mildly. His eyes had a slightly glazed quality that suggested the contents of the hookah he smoked were more than mildly narcotic.

'What do you mean, Janus Darke?'

'I mean, it's not bad enough that you have to weld this blasted gemstone to my forehead so that all my crew look at me like I am a pox-ridden shore boy. Now you have to go and tell my bloody Navigator that I am an Emperor-accursed sorcerer.'

Auric made a pacifying gesture with his left hand, and took another puff at the hookah. Smoke bubbled slowly out from between his lips.

After a moment, he spoke, 'I told Simon Belisarius no such thing.'

'No, but your bloody girlfriend did!'

'Athenys is not my lover, Janus Darke.'

'I don't care if she is your hell-accursed doxie – she had no right to go telling him that!'

'Be calm. Are you sure that she told him that?'

'Simon says she told him my soul was in peril from the creatures of the warp. Just the thing to be telling him a few hours before a warp jump.'

'And you take that to mean that she told him you are a psyker?'

'No. She told him I am Alderanian bloody cat dancer! Of course, I take it to mean that. What else could it mean?'

'She told him your soul is in peril. It is nothing less than the truth.'

Janus shut his mouth. He realised that his anger came from the fact that Athenys had told Simon his secret. He had half expected the Navigator to turn the ship around there and then and take him back to the Inquisition. Hell, he might be doing that right now. Janus had not waited to learn what else she might have said. As soon as Simon had told him the part about souls and peril, he had stalked from the room and come right here.

A lot of his anger came from his guilt about keeping secrets from his crew and leading them into unknown dangers. Still more of it was coming from the strain of learning so recently what he had become. More of it came from his memories of what had happened in the meat-packing plant on Medusa. What if he lost control now and did that here? He might slaughter everybody on board. The farseer raised an eyebrow; he seemed to be reading Janus's mind.

'She had no right to do that,' Janus said weakly.

'Perhaps. Perhaps not. Perhaps it is better for your Navigator to know some of the perils that await him. He must be prepared for what might happen.'

'And what exactly might that be?'

'This ship is about to travel through what you humans call the immaterium, and which we eldar call sha'eil.'

'So?'

'It is more truthful to say we call it hell.'

'What do you mean?'

'Things live in the immaterium, Janus Darke. Frightful things. Things you could not, in your wildest nightmares, imagine.'

'I have some pretty bad nightmares,' said Janus in an attempt at humour. Once again the eldar seemed to have turned the tables on him. He felt his anger begin to dispel to be replaced by a feeling of nameless dread.

'I imagine you do. But nonetheless, your worst fears are but pleasant daydreams compared to what lurks in sha'eil.'

'More vague warnings.'

'No – a very concrete and explicit warning. Whatever you do, whatever you see, whatever happens, however you feel – once this ship enters the Beyond, you must not for any reason tap the powers you possess.'

'Why?'

'Because if you do, it will be like lighting a beacon for whatever awaits us. It will be like throwing blood into a sea full of sharks. There are things out there in sha'eil to whom your soul would be a feast, and to whom your use of power would simply be a signal to come and feed.

'Moreover there are things that hunt for you. They might find you if you give them a sign.'

Thinking back to what happened on Medusa, Janus sensed that Auric was telling him nothing less than the truth. 'I think whatever it is you fear has already found me.'

'No!' The vehemence of the eldar's response surprised Janus. 'That is not true. When you used your powers to kill those men, the evil you sensed came from within you. The evil that waits cannot take you without your consent – not yet, and not here anyway. What happens when we enter what you call the warp is a different thing.'

'What do you mean?'

'I mean if you draw on those powers of yours in any way, you will set off a flare that will attract the attention of daemons. You will invite them to a banquet, the main course of which will be your soul.

'More to the point, knowing that there is such a tasty morsel here they will stop at nothing to get at it. The primitive shields on this ship are most likely sufficient to keep the denizens of the other world at bay under normal circumstances, but these would not be normal circumstances. They would gather together and unite in their power until they could crack this ship like a man would crack open an egg.'

'You are not telling me everything.'

'Good – you are already becoming more acute.'

'What is it you are hiding? Why did Athenys tell Simon what she did? Would it not have been simpler just to warn me? What sort of game is it you are playing?'

'I am playing no games. What Athenys does is for the most part her business.'

Janus looked at the farseer and felt his head spin. He was still weak from the after-effects of his actions on Medusa and the fumes from the hookah were fuddling his mind. He slumped down on a cushion near the eldar and tried to guess what was going on behind that blandly inscrutable alien mask.

What Auric had just said suggested that he and Athenys might be working at cross-purposes. No, that was an assumption he was making. He was claiming that he had nothing to do with this business with Simon. Of course, he might be lying. Janus shook his head.

Dealing with the eldar was starting to feel like walking through a peat-swamp back on Crowe's World. Ground that looked as if it would be stable under your feet, turned out to have the consistency of jelly; paths you thought you knew shifted in the slow swirl of currents. Briefly, he considered ordering his crew simply to execute them, and push their bodies out the airlock. Perhaps that would be safest.

And yet, maybe not, for the farseer did seem to know something about what was happening to him, and might be able to save him from his daemons. No, not a swamp, he thought, a devil-spider web, one of those cocoons that look as soft as silk yet grow tighter as the prey struggles to escape.

Memory reminded him of how beautiful the devil-spider was too. Eyes like jewels, chitin patterned like a hallucinogenic flower. Mandibles that dripped a venom that caused ecstatic death.

'You are thinking of spiders,' said Auric and smiled. 'Spiders and childhood.'

'Can you read my mind then?'

'Only because you broadcast your thoughts so strongly they are almost deafening. You must learn control, Janus Darke, and you do not have much time.'

Once again Janus sensed deception. There was something Auric was not telling him, but he could not work out what. He also realised that earlier the eldar had managed to distract him from what he had wanted to find out. He must be more tired than he thought, or somehow they had fuddled his thoughts.

Determination filled him. This time he would not be put off.

'Will you teach me how in the time we have left before the jump?' Janus asked.

'That is not possible. However, I have medicines that will… dampen your power.'

'Why are you so interested in what happens to me?'

'You mean other than to preserve my own life?'

'Yes.'

'You would not be happy if I told you.'

'Try me!'

'You possess a very great power, Janus Darke, the like of which is manifested in your species perhaps once in a thousand years. That alone makes you a prize worth having for many creatures of the Old Night.'

'A prize?'

'Beings of power are always useful to the creatures of sha'eil. They are a link between the two realms, the realm of mortals and the realm of Chaos.'

'You are saying psykers somehow stand between these two planes of reality–'

'I am saying that they draw their power from it, and not just power. They can draw other things too.'

'Like daemons?'

'Yes. Your Inquisition is not so wrong with its tales of daemonic possession. Daemons can reach through and influence the thoughts and minds of unguarded psykers–'

'The voices,' snapped Janus.

'I fail to understand you, Janus Darke.'

'Sometimes...' Janus was suddenly embarrassed and ashamed. 'Sometimes I hear voices in my head, whispering, telling me to do things, bad things...'

'Go on.'

'The priests say this is a sure sign of possession.'

'They are close. Sometimes humans think they hear voices when sometimes it is only their own repressed desires seeking to get out. And sometimes–'

'Sometimes they really do hear voices, right?'

'Yes. That is how it always begins.'

'What begins?'

'The process of possession. Then they are seduced into using their power more and more, strengthening the link between their souls and the warp, and then when the link is strong enough, they are devoured.'

'What exactly do you mean by that?'

'The thing that wants them can reach through the link and consume their soul. It is worse than that though for they then have an empty shell of a body and a mind which is capable of being a vessel for a power.'

'Possession.'

'Precisely, Janus Darke.'

'You are saying that this will happen to me?'

'It may happen to you. I fear though that–'

'You are telling me there is something worse!'

'Unfortunately, yes. Normally a human body is not strong enough to hold the essence of even the least of daemons for long. Even with the darkest and most potent rituals of sorcery, the stress ages it and consumes it very swiftly. The body grows older at an accelerated rate, mutation occurs, stigmata appear.'

'I have heard of such things.'

'Such would not be the case with you.'

'Why?'

'Because you are so powerful. Your body is a vessel fit for a daemon prince. It could hold his essence for a very long time without showing any sign. A daemon could wear your flesh and walk among men and do untold harm.'

'Why is this of concern to the eldar?'

'It is not. At least not yet. It is of concern to me.'

'Again I ask why?'

'Because I know the name of the thing that wants your flesh and your soul. And he is concerned with the eldar.'

Janus felt numb. It seemed inconceivable that he should be sitting here discussing such things as daemonic possession and the nature of daemon princes so calmly, but there was something about Auric and the drug-fume filled air, and the quiet musical sound of chimes in the background that made it seem very natural. Slowly, realisation dawned. Perhaps there was some sort of spell at work here? Perhaps the eldar was using some sort of psychic sorcery of his own.

He made an effort to rise, but somehow it was too difficult and the eldar's soft beautiful hypnotic voice continued to speak: 'The greatest of daemons are bound by strange laws. They can manifest themselves only at certain times and in certain places. But for the one of whom I speak such a time is close, and you are to be his chosen vessel.'

'Surely there must be others?'

'Oh yes, many others, but such a form as yours so perfectly adapted to his purposes, so blessed with the ability to wield power would be his first choice.'

'So you have taken me under your protection then,' said Janus ironically. 'You have spirited me away from his clutches.'

'I doubt that I or anybody else would be able to protect you from Shaha Gaathon. Not without a far more potent weapon than I now possess.'

'But even if he does not possess me, there will be a daemon prince walking the realms of men in mortal form.'

'Perhaps – but his power is limited unless he can find a sufficiently powerful vessel. He will only be able to leave the daemon worlds for short periods, as indeed he can even now. But if he wears your flesh, he will become terrible. The harm he will wreak will be incalculable. The destruction beyond comprehension.'

'Forgive me for saying so but dreadful as this would be for mankind, how would it affect your people? I don't think you are helping me out of altruism.'

'Shaha Gaathon is one of the greatest of the servants of He Who We Do Not Name. He existed before the Great Enemy came. Since before the birth of his master he has a terrible hatred for the eldar, and, I believe, he wishes to use your people as a weapon against mine.

'There are futures waiting to be born in which the followers of the Emperor will turn on my people and destroy them utterly. There are timelines in which the eldar respond with our forbidden and ultimate weapons and both races are so dramatically weakened that Chaos overwhelms them.

'Your people are numberless as the grains of sand upon a beach. It does not matter how powerful our weapons are, you will eventually overwhelm us, for the Harbinger of the Lord of all Pleasures knows the location of all our hidden home-vessels.'

'Why do Shaha Gaathon and his master, the Unspeakable One, hate you so?'

'There is an ancient link between my people and the Unspeakable One. We do not often talk about it, but since it is necessary, I will tell you that the Unspeakable One is our own creation. He was born from our lusts and our passions, shaped by our ancestors' use of what you would call psyker powers and technologies.'

'You are saying your people created the daemon gods of Chaos?'

'One of them.'

'That is not possible.'

'It is if you sacrifice an entire race.'

Janus considered what the eldar was saying. He simply did not believe it. It was pure madness, the drug-dream of an insane sorcerer. Seeing his bewildered expression, Auric smiled. 'It was a horror on a cosmic scale.'

'Who did you sacrifice?'

'Ourselves.'

'I do not follow what you mean.'

'Yes, you do. I mean my people willingly gave themselves over to the evil one.'

'Then you are everything the Inquisition say, and worse.'

Auric shook his head. 'I believe my people were deceived, just as yours might be. They thought they were creating a new god, one who would lead them into a new age of universal peace, plenty and harmony.'

'You believe–'

'I do not know for certain. No one can now. So much was lost when our civilisation fell, when our worlds were despoiled, and our souls devoured.'

'Devoured? You are saying that Sla… the evil one devoured your people, the way Shaha Gaathon proposes to devour me?'

'In a similar way.' Auric reached within his robe and produced a glowing gem on a chain of silver metal. Strange runes glowed on it. It appeared to be glow with all colours and none. 'This is a waystone. Every eldar carries one. It is grown from the same stuff as dreamstones. And for a similar reason.'

'I am sure you are going to tell me why.'

'It is a haven for my soul. When I die, my spirit will take refuge within it, and the stone will be returned to my craftworld for inclusion within the infinity circuit where it will join the surviving spirits of my ancestors.'

Janus considered this piece of pagan eldar theology. He supposed it made sense. He doubted the souls of the xenogens would be in the keeping of the Emperor as humans' souls were. It was a strange idea though.

'Why do you need to imprison your soul within a machine?'

'It is not a machine as you understand it, but that is beside the point. If I were to die and my spirit was to walk the paths of sha'eil, as our ancestors did in ancient times, it would be devoured by He Who We Do Not Name, and as he consumed it, the evil one would become that fraction stronger, just as he did in days long gone.'

'Why does this not happen to humans?'

'How do you know it does not?'

'The Emperor protects us.'

'You have answered your own question then,' said Auric nastily. 'Or perhaps once the eldar fall, Shaha Gaathon will lead your people into an age of darkness from which they never emerge. Puny as most human souls are, they will provide the evil one with some nourishment.'

'It has been tried before. Other Chaos worshippers have arisen. Daemons have been vanquished. The forces of the Imperium have triumphed.'

'The worshippers of the Lord of Pleasure are subtle. They will not face you in open battle, and you will discover that pleasure can be as mighty a weapon as the bolter or the blade. If they were too subtle for the eldar, they will surely be too subtle for you.'

'You are being too subtle for me,' Darke said.

'Already the agents of the Unspeakable One are abroad among your people. Their weapons are corruption and the easy path. They peddle drugs to your youth that make them vulnerable to the psychic influence of daemons. They lure them from the path of virtue into indolence and vice. They tempt your leaders with promises of pleasure. They wield more power than you can guess.'

'You seem unnaturally well-informed for one who does not dwell among humanity,' said Janus sarcastically.

'I but echo the words of some of your inquisitors who are far closer to the truth than ever they would guess.'

'Perhaps you should be telling them this, not me.'

'Now you are being wilfully foolish, Janus Darke. You know that your Inquisition would never listen to one such as I. They are more likely to believe me a follower of the Unspeakable One than a foe.'

'You still have not told me why we are going to Belial.'

'I am hoping to acquire a weapon there that I can use against Shaha Gaathon. A weapon created in ancient times to slay beings of such power.'

'Hoping? You are not showing your usual certainty, Auric.'

'You can be an unpleasant man, Janus Darke.'

'You're not the first to tell me that.'

'My gifts are not as infallible as you or many of my own people seem to believe. I see possibilities only. There are billions of untold billions of probability paths that lead just from this day. The futures they birth are myriad and uncertain until the day they become fixed and concrete, a process of alchemy as subtle and complex as any magic spell. I am granted glimpses of what might be, or what may come to pass. Sometimes the things I see are warnings, sometimes near certainties unless actions are taken.'

'So you can try and shape the future.'

'That is the nub of it, Janus Darke. I can try and shape the future. But I am not the only one who can do this. There are many others also trying to see that their visions come to pass and many of them are far stronger than I.'

'Other farseers?'

'Yes, among others. Not the least being our enemies.'

'Why would other farseers try to prevent you from succeeding?' asked Janus, unwilling to give up the point now that he sensed some weakness in the eldar's otherwise impervious façade.

'Because the future, and our vision of it, is conditional, and subject to manifold interpretations. Some claim that my actions may bring about that which I strive to prevent. Some even claim that I may inadvertently be a tool of the Darkness.'

'Could they be right?'

'In all predictions, there is a margin for error, Janus Darke, and it is a foolish prophet who does not realise as much. There is indeed a possibility that it is so.'

'So even now you could be leading us to our doom?'

'That may yet be.'

'What is this weapon you seek? What can it do?' Even as Janus asked the question the alarm klaxon sounded. Simon must be preparing to make the warp jump to Belial.

'Quickly, Janus Darke, you must drink this elixir and I must ring you with spells, or you will not survive.'

Such was the urgency of the eldar's words that Janus obeyed.

The liquid in the flask was sweeter than honey, and as he drank it, numbness stole through his muscles, and darkness crept into his brain.

FOURTEEN
INTO SHA'IEL

NERVOUSLY, SIMON BELISARIUS strapped himself in to the Navigator's throne. He passed the leather harness across his chest and made sure it was tightly attached to the cast iron restraining hoops on the stone of the chair. Many a Navigator had acquired crippling injuries when thrashing around in the immaterium, and he did not intend to join them. He tried not to think about what Athenys had told him. By the Emperor, jumping into the Eye of Terror would be difficult enough, if they were to be prey to daemons…

Don't think about it, he told himself. Concentrate on the task at hand. Take things one step at a time.

He attached the pressure pads to his forehead and felt a tingle as he made contact with the central nervous system of the ship. He ignored it for the moment, knowing the time would soon be near when he would have to concentrate and interface with it fully.

He glanced backwards and upwards to the vast spider-web of brass and copper and ceramic that would link him to the ship. He touched an embossed rune on the armrest and it dropped into place. Coolness squirted across his skin as analgesic sprays prepared him for what was to come. Despite having done this a thousand times, involuntarily he flinched. Snakes of cable, needle-tipped, crawled across his flesh and attached themselves to veins and glands. He closed his eyes and tried to relax as they bit into his flesh.

Where were the eldar now? The thought slipped into his mind stealthily. He dismissed it. They must be in their cabin, along with Janus Darke. Why would daemons come for the rogue trader? They were only supposed to be interested in the lost and the damned, in psykers. Could she have meant that? Was it possible? Certainly according to Imperial doctrine it was. You had to be constantly on guard against sin, for the slightest thought could lead you down into the paths of darkness. But surely not Janus. He did not believe it. To keep the dark thoughts from his mind, he concentrated on what was happening around him. Supervising the familiar procedures gave him some reassurance in a world that seemed to be going swiftly mad.

First came the saline drips that would keep him from dehydrating if the trip should prove to be a long one. Next came the nutrient fluids to keep him from wasting away. Then came the other ones, the ones to prepare his mind and body for the task at hand.

Warmth flowed through his veins and brought with it a sense of well-being. Simon was skilled enough at his job that he did not need the aid of drugs to enter temporal meditation, but you could never tell what accidents might arise to snap you out of it; sometimes artificial aids were needed. Now his skin tingled as various potent psychotropic agents were added to the mix, heightening some of his senses nearly unbearably while others were turned off. His tongue and lips went numb. His sense of his own body receded. Now he felt like he was in control of a flesh puppet, tugging its strings from a very long way away and watching it respond to his commands.

Information from his other senses became strangely garbled. He felt, rather than heard, some of the murmured conversations on the command deck. When he looked down on the crew, they seemed at once very distant and very close, flickering from one to the other almost in time with his heartbeat. It was not that their positions changed or even that the appearance of their positions changed, it was merely that his perceptions of their positions did. The drugs had started playing their tricks on him, shaking his senses loose from their mortal framework of preconceptions, preparing him for what waited in the immaterium.

His heartbeat thundered within his chest. His breath roared like a hurricane through his mouth and nostrils. He swallowed and forced himself to nod to the crew. They responded at once and the preparations for the jump began. All over the ship, warp-shutters slammed into place, blocking all views of what was to come. Klaxons wailed to warn the inmates to prepare themselves for what was to come.

Tension mounted. No one was ever sure what might happen when a ship entered the immaterium. No one could ever be certain that he would emerge again, or emerge unchanged. Terrible things happened in the other space, in that realm where the normal rules that governed the cosmos did not apply.

Simon's distant fingers stabbed at the control runes once more, and the Navigator's chair and the platform on which it rested rose smoothly upwards into the dome, that small ultra-hard sphere of translucent crystal that was the only place on the ship any human would be able to look out onto the warp.

The crystal was harder than any substance known to man, tougher even that duralloy or ceramite. The disc beneath his throne fitted into the opening perfectly and now Simon knew he was truly alone. He gazed out into the darkness of space, saw the cold brilliant light of the stars, and the deceptively enormous sweep of the *Star of Venam* as it aimed for them. He breathed deeply and concentrated as his masters had taught him to.

He reached out with his disjointed senses and made contact with the ship. Strangeness flowed over him. He sensed other presences, echoes of old thoughts, shadows that might be those of ghosts. He knew that he was encountering psychic debris, residue of those who had occupied the throne before him, just as those who would come after him would encounter the shade of what had once been Simon Belisarius.

These presences were not without utility. They whispered old secrets in his brain, fed him the slimy residue of long forgotten memories, gabbled warnings and lies and pleas and welcomes. They thought they were real, but they were not, they were phantoms looking for lodging in his brain, and the only reality they had was that which he gave them. After a moment they stopped and he seemed to be looking down a long avenue at a near endless procession of men and women. Those nearest to him were clearest, for they were the most recent. Those in the distance were vague and formless as blobs. As one, they whispered.

Trust not the eldar.

Simon nodded, wondering whether this really was the consensus opinion of the ghosts who inhabited the ship's datacore or whether it was merely a projection of his own doubts and fears. He shrugged as well as he could, immobilised as he was by the harness, and ordered the ghosts to disperse to their places. Obediently they went, and he continued the process of easing himself into control of the ship.

He breathed deeply, and his awareness receded from the envelope of flesh he wore and extended itself along the cables that were the nervous system of the ship. Simultaneously he became a man with a body of skin and bone and muscle and blood, and a ship with a body of steel and duralloy and ceramite and countless other materials.

His heart was an ancient fire, hot as the sun. His eyes were replaced by divinatory probes allowing him to see far

higher and lower into the spectrum than ever his body's
eyes could. He extended his range of vision until it encom-
passed everything within a hundred thousand kilometres.
He was aware of meteorites centimetres long, and ten million tonne chunks of cometary ice tumbling through the
endless cold darkness. He looked around with greater
senses and saw nothing. No pursuers, no trading ships, no
vessels of any kind. Hardly surprising; the jump point he
had chosen was not one most people would have picked.
It was the easiest route to a path along which no one sane
wanted to travel, to a destination none but a madman
would want to go.

Briefly he wondered whether he was making a grave mistake in helping the eldar. He doubted that anyone who
wanted to go to Belial IV could be up to any good. *Remember your oaths*, whispered the ghosts, and he did. He was a
Navigator. He had in his time, like many a Navigator
before him, carried cargoes he had not wished knowledge
of. It was not his job to pass judgement on what his ship
was used for. It was his job to see that it got safely to its
destination, and that was what he intended to do.

He considered the charts he had studied. He was certain
he had chosen the correct vector. Now it was time to begin
the task of travel. He closed both of his natural eyes and
opened his pineal one. At first as always, he saw almost
nothing. Even for a trained Navigator, making an instanta-
neous transition from perceiving normal mundane reality
to perceiving the pathways of the immaterium was near
impossible.

He drew on some of his inner strength and opened himself fully. Slowly things started to resolve themselves. He
began to perceive the faint flaws on the surface of reality,
tiny scratch marks where the stuff of beyond seeped into
the normal universe. He saw the line of attack the ship
would have to be forced into to achieve his chosen path.

He fed power to the engines for the first immersion, that
brief submersion into the warp that would enable him to
see that all was well or, if it were not, to abort the whole

process of making the jump. He saw faint streaks appear
on the horizon as the ship began to sink out of normal
space.

This was the tricky part, getting things just right, so that
if they hit a rip or a temporal whirlpool, he would still
have a chance to pull the ship free before any real damage
was done. He knew the chances of such a thing happening
were thousands to one, but a good Navigator took no
chances. He applied full power to the drives.

The ship screamed as it slid down the pathways out of
reality. In Simon's third eye, the black of space began to
curdle as tendrils of multi-coloured light reached out to
grasp the ship. He saw that they were slipping out of normal time altogether into a realm where everything was
different. As always it took moments for him to adjust. For
a second he felt a flash of pure nervous fear. This was the
time all Navigators dreaded, when they were almost blind,
like a man who has been kept in a dark pit having to adjust
to sudden brilliant light. Perceptions other than hearing
let him perceive the keening whine of the engines, a wail
like that of lost souls, and the first faint echoes of the celes-
tial song of the psychic choir that surrounded the Emperor
and powered the mighty beacon of the Astronomican.

So far, so good, he thought. The ship slid along the very
brink of the abyss, at the gateway between the two realms.
He slowed the flow of power to the drives with an impulse
of his will, and let the ship glide along the boundary. By
cutting power now, he could still abort the departure. He
opened his pineal eye to the fullest and took stock of his
surroundings.

He saw the vast slowly rotating constellations of energy
that were the great warp storms of the Eye of Terror. He saw
the tiny calm flows of current that pulsed between them,
moving first in one direction and then in the other. He
checked his visualisation of them with his memory of the
star charts and found slight deviations, but not enough to
worry about. He could find a path, he was certain, providing all went well and nothing untoward happened. Don't

be too certain, he heard old Caradoc's voice murmur in his ear. Strange things always happen in the immaterium.

Things were as he expected. There were no obstructions, no probability wakes from other ships to drive him off course, conditions were as propitious as they were ever going to get. Now was the moment of truth; now he had to decide whether to commit the ship to the jump.

His mistrust of the eldar flashed through his mind, and along with it came vague dark premonitions concerning the future. He was enough of a Navigator to listen to his misgivings seriously, but he could not find in them enough of a reason to abort. Briefly he considered abandoning the jump and telling the xenogens it was impossible. It took him mere moments to dismiss the thought. To give into it would be a slur on the honour of his House, and he was not going to allow that to happen.

He sent a finger that weighed as much as a planet stabbing at a command rune on the armrest of the throne. A klaxon sounded throughout the ship warning all of the crew and the passengers that they were about to make the jump. In his mind's eye, he saw men throughout the ship scuttling to strap themselves in, to make themselves ready for the indescribable sensation of leaping out into the void, possibly never to return. He imagined men invoking the Emperor in a last prayer and decided to join them himself.

Prayer completed, he pulled the brass lever that would feed full power to the drives. The ship began to race forward, sliding down through the flaws in the surface of reality, immersing itself into the vast sea of the warp. Simon felt a glorious surge of acceleration and a spurt of sheer stark terror as the ship hurtled out into the void. This was no tentative touch but a full thrust through the fabric that joined two universes.

Suddenly they exploded out into the immaterium. Simon felt the ship buck and writhe as it hit a current. He opened his pineal eye wide and cast his gaze outwards. At first, as always, there was only formless primal Chaos, a jumble of shifting energy patterns. A kaleidoscope of intricate colours played across his vision, until his mind began the process of adjustment to its new surroundings.

While he did this, he wrestled to keep the ship on a clear path, more by instinct than anything else. Slowly, the random patterns subsided as his brain projected its own framework of understanding onto the immaterium. Now he saw it as something like real space only in negative. Black stars glittered against a background of grey and white. Huge nebula of darkness rotated above him.

As he adjusted, more colours became visible and the scale became more intimate and more turbulent. He began to perceive patterns within patterns. The ship drove forward now through shifting shoals of lights. The denser shifting spheres were clusters of worlds and solar systems. His sense of the size of things had altered. He felt like a giant who could see halfway across creation. He saw the currents of the warp, those secret roadways of the cosmos that could lead you anywhere at all if you were not careful.

He remembered old Caradoc's words: Heaven, hell, the past, the future, Navigators have claimed to have seen them all, and the strange thing is that they probably did.

Some theorists had posited that these were merely hallucinations, strange dreams drawn from the depths of the Navigator's brain and painted on the blank canvas of the void.

Others actually held that the immaterium was the primal Chaos on which the universe was built, and that what the Navigators saw actually came into being somewhere at some time. And that being the case, since it actually did or would exist, a path could be found to it. Some held that this was the way Navigators actually found their way through the void.

As always, Simon found that theory did not exactly match reality. The void was there and he saw things swirl within it. He saw portents, omens and pathways and wild, hallucinations like the worst fever dreams of a weirdroot addict. He could by dint of prodigious concentration alter them slightly, but he found that they interacted with him in strange ways. Images he saw would suggest something to his mind, and thus alter his visualisation of his path. If he was projecting his will onto the immaterium, he felt that no less was it projecting something of itself into his mind. It was an experience too complex to be accounted for by the dry theories of the scholars. It was too real, too vivid. Ultimately you had to go through it to begin to comprehend it. No simulation, no lectures, no training could prepare you for the totality of the experience.

He focused his mind, seeking the one fixed point of stability, the mighty beacon of the Astronomican. It took him some time to lock on to it. It seemed very faint and far away. Somewhere far off, he heard the faint chorus of the psychic choir, then he heard the first faint pulse of the Astronomican as the mighty psychic beacon's signal echoed down the canyons of infinity.

The voices of the choir were almost drowned out by the thunderous roar of the Eye of Terror. The signal seemed weak and distant. He paused for a moment, to make sure that he really had fixed his position with relation to distant Terra. Many a ship had foundered when its Navigator took position from something he thought was the beacon, and was in fact some other astral phenomena or worse a lure set by pirates, wreckers or the spawn of Chaos.

He listened with his psychic senses, catching the regular pulse of the chant, the weird eerie sound of psychic plainsong echoing down the corridors of time and space in time to the pulse of the beacon itself. To him, the pulse of the Astronomican was like the tolling of a great bell in a vast cavern. He looked within himself as he had been taught and found truth. It felt right. That was the great beacon.

From the hidden sub-basements of his mind he brought up pictures from the charts he had been studying earlier. Now, superimposed on his view of the warp, they made far more sense. Triangulating from his entrance wake at Medusa and the position of the Astronomican, he located

Belial IV. It did not look good. The world lay somewhere within the edges of the Eye, and the Eye did not feel calm today.

Now he gave his attention to the thing he dreaded. He cast his gaze ahead along the path he had chosen. There lay the mighty spiral vortex of the Eye of Terror, a huge whirlpool of energy, a massive unending sea of warp storms. The best he could hope to do was to find a patch of relative calm and guide his ship through the eye of the storm. It would be a feat worthy of a master Navigator.

Somewhere far off the puppet that was his fleshly body touched the controls in the arm of his throne. The ship yawed as he sought the first of the warp streams that he hoped would carry him to his destination. He felt the tug of the current as it bore him towards the Eye of Terror. For a brief insane moment, he felt like he really was looking into a giant eye, the mad malevolent orb of an insane god. It seemed to bore into his very soul. Illusions, he told himself, or perhaps omen or portent. Ignore it. Concentrate on the ship.

The vessel shook now as the current took hold. He communed with the spirits of the datacore. Fair going, the electric ghosts whispered. The ship can take it. Well within the tolerances she was built for. The sense of speed built within him as the ship accelerated towards the Eye. He guided her gently, moving into midstream, trying to avoid the worst of the turbulence in the current. It was not easy. Here at the edges of the Eye disturbances were far more common and violent than they normally were. There was a sickening lurching, bumping sensation as they hit some distortion pattern, but Simon righted the ship and they clove on through the eternal void. He kept part of his mind focused on the Astronomican, keeping himself always oriented towards it.

The Eye swelled in his view, losing all outward appearance of form as it grew so large it filled the entire field of his pineal eye. The roar of the void all around him had taken on a terrifying sentient quality. It was the voice of an army of hungry daemons chanting for a soul they could sense but not quite perceive. He tried to ignore them and concentrate on the ethereal song of the Astronomican, but the voice of distant Terra was hard to hear now. Behind him, he knew, desperately locking on to its position.

The ship shook more as the current grew stronger. Simon studied the warp around him. Vast tendrils of power reached out from the edges of his vision, attempting to grasp the *Star of Venam* as it passed. Simon corrected his course for what he hoped was a passage between them, then realised that he was heading towards a fast-forming temporal whirlpool. Here the energies of the immaterium were being sucked out into real space somewhere in a swirling vortex of madness that could easily destroy a ship that fell into its clutches. Worse, such vortices often led directly into long fast-flowing tunnels that could emerge almost anywhere, including, it was speculated, the heart of a sun. Frantically, he wrestled the ship away from the deadly current.

He almost managed it. The *Star* clipped the very edges of the vortex and began to spiral inwards. Simon cursed the mad flows of the immaterium through the Eye. He was encountering more hazards on this one trip than was normal for a year in normal travelling.

He pushed such thoughts aside as a pointless distraction; he needed to keep all of his wits about him if they were to have any chance of survival. Already the hull echoed as the maelstrom of wild energy smashed against it. Once more Simon thought he heard the howl of daemon voices.

There was only one chance now. He allowed the ship to go with the flow, cutting all power for a few moments, and letting it orbit around the edge of the whirlpool. As they reached the point where they had been sucked in, he applied massive amounts of power to the drives, hoping to slingshot the vessel outwards.

We are close to destruction, whispered the ship's ghosts. Our end is nigh. Somewhere in the distance, he thought he heard the spirits screaming. You have doomed us all, said a sad, desperate voice which bore some resemblance to his own. Somewhere in the distance the Astronomican pulsed.

The hull resonated as the huge reinforcing struts flexed under the strain. Somewhere down in the bowels of the ship, emergency generators were coming online in a crackle of thunderbolts and an eruption of ozone Simon could almost taste. He focused on the Astronomican and kept the ship on course, aiming for a small window of calm he could see in the warp flows. The ship leapt forward, pulling clear of the terrible suction of the temporal whirlpool, and sped like an arrow towards its goal. Simon offered up a prayer to the Emperor, hoping that the spirit that ruled the Astronomican could hear him.

The ship slid into the chosen channel. The retreating warp current carried it through the tempests of energy. Now the flows were behind, adding their own power to the engines of the ship. The *Star of Venam* hurtled through the immaterium towards its goal.

He became aware of other things around him now. He could hear something above the roar of the warp storm and the song of the great beacon. This was another song, astonishingly sweet and pure, its very beauty demanding all of his attention. Simon ignored it. He had been warned of such things, the sirens of Slaanesh, as they were known to Navigators. He had no idea what they really were. Perhaps they were indeed daemons that sought to lure ships to their doom. Perhaps they were simply some strange form of astral phenomena. It did not really matter at this moment. All that counted was that he did not succumb to their wiles.

He concentrated on the Astronomican, praying for the salvation of his ship and his soul, wondering whether, even if the Emperor heard him, he would grant them succour. They were after all heading directly into an area forbidden by his Ecclesiarchy, and marked as under interdict on all the navigational charts of the Navis Nobilitae. Perhaps by offering up a prayer in such blasphemous surroundings, Simon was bringing doom on himself and his ship. This was an eventuality that had not been covered in his training. Still, his instincts told him to do it and he listened to them.

Suddenly, the ship emerged from the battering stressful current and entered an area of relative calm. Now the huge flows pushed them peacefully onwards. It seemed like they had passed out of an area of extreme turbulence into an area of utter stillness. The realisation struck Simon that he had never quite seen the immaterium like this before, but then that was hardly surprising since he had never passed through the Eye of Terror before. The very fabric of the warp felt different, thicker and more viscous, yet at the same time hinting at hidden depths. He felt that if he turned the ship into the current here and forced it downwards, he might emerge at the very birth of the universe, in the formless primal void that was said to exist before being. More than that, here in this place, more than anywhere else he had ever been in the immaterium, he could feel a sense of wrongness.

The very stuff of the warp felt corrupted somehow. He recalled tales of how the Chaos stuff of the Eye of Terror often overflowed into worlds.

Was it possible, he wondered, that matter from the material universe had somehow invaded this place, and transformed it? Could there be all manner of stellar reefs and shoals here, the like of which were not to be found elsewhere?

He kept every pineal sense strained, watching the void around him for any danger. Slowly as he did so he became aware of things that either he had never encountered before or never truly noticed before. All around him flowed lattices of energy, small permanent disturbances in the immaterium. They pulsed and moved of their own accord, and as he watched he noticed that they seemed to be performing regular actions. Some of them engulfed each other, devouring and absorbing like huge amoeba enveloping their prey, while some danced around each other like performers in a strange ritual. Suddenly some hurled themselves against the ship, slamming into it and screaming their frustration.

Those things over there were sentient, Simon thought! Perhaps this is what daemons are made of. He brought his gaze back from infinity and cast it along the length of the ship. Three mighty glowing lights shone from within the *Star of Venam*. So brilliant was their illumination that they were visible as a dim glow even through the duralloy walls of the hull and its enveloping psychic screens. What was going on here, he wondered?

More and more of the alien shapes hurled themselves onto the *Star of Venam*. At times he thought he saw strange humanoid shapes crawling all over the ship, banging at it with weapons and pincer-like claws, seeking to gain admittance through any entrance or weak spot they might find in the force fields surrounding the ship.

Madness, he thought, the effects of the Navigation drugs and my own mind projecting its fears onto the warp. Yet somehow he knew that it was not. Those things out there were real and becoming ever more concrete as if his own terror gave them form. Did they feed on strong emotion, he wondered, or was it something else? Were they taking shape in response to the fears of those within the ship or was it just that now he was seeing them as they actually were? He gazed on them, afraid that they might notice him, but they did not.

Some of them gazed right through him, as if he were invisible, although he was aware of their presence. He had heard it said that the daemons of the warp devoured any souls they encountered save those of Navigators. Somehow, it seemed that his people were invisible to the creatures as long as they did nothing to attract their attention. Had he discovered one of the secrets of why his people could live where others could not? Why of all the sub-races of humanity they did not go mad after prolonged exposure to the warp? He watched in panic as armies of the things appeared to swarm over the craft, gnawing away at its protective spells and runes.

It seemed like the whole outside of the ship was a seething mass of daemonic flesh, drawn to whatever was inside, battling with each other for places, like miners staking out a claim. Suddenly Simon was certain he knew what had happened to the ghost ships, those vessels whose crew had been found insane within gibbering tales of monsters, phantasms and devils. These were creatures of nightmare, and they lusted for something within his ship.

Three things, he thought, those three mighty glowing lights. What could they be? What made his ship different this time from all of the other times? Was it simply that they were now within the Eye of Terror and the power of daemonkind was stronger, or was it something else, something connected with his quest or his passengers? Three lights – Auric, Athenys and Janus perhaps?

He thought about the eldar. It was virtually unheard of for them to take passage on a human ship. He thought about the argosy ships and the disaster that inevitably overtook them. Was there a connection between these two facts? It seemed likely.

Right now, though, he had a decision to make. He needed to work out a way of saving his ship. In his ears the ghosts gibbered, shrieking warnings. This ship was now the only home they would ever have, and if it died, so did they. It did not matter to them that they were merely resonances of dead men within the ship's datacore. They were afraid, though they did not know of what, and Simon did not blame them.

He attempted to gauge how long the shields would hold. Not much longer against the horde of things assaulting them. Would it make sense to try and tear the ship from the immaterium now, cast it out of the warp before it achieved the angle of exit he had decided upon? That strain also might destroy them. And if the ship were damaged by a forced exit, then there would be no drydock in which to execute repairs here in the Eye of Terror. That would leave the choice of trying to make another jump with a crippled ship, or being stuck within the realm of the Chaos lords. Not really much of choice at all, he decided.

How much longer till they hit their exit vector? Judging as best he could by the position of the Astronomican, not that much longer in the subjective time of the ship. He could almost see the dull cluster of lights that he guessed was Belial system. He made up his mind. If he crippled the ship coming out of the warp prematurely, there would be no chance of survival. They would simply have to repeat this performance in a ship already partially broken. He decided to stay running with the warp current for the time being. If it looked like the shields were going to give way, he would make the break then.

At least that way they would have a chance of a clean death, starving or suffocating as the ship's systems slowly failed in real space. He offered up a prayer to the distant Astronomican and fed more power to the shields.

He sensed the daemons' frustration as the resistance increased. Their efforts redoubled. The ghosts whispered frantically that the shields had given way in a dozen places. They were down to the ship's armour. There were times when he was certain he heard the scrape of claws along the hull. It did not matter how often he told himself that was impossible either. He still felt it was the case.

Fear gnawed at his vitals now, the stark fear of the unknown. He had no idea what might happen if those things out there breached the hull, but he knew it was not good. Perhaps some future starsailors would be destined to come across the *Star of Venam*, a ghost ship, peopled by men who had died in mysterious ways, or worse yet inhabited by walking corpses possessed by the malevolent spirits of daemons.

He checked his position against the Astronomican. Not much further now. The current had carried them a long way into the Eye, and their exit gate should be upon them soon. Briefly he wondered how the others were taking this. At least he had some idea of what was going on; the people within the ship, sealed within their vessel like corpses sealed in a tomb, had no knowledge. They could only wait and pray and imagine the worst.

Ten more pulses of the Astronomican, Simon decided, and he would angle the ship upwards and outwards. He cursed himself for ever being foolish enough to agree to take the eldar anywhere. What if he had simply refused to acknowledge the coin they had presented? Perhaps others had in the past. No, that was not at all likely; he would have heard of such a vast breach of trust. House Belisarius prided itself on its honour.

Nine pulses. He wondered if he would ever see the distant world of Terra with its sculpted hanging gardens and its city-size palaces ever again. He doubted it. A pity he thought, he would liked to have looked on the Sanguinean Gate once more, and see the palace of the Emperor rise in the distance above the lesser mansions of the great lords.

Eight pulses. He gazed out of the observation portal at the seething mass of creatures that had attached themselves to the hull. He could make them out better now. Some were lizard-like things with long snaky tongues and eyes that reminded him of a beautiful woman's. Some looked like beautiful women, only with a single breast and pincers instead of hands. Madness, he told himself. Hallucinations induced by the warp. The women fought with enormous reptilian hounds with collars of brass and teeth like crocodiles. Their psychic howls reminded him of starving beggars fighting to get at a feast. Their jaws slavered. Their eyes were bright with mad hunger.

Seven pulses. One of the clawed women scratched away at the crystal of the observation dome. Her single breast was flattened against it. He could see her head was bald. She wore a necklace that bore the sign of one of the Dark Powers. She gazed straight at him without seeming to see anything. How was that possible, he wondered, as her claws drew a neat line across the supposedly impermeable crystal? What would she do when she broke through? What would happen to him? Would he be sucked out into the warp?

Six pulses. He saw something monstrous and slimy, all tentacles and teeth, throw itself on the woman. They fought with an insane ferocity. Simon had once seen sharks in a feeding frenzy; this was worse. They lashed at each other until it looked like they would be hacked to pieces.

Five pulses. The woman slashed her assailant in two and returned to her task. Simon was sure he could hear the scratch of her claws on crystal now. He fought down the urge to begin the ship's exit from the immaterium. This was the critical time.

Four pulses. He felt certain that the armoured crystal was about to shatter. The whole structure rang with the force of the daemonette's blows. He found himself unconsciously holding his breath. The ghosts gibbered crazily in his ears. *Spawn of Slaanesh*, they screamed. *Child of Chaos. You will die horribly but in ecstasy.* Simon wondered where that knowledge came from. Some long dead ancient, he judged, for he could put no face to the voice.

Three pulses. No doubt about it, the crystal was giving way. Simon could see shards of the stuff drift past the she-daemon's head.

He reached down with weakening fingers and found the bolt pistol strapped to his thigh. He was not sure whether he intended to use it on himself or the thing. He was not even sure he would get the chance if the warp burst into the vessel.

Two pulses. Simon poised his fingers over the activation runes and tried to drown out the fearful shriek of the ship's ghosts. His fingers grew tense from an eternity of waiting.

One pulse. They stabbed downwards. The ship heeled and rocked. It began to move in a direction that Simon could only describe as upward, heading away from the depths of the immaterium, up towards the light of the real world. The current fought against it, and the daemons fought against it, but Simon knew they were fighting now against the natural tendency of a product of the normal sane universe to return to its point of origin. It bobbed upward like an air-filled bladder heading towards the surface of the sea.

The daemons screamed in frustration as they reached an area where the immaterium was too thin to support all but the most powerful of them. A few clung on, chipping desperately at the side of the ship, determined to get at their meal no matter what.

Simon saw a look of fear, frustration and apprehension on the daemonette's face. He could almost tell what she was thinking. She had come so close, and she did not want to let go. Then it was suddenly too late, the ship had settled into the groove that would take it out into normal space. It raced up and away. The daemon let go and he saw her drift downward and away, dwindling into the distance of the abyss far, far below.

He gave his full attention to the controls as he wrestled the ship into her final approach to the exit gate. It erupted into night and space and cold, and looking at the strange stars, Simon knew with dread that they had emerged deep within the Eye of Terror.

FIFTEEN
REPORTS

SIMON BELISARIUS RELAXED as the ship emerged from the immaterium. Nothing to it, he thought sardonically, knowing that memory was already doing the work of smoothing the rough edges of the jump. He forced the images of daemons and disaster from his mind. There would be time enough to think about what he had seen later.

He snapped open his eyes and exhaled, then glanced at the chronometer on his wrist. The hands indicated that eighteen hours had passed in subjective time. He would need to wait until they contacted another ship or world to find out how much time had passed in reality. The discrepancy could sometimes be immense. He remembered one trip in which two weeks had passed aboard ship, but only two days in real time. There had been another when he had been in the immaterium for barely two hours according to the ship's chronometers, but three months had passed in the real universe.

And of course, such time, measured in the ticking of clocks, the beating of hearts or the atomic pulse of ancient

169

artefacts, bore no relation to his own experience of time. A
Navigator in a jump was always in the 'now'. Time seemed
infinite until the experience ended. Something he knew he
never could and never would be able to describe to any of
the ancestrals.

He unhooked the command crown from his head and
began the long and nasty process of detaching himself
from the Navigator's chair. He unhooked the drips that
pumped fluid and nutrients directly into his system. He
unscrewed the life support tubes. His body felt weak, as it
always did after a jump, and his stomach growled, wanting
something solid. He knew that his legs would still be too
rubbery to let him stand, so instead he closed his eyes,
breathed deeply and tried to relax.

It was not easy. The strain of piloting a ship through the
immaterium took a terrible toll on the body and mind at
the same time as it flooded the system with adrenalin. He
felt tired and weak. Human bodies were not meant to
endure what his just had, just as human minds were not
meant to experience all of the things his had just under-
gone.

He reminded himself that he was not a human. His
people had risen above the ancestrals a long time ago.
Even so the images of the journey were starting to fade, as
if his mind did not want to hold onto them, or simply
could not.

He took another breath and began to tense and relax his
muscles. At the moment, even the pain in his arms, legs
and hips was almost welcome. It was a reminder that he
was back in his body, back in the flesh, not linked to the
enormous inhuman bulk of his ship. He hit the command
button and the navigation platform lowered back to deck
level. The crew looked at him, awed and a little shaken.

As always there was a tangible sense of relief in the air.
The jump had been made. The ship had not foundered.
They were all alive, or at least he hoped so.

'Reports,' he said. His words came out a hoarse whisper.
It took a near super-human effort to voice them. His voice

seemed crude and strange after the supernatural beauty of listening to the psychic choir of the Astronomican. Even now the last faint echoes of their plainsong were only just fading from his memory.

The master helmsman studied his control altar. The divinatory runes flickering on the viewscreen below him were mirrored on his face. 'Shields down to fifty per cent. Some hull damage. Engines at optimal magnitude. Location: alpha null two two one, omega pi five six zero.'

Simon allowed himself a satisfied smile. Point of emergence was only a few hundred thousand kilometres off, which was nothing in terms of the cosmic magnitude of the jump. The shields had taken more wear and tear than he would have liked. Still, considering how close they had come to being overwhelmed, they should be grateful.

'Very well, the command deck is yours, Mister Raimes.'

'Thank you, sir.'

Simon felt strong enough to take a stimmtab and lift himself out of the throne. As he did so, the door of the command deck opened, and Janus Darke and the two eldar entered.

Janus looked a little stunned. His pupils were dilated, his movements oddly slow. The two xenogens had a swift eerie electric quality to their movements. They were still far more fluid than a human's but there was a stiff, jerky look to them. Simon at once realised how tense they were.

'What is it?' he asked in eldar, beckoning for them to follow him off the command deck. The crew usually considered it bad luck to have passengers there. Doubtless they would consider the presence of aliens doubly unfortunate.

With their usual awareness, the eldar seemed to sense his reservations and held off responding until they had crossed the corridor and entered the small cabin that was usually kept empty for him when he came off the navigation throne. There was a bunk, a couple of chairs and some food. Little else.

'Something came for us,' said Auric. 'I felt it.'

From the tension in their voices, Simon guessed that they were afraid. 'Nonetheless we made it,' he said.

The two eldar considered this for a moment. It was like watching them draw a cloak over their feelings. Slowly all of the tension subsided from them and they became their usual calm and inscrutable selves once more.

'You are correct, Simon Belisarius,' said Auric. 'We have survived the journey and done something few eldar have done in ten thousand years. We thank you.'

With that he turned and left, Athenys following after him.

'What was that all about?' Simon asked.

'I do not know,' said Janus. 'All I know is that there is something about the warp that terrifies them. I get the sense that no eldar would ever travel through it save at direst necessity.'

Simon nodded. 'I agree.'

He studied his friend. Janus Darke's speech was slow and his manner listless. That odd eldar jewel glittered on his forehead. He thought back to the farseer's foreboding words before they had made the jump. It seemed that they had indeed taken precautions.

'Are you all right?' he asked. Janus nodded groggily. 'I slept through most of the journey. I had strange dreams.'

Simon did not like the sound of that at all. There was something going on here. His instincts, honed by years of growing up within the political whirlpool of a Navigator House, told him that the eldar were playing a far deeper game. He was going to ask Kham Bell and Stiel to keep an eye on them. Right now though he needed sleep himself.

'How long till we make orbit over Belial IV?' asked Janus.

'Two days or so. I had to bring us in at the edge of the system, and there was a little more deviation than usual in the jump.'

'Was it bad?' Janus asked.

Simon surprised himself by answering.

'It was very bad. We should not have come here. There are more hazards in the immaterium of the Eye of Terror than anywhere I have ever been. I am not looking forward to taking us out of here.'

'Assuming we survive what is waiting for us down there.'

'Do you have any idea what it is they are looking for yet?'

'They are seeking some ancient weapon.'

'Why?'

'They think they can use it to kill a daemon.'

Simon could see that Janus was being evasive, that he truly did not want to answer him. He considered pressing the matter for a moment, but he was too tired. 'They have certainly come to the right place, if they are looking for those.'

Janus lurched to his feet. 'I will let you sleep now,' he said.

Simon slumped down wearily on his bed. In moments, his mind sank into slumber with the speed of a foundering ship. His dreams were troubled by images of things rising from the warp to devour them all.

JANUS FELT A little better. The caffeine had tasted good, the food had settled in his stomach. The tranquillising effect of the eldar medicine had almost worn off. A pity, he could have used some more of its artificial calmness. This was a moment he had been dreading. His fingers toyed with the amulet Justina had given him. Just get it over with, he told himself, and then you can rest.

He leaned against the lectern and looked around the briefing room at his chiefs. He could almost ignore the glances they gave to the jewel in his forehead. He could see that they all wanted to probe, to ask more about it, but as yet none of them had summoned the courage. They still had that much respect for him at least.

The briefing hall looked empty. There were only two of the ship's officers and the three sergeants present, along with Stiel. This chamber could have held ten times as many.

'Reports,' Janus asked.

'The men are ready for action whenever you say so, captain,' said Kham Bell. 'I'll have them going through the drills ten hours a day.'

Janus nodded his approval. Exercise would stop any slackness slipping in and help keep discipline among the men.

Ruarc, the narrow-faced chief tech-adept, looked at Janus. As ever his robes seemed two sizes too big for him. He rubbed his nose with his sleeve. 'I have engineering checking the hull for breaches and weakness. It was a rough passage, as the Navigator said.'

'Are you going to tell us where we are and what we are doing now?' asked Kham Bell.

Janus gave it to him straight. 'We're in the Eye of Terror.'

Silence filled the room. He guessed a lot of them had already worked this out. Most of the men present could have done so by taking a sighting through the observation windows. He wondered how they were going to take this admission. If there were going to be a mutiny, now would be the time. He waited; the silence lengthened. As ever, Stiel's eyes raked the crowd, then he looked at Janus reassuringly. If things came down badly, Janus knew he could count on the assassin. He might need to.

The men looked at each other and then at Kham Bell. He would be the spokesman. He could almost see the wheels turning in their heads as they made the calculations. They were here, and they were stuck unless Simon Belisarius took them out. And it did not matter now if he had misled them about their goal – to the Inquisition it would all be the same. They had broken the interdict, they had gone where no man was supposed to go. Their lives would be forfeit whatever they did. The best they could hope for would be a painful death on their return – even if they rebelled against him now. Fear spread across the room marking every face.

'What are we looking for?' the sergeant asked. Janus relaxed a little. They were not going to rebel, at least not until they had heard what he was going to say.

'Eldar treasure,' he lied. Some of the men relaxed a little. This was something they could understand: the riches of an alien race.

'Very good,' said Kham Bell. 'But how are we going to live to spend it?'

'To begin with, tell no one what I have told you. When we are done every one of your men will be sworn to silence,' Janus said. 'They will all know the penalties for loose lips.'

'What of those who won't swear?' The sergeant was determined to push this. And Janus understood why – there would always be some Janus knew, religious fanatics who feared more for their souls than for their bodies. He knew what he had to say, but he still found himself reluctant to give the order. After all, these men had followed him here on trust. He had not given them any choice. He was making them take risks in what might be a futile effort to save his own soul.

How had things come this far, he wondered – but he already knew the answer. He had just let himself be swept along by events. Things had happened so fast that for once in his life he had not been able to take control of them. The eldar had always held the initiative. He was going to have to do something to change that.

'What about those who won't swear?' Kham Bell asked.

'Make them see reason,' said Janus. 'Otherwise…'

He drew his finger across his throat and looked meaningfully at Stiel. He felt more like a traitor with every moment that passed. 'I'll brief you more when we arrive. Until then everything is on a need to know basis.'

The men nodded and departed, until only Stiel and Janus remained.

'You want me to keep an eye on the eldar,' said the assassin.

Janus nodded. 'And be ready to kill them if I give the command.'

'I have always been ready to do that,' said Stiel sombrely.

ZARGHAN, ONCE A Space Marine of the First Founding, looked into the mirror and on Shaha Gaathon's beautiful, evil features. The daemon wore nothing save a translucent diaphanous gown, and she appeared to be reclining on a couch that consisted entirely of writhing naked human beings. An interesting effect, thought Zarghan. The fleshy walls of her chamber were a bit tasteless though. As he watched the whole scene changed colour. Was that his eyes again, he wondered, or was it some peculiar effect of the mirror? He supposed it did not really matter.

Shaha Gaathon continued to speak in that husky sensual voice, but he did not pay too much attention. The music in his head was too loud and too entertaining. Although she was technically his superior, and he was supposed to obey her, it did not come easy to Zarghan. After all, if it had, he would still be serving the Emperor of Mankind, as he had done ten thousand years ago.

Pride – that had always been his greatest flaw, he decided, with the insight of a man who has had ten millennia to contemplate his many character defects. He had been unable even to obey his own primarch in the end, or see eye to eye with his own captain. To tell the absolute truth, he had trouble even getting along with his own battle-brothers, even linked as they were supposed to be in the service of the Liberator of the Flesh and Spirit. And lovely and vicious as she was, Shaha Gaathon was probably not even the equal of one of those. Alas, he thought, so few were – the Emperor's Children had always been special.

He took another puff from the hookah of crystal and black iron and let the pleasure smoke enter his atrophied lungs and then his brain. His mind pulsed with chemical joy in time to the changing colours of the walls of his cabin. The music in his head reached a crescendo. Outside the depths of space were cold but here in his great warship, things were just fine.

'Are you listening to me, Zarghan Ironfist?' asked Shaha Gaathon, a note of anger tinkling in her wonderful throaty voice.

'But of course, great mistress,' said Zarghan in his oiliest tones, not bothering to conceal his contempt. 'Every word. Should I repeat them for you?'

If necessary, he could have, too. His mind had that capacity, along with many others. It had been there ever since the Emperor and his primarchs had altered Zarghan all those thousands of years ago. He inspected the silver filigreed gauntlet that covered his left fist. The metalwork looked a little chipped, he thought, best get Gormar to replace it. Then he realised that it would be impossible: he had ordered the armourer thrown out of the airlock without a suit for some infraction of discipline. He could not at this moment recall exactly why, but he was sure it would come back to him.

'That will not be necessary. Simply see that your orders are carried out. You and your crew of scum will go to Belial IV and capture the man, Janus Darke. Kill all who are with him. There will be two eldar. Make sure they die.'

'My crew would be… very hurt to hear you speak so disparagingly of them, great mistress,' said Zarghan, allowing just enough mockery to show in his voice to goad her, not enough to drive her to outright rage. 'They are very sensitive souls, really. Poets, in their own way. Poets of violence and blood.'

Poetry – that was it. Gormar had composed some exceptionally tedious verses in honour of his captain's latest victory. The metre was off, the rhyme scheme atrocious and the imagery quite frankly stale. Zarghan stifled a yawn with his fist of iron. Of course, when you had endured ten thousand years of indulgence almost everything was inclined to seem stale. Perhaps he had been a little harsh – death was so irrevocable and mortals were so frail. Still, no use crying over spilled milk. He would just have to go a little easier the next time one of the crew decided to sing his praises. Well, he would if he remembered. A thought sidled into his mind. There had been something about one of those names…

'Janus Darke – that is a familiar name, milady. Was he not the owner of several of the vessels I pillaged for you?'

'Your insight is remarkable considering how much of that vile weed you smoke,' said the she-daemon sardonically. 'I am surprised that ten thousand years of it has not reduced your brain to mush.'

'Great mistress, I was, and am, a Space Marine of the Emperor's Children. My geneseed is of the earliest and most potent generation. My body was designed to be able to process any level of toxicity. It would take more weed than you could grow on a jungle world to begin to impair my mental functions.'

It was true, too, thought Zarghan, although there were times when he did feel like he was paying the price for all of those centuries of indulgence. It was impossible to understand what hell was until you had suffered the hangover brought on by a decades-long spree. There were times when even his Emperor-designed frame, reinforced by all the gifts the Liberator had lavished on him, felt like it was unable to endure. Fortunately, today was not one of those times. The music in his head faded, almost as if it was in agreement.

'As I recall, you are no longer one of the Children,' said Shaha Gaathon. 'They expelled you after your last infraction of discipline.'

Always, she brought that up. He hid his anger well. 'A minor misunderstanding, great mistress. I will eventually make peace with my peers. After all, we have all eternity. A little enmity adds spice to the otherwise dull millennia.'

'I would not call mounting a surprise raid on your captain's palace and crucifying all of his pleasure-slaves a minor misunderstanding, Zarghan. I do not think Vilius thinks that way either.'

'He was a little piqued, I will admit. Still, he did owe me several farthings over a wager that–'

'I am not interested in your wagers, Zarghan. I am interested in Janus Darke. You will find him and bring him to me.'

'How will I find him?'

'He will be at the Palace of Asuryan on Belial IV. Just put yourself into orbit and scan for life-signs. You will find him.'

'What if the warp currents are not propitious, great mistress?'

'They were propitious enough for a human to make his way into the Eye. They should be propitious enough for you.'

Zarghan was impressed. Very few mortals had the courage to attempt to enter the Eye, let alone the skill to navigate the great warp storms that guarded it. Navigate, yes, that reminded him of something. Oh yes...

'I am assuming that he got there by ship, your unspeakable greatness.'

'That is a fair assumption.' For some reason she sounded a little exasperated.

'I will plunder the ship and add it to my fleet.'

'As you wish, although I am given to understand that your fleet currently consists of only one vessel.'

'A minor and temporary setback, most beauteous of immortals. Khârn the Betrayer surprised me off Altarak.'

'Succeed in this and I will ensure that you have the power to repay him in full measure and with interest.'

'I am sure that you will, great mistress,' said Zarghan, 'and maybe I will also pay off my score to you as well, if I play the cards I have been dealt with correctly. A look of devastating anger played over Shaha Gaathon's face and Zarghan wondered if he had been foolish enough to speak his thoughts aloud again. Surely not! He was a Space Marine of the most ancient order after all, and such a thing could not happen to him.

'Just get that man and I will see that you are paid in full for your service.'

'As you desire, great mistress,' said Zarghan as the image in the mirror faded and went black, leaving him gazing upon his own rather surprised reflection. Looking at himself, he was forced to admit that even after a hundred centuries, he was still a handsome devil. Pride, he thought, my besetting sin. Or perhaps it was vanity? The Emperor had told him that once long ago, or so he seemed to recall. Anyway, it was a long time ago.

He strode from his perfumed chamber towards the command centre. The crew had been redecorating again, he noticed. Those severed heads set off the black and red swirls on the walls quite nicely. Now where was it he was to go again? Oh yes – Belial IV.

Capture the man, Janus Darke. Kill the rest. That seemed simple enough. He just hoped his crew did not make any of their usual mistakes. The music in his head returned, a throbbing, pulsing sound that spoke of imminent violence.

SIXTEEN
VISIONS

Janus Darke knew he was dreaming. He was not certain how he knew, he was just certain he was. At first, it seemed to him that he lay on his bunk in his cabin. It was almost like being awake, until he noticed the strange quality of the walls surrounding him. He sensed their age. He had always known the *Star of Venam* was old, but this was the first time he had ever realised quite how old.

It was as if, for the first time, he was aware of the corrosion caused by the moisture on the breath of every man who had ever breathed her air. It was as if every soul who had passed through her duralloy corridors had left some trace of its passage. And there had been many, many souls he realised in the long millennia since the ancient starship had been built.

Images seeped into his mind. He saw the previous captains in the uniforms of the Imperial fleet. He saw the battles they had fought and the trips they had made. He saw back to the original creation of the ship back in the forge yards of Sidon 452 almost two thousand years ago.

He sensed the spirits who slept within the datacore of the ship, echoes of past commanders, shadows of Navigators long gone, and he saw that they were restless.

Not possible, he told himself. It's my imagination, a product of sleep and the strange drugs the eldar gave me, and my own overwrought brain. And yet, he knew that part of what he was seeing was, in a sense, the truth. Every man who commanded the ship, every man who patched himself into its internal systems, did leave something of himself there, a psychic residue that those who came after would touch and feel and join in their turn.

Now the great walls became translucent. Not even their massive age-corroded quality could halt his vision. He could see the armsmen coming and going though the walkways, tech-priests working on the data-cables and engines and welding weak points in the hull. He saw Simon Belisarius asleep on the cot of his small cabin, and Kham Bell bellowing orders to his sweating soldiers as they went through their exercises in the great assembly chamber. He saw Stiel bent over a great ledger inscribing something in his tomes, a small smile twisting his lips.

His soul seemed to roam the corridors of his space-going domain. The only thing that remained impermeable to its eyes was the outer walls of the ship itself. It was hardly surprising, they had been embedded with the strongest psychic runes to resist the daemons of the warp, and forged from triple-layered truesilver and duralloy to prevent the incursion of evil psychic forces from the warp.

He felt something burning on his forehead, and he reached up and felt the eldar jewel there. At first he could not tell whether it felt hot or cold. It burned, but he knew only too well that the chill of space was as capable of burning as the hottest of infernos. Burning or not, though, he felt only a mild discomfort, a nagging sense of something pulling at him, the touch of premonition's ghostly fingers running through his brain. He allowed himself to drift, and, like a fish being reeled in on an angler's line, he was drawn forward. It did not surprise him in the least to see he was being pulled towards the eldar's chambers.

What was going on, he wondered?

He passed through walls with all the ease of a ghost, drifted across rooms in which men worked, slept, ate or played chess. The closer he came to the place where the xenogens rested, the more strained he could see were the looks of his followers. They too could sense something ominous was happening.

He came to the doors of their chamber; saw Athenys was standing guard outside them. She held her weapons ready, but appeared completely at ease. She did not seem to notice him as he moved past. The chamber was warded. He could see the bright patterns of energy swirling in the air, knew they would be invisible save to those who shared his odd vision. He floated towards them and knew that the runes were potent enough to kill almost any creature that encountered them. A brief surge of nervousness and fear filled him, but he could not stop himself. The force that dragged him onwards had all the irresistible power a planet's gravity well exerts on a meteor blazing down through its atmosphere.

He tried to back away, exerted all his will, but, as in a nightmare, he was drawn inexorably onwards, while the blazing gem on his brow grew hotter and hotter or perhaps, colder and colder. He thought he could see faint lines now running out from the room and connecting to the gem on his forehead. He touched the wards on the door and felt a brief flare of power. He entered the eldar's chamber and was surprised by what he found there.

Auric was present. Instead of his normal garb he was clad in full ritual vestments. A huge black cloak trimmed with white fur was flung over his shoulders. A mask of some burnished metal covered his face. From a complex shoulder piece three large prongs, the highest topped with the head of a phoenix, emerged. In one hand the eldar held a blade of power. In the other, he held a satchel of leather that seemed to contain something of as much power as the sword.

As Janus entered the eldar looked up and the man sensed his surprise. Obviously he was not expected. There was a pause in whatever ritual the xenogen was preparing for. Janus now saw the burning censers on either side of the room from which multi-coloured incense billowed and swirled in uncanny patterns. After a heartbeat Auric appeared to come to a decision and began anew.

Without being able to hear the words, Janus knew that the farseer was chanting, or singing, or some mixture of both. Without hearing any sounds, he was yet aware of a distant throbbing of energy and the beat of rhythm, and the surge of power in response the farseer's song. He was aware that powerful forces surged through the sealed chamber and wondered how they would affect him. If, as he suspected, his spirit had been torn from his body, was it possible it could die here? Briefly he wondered what would happen to his body, and then he dismissed such speculation as futile. Doubtless if it happened, he would not be around to be concerned.

Auric swept his blade through a complex pattern of cuts. He had begun to move in a pattern that resembled a dance, and yet suggested some form of martial practice. The sound of his singing became clearer. It resonated within Janus with near unbearable keenness and beauty.

Suddenly Auric stopped, turned to face each of the four corners of the room, and to each in turn performed a complex salute with the blade. Afterwards he spun it back into its scabbard. Whatever purification ritual he had performed seemed to be over. He was ready to begin in earnest.

With his right hand he reached into the leather sack and produced a glittering stone. Using thumb and forefinger he held it before his masked face. It was a crystal of some sort which pulsed with its own internal light, sending glittering beams out to reflect on the eldar's mask. Janus inspected it and saw that the crystal bore a rune. It was a stylised representation of something, a scale or balance, of the ancient sort, the kind that certain merchant guilds still used as a symbol of truth, honesty and fairness. Without having to be told, Janus knew it symbolised something different to the eldar. It was a sign of powers in mutual counterpoise, of events balanced on a knife-edge that could go in any direction. Auric nodded as if this was something he had expected.

He cast the stone into the air. Instead of falling to the ground, it hung there for a moment and then began to spin, holding its position immediately before the eldar's head. The xenogen reached into the pouch once more and withdrew another stone. This one bore a symbol of a stylised human with an elongated ovular head. The sign was a symbol of the eldar race. Janus wondered where that knowledge had suddenly sprung from. From the stone itself, from Auric, or perhaps from the gem in his forehead? There seemed to be some sort of link here.

The second stone started to loop around the first, orbiting it like a small multi-faceted moon. The ritual continued. A third rune was drawn – this one bearing a stylised figure that Janus did not need to be told represented man. A pulsing reddish gem that seemed in some way fraught with menace swiftly joined it. The enemy, Janus thought. These two stones took up a close orbit circling the first rune, with the evilly glowing gemstone following very close on the track of the human. An image of himself followed by the powers of darkness flickered before Janus's eyes.

As more and more runestones were added to the viewing, he began to get a sense of Auric's increasing disquiet. More than that, he began to perceive more and more about the pattern of stones. He could see that faint, near-invisible lines of psychic force joined all of them, and that they formed a lattice of energy that was somehow connected to Auric. He knew that the eldar was using this as a focus for his visionary powers, trying in some way to steer a safe course into the future in the manner similar to the way Simon guided a ship through the immaterium.

The pattern pulsed with possibilities, was pregnant with many futures. It had a hypnotic fascination for him. The vortex of energy inexorably drew him closer, until he hovered a mere arm's span away. Looking now at each jewel in turn he began to see that the lines of force were not only connected in some way to the farseer but also to the gem on his forehead. What had Auric done?

The suspicion blossomed in his mind that the dreamstone fused to his flesh was more than merely a protective talisman. The eldar had done something else. He sensed plans within plans, and hidden motives behind hidden motives. Anger touched him then, and fear. He saw that these hovering jewels were more than merely a focus of psychic power, more than a means of viewing potential futures. In some strange way, they represented a vast gameboard. The rules applying to it were ones he could not even begin to guess. These gems were also a way of influencing the future.

No! That was incorrect. What they represented was a way of influencing the future. The act of prophecy itself shaped things. Seeing parts of the pattern allowed you to take action to change that pattern, and that added an element of uncertainty to the entire pattern. By taking action on what he saw here, Auric sought to influence the future. He could gauge his own responses and shape what he wished to happen.

It was something akin to using a small pebble to start an avalanche. Or perhaps it was like the example the ancient philosophers had been so fond of, where the flapping of a butterfly's wing on one side of a planet caused a storm on the other, simply by affecting the complex interacting currents of the air.

And the stones were not just connected to Auric and to him. In some way they were connected to everything, to the whole vast ebb and flow of events across the universe. His head spun. It was too big for him to begin to comprehend. Instead, he chose to concentrate on individual stones, to try and see what he could perceive himself.

Naturally the stone that first drew his eye was the one that represented man, and in some way, himself.

Looking into it, he saw himself, not just as he was now, but as he had once been, and perhaps one day would be. He saw himself as a child on Crowe's World, an orphan apprenticed to the trading houses. He saw himself attend the mission schools. He saw his first day at work and the great battles in which he had fought, and he saw his rise to power and fame. Now though for the first time he sensed the presence of the thing that had dogged him. He saw what he owed to it, and to his hell-accursed powers.

He saw now that the luck he had possessed was a product of what lay within him. He saw the insight he had been granted into the motives and tactics of others had come from his latent psychic powers. He saw that always something within him had shielded him from detection from the forces of the Imperium, but whether it was a natural gift or something reaching out to cloak him from beyond he could not say. He saw too that there had been shadows dogging him, creatures of evil that had watched him and waited. Faces he recognised and faces he did not crowded his sight. He saw Justina and her servants; he saw a man he had worked with in the offices of Sansom & Sansom on Crowe's World. He saw men who had been his business partners and warriors he had fought alongside. All of them had helped shape his life and wittingly or unwittingly had driven him onto the path he had taken.

He became aware that something snuffled on his trail even now, that malign intelligences sought him and were for the moment baffled by the shields the eldar had laid about him. He saw too that it could not last for long. Those who wanted him were too powerful and too driven to be thwarted by even the most potent of magics. He became aware that this was all part of a greater pattern that involved him and the farseer and many others.

Now inexorably his eye was drawn to something else, to the stone that represented the Great Enemy. Other stones orbited now, gems that represented women, men, ships and events, all of them somehow familiar, but it was the central gem that attracted him. His attention fell towards it, drawn once more like a meteor into a gravity well.

He saw things now. He saw worlds of terror ruled over by beings of daemonic power. He saw things that feasted on the darkness that lurked in the human soul, and not just the human soul, but the souls of all sentient beings. He saw scorpion-tailed women and monstrous crab-clawed daemons. He saw things that were not even remotely humanoid and things that wore the shape of men, and to his horror he saw that one of them was himself. The vision swirled and he saw something that might have been a beautiful woman or man. And as he watched it began to change until it was himself. He knew that in some strange unclear way, he was looking into a future.

The thing looked like him. It dressed like him. It had the same scars, the same voice, the same mannerisms. Only that which lay behind its eyes was not human. The soul that occupied the body was not his. Perhaps once it had been him, but something had battened onto it, sucked the energy from it, left it a cold husk and then took over his shape. It wore his flesh and his memories like a man might wear a suit, but it was not him.

He saw this being occupying his life, like a squatter in someone else's house. It rebuilt his fortunes. It made its name among men. It rose high in the councils of the great. It gathered men and wealth and power to itself. It maintained a façade of the utmost respectability, and behind that façade lived a life of the utmost debauchery and wickedness. And all the while, as the span of its years lengthened, it worked on its great plan. It became wealthy beyond the dreams of avarice, using means too despicable to contemplate. It used its money to buy machines and weapons and men. It used the levers of political power to steer the worlds into conflict, and man and eldar into war.

Janus saw now what Auric feared. Part of him wondered if what he witnessed was merely the farseer projecting his own thoughts into his mind, but he felt that this was not the case. He felt like he really had tapped into the farseer's powers and was witnessing a possible future. Not that he was in any position to be able to judge, he thought sourly.

Other futures fanned out like a peacock's tail. In some of them, the humans won their war and destroyed the eldar of Craftworld Ulthwé. In others, they were themselves destroyed when the xenogens deployed weapons of apocalyptic power. In all of the timelines though, destruction was wrought on an enormous scale by the thing that wore Janus Darke's body. Was it possible that one entity could create so much devastation, Janus wondered? A stone starts an avalanche, he thought; a butterfly's wing begets a cyclone. Yes, it was possible.

He felt his sanity teeter on the brink. He had gone his entire life without realising all of the possibilities that lurked in his future waiting to devour him. It was as if he had been blind all of his life and suddenly been given vision. How could he have known his decisions could have had so great an effect? He had blundered blindly along his path, unaware of all the people he had affected and all the things that he might have done. It was possible that somewhere in the past he might have taken a different route, might have avoided this altogether, but such thoughts were senseless now. It was too late for that. Just as in one heartbeat it would be too late to regret the decisions he was taking this instant. For all of his actions held a decision, he realised, even if he did nothing. He could paralyse himself by indecision, for some of those futures would come about through his own inaction.

Now too he became aware of the fatal flaw in the farseer's vision: it was imperfect. Just as each decision birthed its own future, it also created its own shadows on the mirror of the future. He could not forsee the consequences of all his actions. It simply was not possible for any mortal mind to encompass them all.

And that was not taking into account the fact that some timelines were hidden from view. They folded away into the future, and were hidden behind other events like roads being hidden behind hills, or a ship disappearing out of sight on the other side of a massive wave. For the future was not fixed. It was not simply a choice between linear paths. Every decision held the seed of another decision. Every path divided and divided again at critical points. The whole mass seethed like an ocean in turmoil, responding to the tiniest of stimuli – the way he moved his hand, what he saw from the corner of his eye. An eye blink could spawn a different eternity, he saw. There was too much information, too many stimuli. He felt like he was drowning under a tidal wave of images.

Despair swept over him. He saw too that there were other timelines, currently precious few, in which he survived the coming storm. In most of them, he saw Auric, Athenys and Simon and some of the others swimming against the tidal wave of disaster. But even in those every path eventually led down into darkness. In some, he was gunned down in a pointless petty battle. In some he died abed in old age. In one he choked on a fishbone. In another he was run down by an autocar while trying to cross the street.

What was the point, he thought? All roads led to death anyway.

What did it matter to him whether a daemon took his flesh and created a hell on earth with it? His flesh was doomed anyway. Death's bony claws stretched out everywhere. All of life was a nightmare that ended when breath stopped and the heartbeat ceased. He tried to pull himself away from the gems and their odd patterns, but he was caught in their intricate swirl of power.

Too late he saw another trap, that he could die even here, or at least be reduced to a mindless gibbering thing, his sanity crushed by seeing too much of too many things that man was not mean to see. Too late he saw that if this happened, the daemon that wore his face might be able to reach out and claim him.

He sensed something coming for him, reaching out through the lattice of energy that the farseer had created.

Too late he saw where all of those threads of possibility were connected through. Too late he realised that they all ran through the immaterium. It was the medium that connected all living things and all psychic powers. And it was also the place that held all of the daemons of Chaos including the thing that hunted him.

He felt its searching eye turn on him, saw the face that looked like his smile, and knew that there were things worse than death. Even if all there was to be looked forward too was oblivion then it was still preferable to what might happen to him if this thing caught him. He knew it would consume him, eat the very essence of his being, and yet part of him would live on, imprisoned within it and tormented.

It will not be like that, said a sweet, seductive voice from somewhere. *You will live forever within me, true, but you will experience what I experience, and believe me, that will be an immensity of things. You will know all of my joys and pleasure, partake of an infinity of ecstasies, look out through the eyes of an immortal, see worlds rise from the void, watch the births and deaths of universes. Death need hold no fear for you; contained within me are multitudes that already know this. You will share in my being and my power.*

The voice was the voice of a rebel angel: sweet, reasonable, persuasive, yet knowing and sympathetic to mortal aspirations and weaknesses. It understood him, as he wanted to be understood, forgave him all the things he wished to be forgiven. It knew his sins and his vices and overlooked them – no it encouraged them, for it knew that it was these things that made him human, and different from all others. It took him for himself, warts and all. A wave of joy and pleasure passed through Janus.

This was like looking on the face of the Emperor and seeing there not the stern visage of eternal, omnipotent judgement, but the face of a friend. This was not what he had expected at all.

They lie about us, mortal. They seek to keep you in terror, afraid of sin, afraid of life, afraid of yourself. They seek to keep you under their thrall by making you weak and powerless and small. We seek to set you free and your oppressors would prevent this.

The truth of the being's words seemed self-evident. He wondered how he had failed to notice this all of these years.

Ah, but you have noticed them. I am but telling you what you have always known deep in your heart, what you have already thought and then felt guilty about. Admit it, I am merely putting into words your own thoughts, and telling you that I agree with them. They are the truths of your birthright that your Emperor and all his little minions have sought to deny you.

Janus listened to the voice, seeking any note of falsehood, and could detect none. There was a rightness in the being's words.

They prate of duty, when they mean duty to themselves. They speak to you of honour, when what they mean is that you should honour them. They talk of obedience when what they mean is slavery. They tell you that you should worship your chains, and be grateful for your fetters. I am here to tell you something different. It does not have to be this way. You can join with us, and be free.

Janus almost reached out to the presence, but something held him back. He sensed he was being restrained by something, felt Auric near. He tried to shrug off the restraints but they were too strong. Still, he knew all he needed to do was hold out and the warm reassuring presence would find him. He felt a flow of almost smug satisfaction and wondered if it came from within him.

The presence was coming closer now, his astral senses bathed in its approach. Strange, pleasurable things happened to them. He smelled a perfume so intoxicating he felt like laughing, not only smelled it but tasted it, and felt it within what might have been his bones too. It was musky and hinted at pleasures forbidden and excessive. He felt like laughing. His whole being tingled with life.

Fool, whispered a small, distant voice, *you will doom us both*. Compared to the first presence's voice this was as harsh as stone grating against stone. *Stop fighting me, the daemon comes and now is not the time to confront it.*

The daemon comes, Janus wondered? What daemon? Slowly, the euphoria began to diminish. The realisation came as to what the first presence really was. It was something that wanted to consume his soul, and it did not matter that it promised the experience would be a pleasurable one; in the end all he would be was fodder to it. He sensed this knowledge too flowed from outside him. It was coming from the farseer. With the knowledge came a hint of desperation. The eldar, despite his knowledge and his power, was deathly afraid.

Slowly, that fear communicated itself to Janus, and warred with his sense of well-being. He sensed that the daemon was close now, so close that in moments he would not be able to avoid it even if he wanted to. Finally, he stopped resisting and gave way to the eldar's pressure. He felt himself being swept back to his body and the matrix of energy closed behind him.

Was it already too late?

SEVENTEEN
PLANS WITHIN PLANS

Janus crashed back into his flesh. A great weight pressed down on him. He was drowning in thick, viscous fluid. The thunder of blood through his veins was agonising. After the pure ethereal being he had just experienced, life itself felt like agony.

Desperately he tried to stop breathing in the turgid stuff but he could not, and slowly the realisation came to him that it was merely air. It just felt rough and heavy on his lungs after the lightness of the medium he had passed through as a disembodied spirit. He raised a hand that felt like it weighed a hundred tonnes, pushed against gravity as great as that on the surface of a gas giant. He touched the gem on his forehead. It felt warm and slick as if it were a living thing.

After a few heartbeats he began to tremble. Now that he was wrapped once more in flesh, the siren call of the daemon seemed somehow more, rather than less powerful. Had he really turned down the offer of immortality, of an eternity of ecstasy? Had Auric really prevented him from reaching his personal heaven? How cruel and wicked the eldar was, Janus thought, and he almost felt like crying.

The door of his chamber opened and the evil xenogen himself swept in. He was still garbed in his formal armour, the great sword bared in his hand. Eldritch runes glittered on the blade. A strange gem glowed on its hilt. Auric looked ready to do violence at any moment. Janus could sense the lethal power in that alien weapon. Certain death rode the merest kiss of that keen edge. There was no trace of the urbane aesthete now in Auric. What confronted him was an armoured warrior, dangerous as a daemon, and just as angry.

He moved the blade through an intricate formal pattern and its glowing tip left compelling lines of fire in the air. Janus found himself forced to look at them, and did so without flinching. Auric stood poised and Janus knew that his life was balanced on a knife-edge at that moment. If he did or said the wrong thing, he would die instantly. Suddenly the blade swept forward with the speed of a lightning stroke. Janus could not have avoided it even if he wanted to.

He felt something snap on his chest and looking down, he saw that Auric, with consummate and astonishing skill, had severed the chain holding the talisman Justina had given him, without breaking Janus's skin. The eldar now lifted the talisman, balancing it on the point of his blade and inspected it, like a man might inspect a huge, venomous spider.

'You could have destroyed us all, mortal. This thing is tainted by the power of Chaos.'

Janus thought back to his encounter with the daemon, and his viewing in the stones. It seemed to him that there was a subtle wrongness in the eldar's words. 'No. *You* could have destroyed us all.'

Auric laughed. 'In a sense you are correct, Janus Darke. I misjudged the strength of your power, despite all of my attempts not to do so, and I misjudged the strength of the destiny that connects us.'

'You are not telling me the entire truth, Auric.' Janus knew it was the case. Something had happened during the ritual, something that had granted him new insights into the eldar and his motives; some link had been forged between them. Perhaps it had always been there, and this was the first time he was acute enough to realise it.

The eldar's whole posture radiated surprise. He obviously had not expected these accusations. Janus turned things over in his mind. Perhaps he was wrong. Perhaps this new knowledge came from somewhere else. Perhaps it was a deception from the daemons.

He needed time to think, to consider his options. He felt that he was missing something, that there was a pattern here he might be able to perceive and understand if he was given time. It was how he had often felt before going into battle.

For the first time since he had started hearing the voices, he felt wholly alive and in his element.

'There are some things that it is better not to know,' said Auric.

'You cannot frighten me with hints and whispers.'

'I do not seek to frighten you. I am merely telling you the truth.'

'As you see it.'

To Janus's surprise, the eldar laughed. 'Yes – I tell everything as I see it. That is my gift and my flaw. And worlds have lived and died because of the way I see things.'

'You must be very certain of your gifts, or those who listen to you must be.'

'It is impossible to be certain of such gifts, Janus Darke. There are too many possibilities of error, too many ways for the Great Enemy to manipulate what we see. Hope and fear and desire cloud and shape the visions. What I see, I see only imperfectly. And yet–'

'And yet?'

'And yet, it is better than not seeing at all. Such visions have kept eldar civilisation alive since the dark times. Some of our kind foresaw the birth of the Enemy and

warned our people. Few listened, but those who did lived.
It has lent weight to the words of the farseers ever since.'

'I imagine that it would.'

'You are being very glib about things you know nothing
about, human. These are matters of life and death to my
people.'

'You take a lot upon yourselves,' said Janus with considerable irony.

'We do, and we do not do so lightly,' said Auric. 'We are
the light that guides our people along a dark path fraught
with perils, where the slightest misstep may mean extinc-
tion for all.'

'There is an arrogance about that statement I dislike,' said
Janus.

'We compel no one to follow us; they do so willingly.'

'You compel me to follow you. I do not do so willingly.'

'I have never placed a blade to your throat and made you
do anything, Janus Darke. You have always been given a
choice.'

'It has not felt that way.' Janus considered the farseer's
words and could see that they were true as far as they went,
but they did not tell the whole story. 'Subtle and not so
subtle forms of compulsion have been used upon me.'

'Nonetheless, choices were always yours.'

'That's not how I see it.'

Auric shook his head, like an adult dealing with a wilful
child.

Janus could see he would make no headway against the
eldar; he was not even sure why he was trying. He sensed
a subtle wrongness here that he wanted to probe. His experience with the farseer's runestones had given him some
inkling of the eldar's power, and he felt more than ever like
a fly caught in a subtle web. Or perhaps more like a beast
being herded to slaughter by the presence of dogs on either
side. It was not a sensation he liked.

'What are you doing here, Auric? Really.'

'I am trying to prevent a war, and incidentally save your
soul.'

'I sense that the latter is very incidental.'

'You are correct but it does not change the fact. Now pay attention, Janus Darke. We must soon descend onto Belial IV and there are things you must know.'

As he listened, Janus found some very dark thoughts flickering through his mind. Had the farseer really not known about Justina's amulet until just now? Why had he really performed the ritual without Janus present? Had he known the daemon would appear? Back on Crowe's World hunters staked out goats on the edge of swamps where dragons lived, hoping to lure them onto killing ground.

Janus was starting to feel that he knew exactly how those goats felt.

'WE HAVE ARRIVED,' said Simon Belisarius, speaking into the comm-net. He gazed out of the command deck's observation window down onto the planet below. It looked a cold unprepossessing place, in a long elliptical orbit around a feeble red sun. Sensor divination revealed very little life on the planet. Observation with long range holo-scopes showed many enormous ruined cities and signs of some ancient war or catastrophe. Belial IV must have once been a rich and populous world. Now it gave the impression of being a vast, haunted graveyard.

In the holosphere floating in front of him, he could see Athenys and Auric now wore full formal gear. The farseer was armoured, the woman wore a cloak of black silk trimmed with white fur. 'You have done well, Simon Belisarius,' said Auric.

'Have I discharged my part of the ancient debt?' Simon asked.

'Not yet, but soon. You will be informed. We wish to descend to the surface – order a shuttle readied. Janus Darke and his men will come with us.'

'You are expecting danger.'

'I am not expecting it, Simon Belisarius. I am certain of it.'

'Perhaps it would be best to tell us what to you expect then.'

'Janus Darke has assembled his men in the briefing room. They will soon learn all they need to know.'

'Very good. I will have the tech-augurs prepare sensor divinations of the surface as well.'

THE COMMAND CHAMBER of the *Pride of Sin* was full to the brim with Zarghan's followers. There were at least a hundred of them, and they were not a pretty sight. Most showed the stigmata of mutation or the wasting effects of too great a dedication to the pursuit of pleasure. One or two were quite obviously dying of some of the nastier diseases associated with it. No, Zarghan decided, not a pretty sight.

As he listened to the power chords surging in his head, the Chaos Marine had to admit that Shaha Gaathon had not been wrong when she called his men scum. Looking at them through the halo of curdled lemon coloured light that filled his vision, he had to agree that they were, for the most part, not people with whom he would want to spend eternity with. They were, he decided, the dregs of humanity, which was saying a lot. They were mostly members of various cults dedicated to the Lord of all Pleasure in his more warlike aspects, with a smattering of mutants, abhumans and the odd psyker thrown in. When he measured them against his former battle-brothers they were a tawdry lot. On the other hand, a warrior worked with whatever weapons were at hand, and this bunch was all he had.

His helmsman, old Malarys, who claimed to have once been a priest of the Emperor until his fondness for sacramental wine and other less mentionable things had got the better of him, stood before him.

'Belial IV, great leader,' he said. 'Not a good place. Haunted they say. Spirits of the eldar, they say.'

Zarghan considered this information. He did not really want to kill the old man. He was too useful a host for the

Chaos Marine's pet daemon. On the other hand, orders were orders.

'Perhaps you would like to explain your objections to all-knowing Shaha Gaathon, my friend,' said Zarghan in his most reasonable voice. All present flinched. Some laid off fondling their concubines, a few stopped injecting morphia. One or two even reached for their weapons. They knew that voice. When Zarghan used it it was time to walk very lightly indeed.

'That will not be necessary. As you desire, my lord. As you desire.'

Zarghan smiled. That was more like it. He studied the command deck. The drapes were rich and covered in pornographic images. Censers filled with hallucinogenic incense burned constantly. The far corner was a writhing mass of naked flesh where some of the crew were celebrating one of the major ritual orgies demanded by the Liberator. One benefit of such a profusion of cults was that there was always some holy day to celebrate. He leaned back on his throne and watched the old man begin the first of the ritual human sacrifices that would ensure they passed safely through the warp.

A pity, he thought. The child looked barely twelve and she had such pretty eyes.

KHAM BELL SENT Janus Darke an interrogative look as he entered the chamber. Twenty hard-bitten men in dark uniforms filed in behind him. Janus shrugged. Until an hour ago, he had known as much about what was to come as his master sergeant. In another few minutes, they would know as much as he did now.

He glanced over at the eldar. They stood in the far corner of the room, their black garb blending in with the shadows almost sinisterly. Auric still wore the formal mask and armour he had put on for his ritual. Athenys wore lightweight body armour of a type Janus did not recognise but which he supposed was of eldar make, beneath a coat of black trimmed with white fur.

Janus strode to the centre of the chamber to the command altar where he would be able to control the holospheres. He kept his back straight and his manner crisp and ignored all the stares his men aimed at the gem on his forehead. At least they were not making signs of protection against the evil eye, as the sailors did when they thought his back was turned.

Janus reviewed what he wanted to say, weighing how much of what the eldar had told him it would be sensible to tell his men. Most of them shared Kham Bell's prejudice against the xenogens, and Janus was not sure that he blamed them. He glanced around to make sure he had everybody's attention then stabbed a finger at one of the command runes on the altar. Immediately the chamber became dark, save for the dim glow of the holospheric representation of Belial IV that hovered in the centre.

'This is Belial IV. And yes, before anybody else asks, we are in the Eye of Terror.'

He heard gasps from some of the younger soldiers. He could tell they were shaken. The Eye was a name spoken of in hushed and horrified whispers in any place in the Imperium.

'The world is dead, the population were killed in a catastrophe.'

'Are there daemons, sir?' asked Harker, one of the youngest of the soldiers.

'So far our diviners have found nothing at all. No sign of life whatsoever.'

'Then there might be ghosts,' muttered someone from the back of the room. Janus was not sure who had spoken, but it did not matter. He could hear the fear.

'There might be, but I doubt it. From what the eldar have told me this world has been dead for at least ten thousand years. Any ghosts would most likely have faded long since.'

'They say time flows strangely in the Eye of Terror, sir.'

'Aye, they say. Nevertheless until we find out differently, I think it's safe to assume that we will find no ghosts. And if we do, then the farseer is an eldar priest of sorts. He will no doubt be able to exorcise them.'

'They are going with us, sir?'

'Aye, Sculley, they are. We're taking them to find a treasure.'

Janus paused to give that time to sink in. In a strange way reality had turned his earlier lie to truth. From what Auric had said there would be no shortage of precious eldar artefacts to be found down there, and he needed to give the men something to aim for. Telling them there was treasure was giving them a reason they could understand for coming here. He could almost feel the tension lessen in the room.

'Lots of treasure, sir?' asked Harker.

'Enough to make it worth our while to come to this benighted place.'

'Then it must be big indeed,' growled Kham Bell. Laughter filled the chamber. The sergeant was not laughing. Janus could tell he was still wondering why they had come here without him being told. Janus did not blame him for that either.

'I think I can assure you of that. We have the pick of the plunder of an entire world to look forward to.'

Janus sincerely hoped that this was the case, but he was not so certain. Some of these men would probably die to get Auric where he wanted to go, and he did not feel good about leading them to their destruction. On the other hand, he did not see what choice he had. It was either them or him, and when all was said and done, he was no hero.

'Now if you gentlemen would be so kind as to give me your full attention, I will tell you what we are about.'

He touched the runes again, his fingers flickering fast, as he made changes to the holosphere to illustrate his point.

'This is the southern continent of Astayan.' The globe swelled and disappeared as a massive landmass zoomed into view. Their point of view soared across a desert of ash, a chain of burning mountains and came to rest on a monstrous ruined city.

'This is the city of Zytheraa, once the most populous place in the world.' The towers were smashed and broken now, but even so it was easy to see that humans had not built the place. Even the broken stumps of the buildings looked too fragile and too graceful. Their crystalline forms glittered in the baleful light of the gloomy red sun. They looked more like plants than manufactured structures. They seemed to have grown to fit in with the hills on which they rested, and blend in with the bay around which they lay.

Janus guessed that before whatever catastrophe had struck the city down it must have been a beautiful place. Even now there was something about it that... He forced his mind back to the task at hand.

The viewing perspective swung over a massive bridge that seemed spun from spiderwebs and starlight although it was huge enough to take several super-heavy tanks abreast, and then came to rest in a low, curved structure that overlooked a dried out lake. The hulks of several pleasure craft lay in the dust below.

Janus gestured and their point of view dropped closer. As it did so, he once more began to get some idea of the scale of the building and the bridge. The building was larger than the *Star of Venam*, a city contained within a city.

'This is the Temple-Palace of Asuryan. It was a holy place to the ancient eldar, a place where great wealth and many artefacts were stored. We are going to put down here and enter the temple and find one of those artefacts...'

'What artefact, sir?'

'It is a sword. About the height of a man and made entirely of black crystal.'

'Won't that break on the first swing, sir,' said someone. Other voices laughed.

'Apparently not. Apparently it is hard enough to cut through duralloy and strong enough to endure the destruction of a world. I am quoting our eldar friends over there.'

'Is that what they have come for, sir?'

'It is. Anything else we find is ours. As long as we can carry it out.'

'Surely those ancient people must have left some defences for their treasure?' said Kham Bell. Janus could tell he was thinking about the temple on Typhon and what had lain in wait for them there.

'That would be a fair assumption but it would be a false one. These were an extremely peaceful folk until disaster overtook them. War and crime were unknown.'

'Sounds unlikely,' said Kham Bell. 'I will believe it when I see it.'

'I agree. We will take all sensible precautions. We will go in full battle array, and take nothing for granted. Touch nothing unless one of the eldar has cleared it. There may be some ancient machines still active.'

'How long do we expect to be on the surface, sir?'

'As long as it takes. The palace is a big place, as you can see, and it may take us some time to locate the sword. The farseer hopes to be able to find it swiftly, but there may be complications.'

Janus thought it best not to mention that the farseer hoped to find it by using his psychic powers. The men were spooked enough by the situation as it was.

'How will we get back?' Harker asked. 'To Medusa, I mean.'

'The same way as we came. Simon Belisarius brought us here. He can bloody well take us back.' There was nervous laughter, then Sculley asked the question he had been dreading.

'And when we get back, sir? What then? What about the Inquisition?'

There was not much he could say to that one. The only response was a lie. Janus was pleased that his voice sounded so confident when he spoke. 'This is a secret mission on behalf of the Imperium. Mention it to no one. I mean *no one*. If word of this leaks out, it could mean the death of every man here.'

Heads nodded. Janus was not sure if they believed him or not, but they could all see the sense of what he was saying. They were all in the same boat now. If anybody breathed a word of where they had been been, it was a death warrant for every man aboard this ship. The Inquisition would not care whether they had knowingly broken the interdict. All it would take account of was that they had. No excuses would be accepted. Janus wondered how long it would take the men to work out what he had done to them, and how much they would hate him when they did. Kham Bell's glare told him that at least one man present had already figured it out. Too late to worry about that now, he thought.

Another part of him worried that the Inquisition had good reasons for keeping the Eye of Terror under interdict. In the unlikely event they survived this and returned to the realms of men, who knew what they might take with them? Some daemonic plague, some hidden evil that had seeped into the men's souls, some dreadful thing he could not even begin to imagine.

After all, his own problems had only really hit him after Typhon. Was this the real reason they were here, he wondered, to bring home a shipload of men as corrupted as himself to the Imperium? It was not a pleasant thought.

'Any more questions?' he asked.

'Aye,' growled Kham Bell. Janus flinched wondering what was coming now. 'What are the bonus arrangements?'

'Usual shares,' said Janus. 'Every man on the ground gets a double share. In the event of casualties, the survivors take the dead man's shares.'

'What about them?' asked the sergeant, stabbing a finger in the direction of the eldar.

'They get the sword. They want nothing else.'

Kham Bell sucked his teeth. 'That is mighty generous of them. I wonder why?'

You are not the only one, thought Janus, but kept his suspicions to himself.

'Right, dismissed. I want every man aboard the lander inside the hour. Soonest done, soonest home.'

The men rushed out to get their gear and head for the shuttle. Only the sergeant stayed behind. 'I don't know what they have done to you, laddie,' he said, 'but bringing us here wasn't right. I know it, you know it, and they know it. If anything goes wrong, there will be hell to pay.'

The sergeant got up and stalked to the door.

'There already is,' muttered Janus to his departing back.

EIGHTEEN
THE BIRTH OF A GOD

THE ARMOURED SHUTTLE settled down on the crystal plain outside the enormous temple palace. Janus strode out through the airlock, down the gangplank and set his feet on a new world again.

'I claim this world for the Emperor of Humanity and his Imperium. I bring justice and truth for the loyal. Punishment and death for the guilty,' he murmured automatically, the words of the ancient formula springing to his lips from force of habit. He took a deep breath of the air. It tasted tainted. He tried to dismiss the thought. It simply missed the industrial tang of Medusa, or the faint chemical stench of recycled air within the *Star of Venam*, he told himself, but could not quite bring himself to believe it. There was something about this place that made his flesh crawl and set his nerves on edge.

He strode forward and looked for a place to plant the standard. It would not do to try to break the hard crystal of the pavement and fail. It would be unpropitious. Behind him the boots of his men rang on the duralloy of the gangplank. The sound altered as they hit the eldar material covering the ground.

He glanced back, shocked by the lack of numbers. Only twenty, he thought. Once I would have brought down nearly a thousand. There would have been dozens of shuttles, tanks, artillery, all of the things a rogue trader needed to show uncivilised savages the might of the Imperium. Glancing around, he doubted that the original inhabitants of this place would have been all that impressed. They looked to have been anything but savages.

Even their ruins had a certain grandeur, and there was a sadness as well as an evil that brooded over them. He found himself striding towards an ancient statue of a tall slender robed eldar woman. It had been chipped and its nose and part of an ear as well as most of its right arm were missing, but it was still beautiful.

Some collector back in the Imperium would pay a small fortune for workmanship like that, he thought, then smiled. It seemed that the reflexes of a lifetime of plunder and trade had not abandoned him. He still looked at everything with the eyes of a potential looter.

His men fanned out behind him, looking for threats, finding cover, holding their lasrifles and bolters ready for action at a moment's notice. They too had come like conquerors in their heavy body armour and metal helmets. Suddenly he wanted to laugh.

Twenty men on this dead world and they were treating it like an expedition of conquest. It suddenly seemed like an exercise in futility.

Still, his men were not to blame. Such things were part of the mythology of the rogue trader. Had not Herman Bloch conquered the whole of the Zacatan continent with only 150 men and one Rhino APC? Kyle Langer had brought Kallista into the Imperium with a thousand troopers, and that had been an armed industrial world. In better days, he himself had contributed something to those Imperial legends, and those men over there still believed in him, at least a little.

He found a crack in the paving, wondering what force had caused it, and pushed the standard home, then ritual complete he watched the eldar descend onto the face of Belial for the first time in more than ten thousand years. They came fully armed and armoured beneath their robes of black.

If it was a homecoming for them, it was a bleak one, Janus thought.

THE ENTRANCE BEFORE them was huge and marked with runes in the graceful flowing script of the eldar. Before they entered, Auric knelt and spoke what sounded like words of prayer. The door, which had appeared to be made of some solid silvery metal, flowed outwards like liquid and he passed within. Athenys followed. Janus gestured for his men to follow and then strode into the warm darkness after them.

The ceiling curved above them. Beautiful mosaics, seemingly untouched by time, glittered on the floor. They depicted trees, forests and scenes of great natural beauty. As they progressed through the place, Janus found there was something subtly disturbing about them. In many of the scenes there were hunts, or what looked like stealthy murders or ritual sacrifices. They became darker as they progressed.

As if sensing his mood, Auric turned and said, 'The palace was built late in our history. The great corruption had already begun.'

Janus lengthened his stride, until he walked beside the farseer. 'The great corruption?'

'When my people first encountered the harbingers of the Great Enemy, they did not run from them. Some of them embraced them.'

Janus considered this. It sounded not unlike the Chaos cults that were said to riddle the Imperium. 'Did you not scourge them from your halls?'

'No. Such was not our way. In those days we did not even recognise the enemy for what he was, for he wore our face.'

'He came in disguise?' asked Janus mockingly, for he was tired of the eldar's cryptic games. 'Or he was possessed by a daemon?'

'No. I shall tell you a great secret of my people, Janus Darke.'

'I am honoured.' Sarcasm dripped from his voice.

'More than you will ever know.'

'What is this secret?'

'It concerns the Lord of Pleasure. We are him. He is us.'

'By "we" do you mean all of us?'

'I mean my people, the eldar.'

'I do not understand.'

'Soon you will. That is why I am trusting you with secrets that only a few of my people know.'

'That is not very flattering, particularly since most of my men are within earshot and now also share these close held secrets.'

'They have not heard us. We have not been speaking with our voices.'

Janus laughed mockingly and glanced around to see if any of the others also saw the funny side of this, but he received only curious stares from Kham Bell and the men. Perhaps they really had not heard. Perhaps the eldar had warped their minds with some of his sorcery. Or perhaps it was as he claimed and they had been speaking only with their minds. Perhaps they always had. Perhaps that was why they had been so unconcerned by Stiel's listening devices. Was it possible? Could this have been happening all along without him noticing it?

Just the thought was disturbing.

By NIGHTFALL, THEY were deep within the palace and still had not found what they were looking for. Janus was left with a profound appreciation for just how large this structure really was. They had been on the move for close to ten hours and the ruby red light of the sun had faded in the skylight overhead. The rest of the corridors had darkened into a sort of twilight gloom, as if seeking harmony with the cycle of night and day. It had been a long day, broken by many stops while the farseer opened the huge sealed doors with his spells and Janus was tired.

The men had made camp in a great hall that contained a sunken pit that once might have been a pool. A statue of what looked like some warlike eldar god stood on a plinth in the middle. Sentries were set, camping stoves and field rations produced. Weapons lay close at hand. Janus could understand why. The feeling of gloom had intensified with the coming of night. The sense of melancholy and evil had both increased. It was as if the sadness and wickedness of an entire people had seeped into the very stones, leaving a residue that would taint any who came after.

The long shadows contained a hint of menace. Men talked louder as if to ward off the unnatural silence, then once they realised what they were doing, their voices faded into scared whispers. Several of them cast uneasy glances at the eldar, as if wondering why they had been brought to this place. Most likely thoughts of the bloody sacrifices they had seen depicted on the murals were still in their minds.

Janus himself was uneasy. All day the sense of wrongness had increased and with it the fear inside him had grown. Something terrible had happened here, he thought, and something terrible was going to happen here again. And he knew now that he was going to be part of it. Something told him that it was all part of a pattern as sure as he had seen it laid out in the farseer's runestones. He stroked the smooth flesh where his little finger had been. It was strange how natural it seemed now, and that there was no pain. Remembering the events leading up to the loss of his finger made Janus flinch.

Janus sat down cross-legged between Athenys and Auric. The farseer appeared lost in meditation, crooning a strange song. The runestones orbited him, like tiny moons circling a gas giant. Athenys sat alertly as if expecting danger at any moment. It seemed once again that the farseer was using his powers, although for what purpose Janus could not say.

As he listened, Janus felt heavy with fatigue. His eyelids grew heavy, his head slumped down onto his chest and strange dreams stole stealthily into his skull.

Images began to spin through his mind. He hovered over the city as it had once been, in the days when mighty spirit engines had provided it with power. He saw a wonderful place filled with beautiful, peaceful people. He saw long crystalline ships flying through the sky. He saw sorcerers draw on the energy of massive psychic engines to raise vast starscraping towers whose sides were smooth as glass and stronger than steel. He saw an age of peace and plenty when the eldar dreamed their alien dreams of perfection and splendour underneath the light of an uncorrupted sun.

He saw great webs of energy lace the land. He saw hidden highways being woven between the stars. In a heartbeat he understood the answer to one great mystery – why eldar ships were never encountered in the warp. They used other pathways, built by the ancients, in a time before the Imperium was even born. He caught a glimpse of the arrival of mighty liners and enormous trading caravels from other worlds, and he began to realise the reach that eldar civilisation had once possessed.

Centuries passed, then millennia, and the cities grew. As they did so the images became darker, the people more debauched. More and more power brought greater and greater wealth and luxury, and that in turn, brought spiritual corruption. He saw the eldar grow corrupt. He saw great orgies of indulgence and torchlit rallies where painted prophets spoke words of wickedness to a willing audience. One of them seemed somehow familiar. It was not anything about his appearance: it was his aura. It was the same as the daemon Janus had encountered in his last vision. It was in some strange way Shaha Gaathon or someone possessed by him. He moved through the crowds talking and preaching, hidden by potent spells from even the psychic senses of the eldar. The Harbinger of Slaanesh, come to prepare the way for the god's birth.

He saw the hidden daemon preach. Many listened, perhaps the majority, for his words were persuasive and his presence great.

A few of the eldar had some presentiment of the disaster. Some turned their faces from the dark and prepared to flee their worlds in great arks, but most stayed and so were doomed. Others, the priests who had built this temple, who also saw gathering doom, remained and tried to preach against the corruption. When this failed, they retired to its depths to forge a weapon against what was to come. Using engines of awesome power, they forged a sword that was not a sword, but a captured echo of the death force of the universe bound into the shape of a blade. Then they waited for their doom to come upon them.

The days grew darker, strange savage rites stained the streets with blood, and eldar hunted eldar for pleasure through the streets of the city. Red garbed priests rose, preaching the coming of a new god, a deity created by the eldar themselves, who would lead them into an age of ever greater wonders and life everlasting. Janus did not know how he understood what was going on, but he did. It unreeled before his eyes like scenes from a vast pageant. Over it all brooded the smiling enigmatic face of Shaha Gaathon.

There came a day when a mighty ritual was performed under the supervision of those perverse and dedicated priests, the ritual they promised would usher in a new age of even greater splendour and pleasure. He saw the faces of the crowd aglow as they watched the rituals being performed. He saw the creation of mighty vortices of energy linked between many worlds. He saw the pride and the power written on every face, and then saw the horror enter their expressions as the watchers realised that something had gone wrong.

Lightning flickered, black clouds raced across the sky. The sun's rays reddened and a blood-coloured light illumined the crowds. Janus sensed something grow. As the ritual took place, something was born: something dark and evil and terrible. From the vortices, shafts of light lanced out, striking at every eldar, extending tentacles into every soul, reaching out to grasp every being on the surface of the planet. He saw the eldar scream with a mixture of pleasure and horror as the summoned thing drew the very life from them, consuming their souls and their bodies, reducing them to a fine powder of ash that blew away in the wind. With each death, with every soul it absorbed, the dark thing grew stronger and stronger.

The priests emerged from the shrine of Asuryan, armed with their weapon that had been so long in forging. It was a blade that glowed brighter than the sun, and was pregnant with the power of death, a blade powered by the mighty spirit engines that slept beneath the temple. They came for Shaha Gaathon, the dark prophet. The leader of the priests cut and wounded him, and the prophet vanished, fleeing beyond their reach. Filled with triumph the eldar high priest turned on the newborn god.

He struck the growing thing and wounded it, but it was not enough. The new being was too strong. It threw itself at the priests and consumed them, and they died screaming in ecstasy and horror. The few that survived snatched up the sword and were driven back within their fortress temple. They forced closed the doors, but not even the mighty seals they invoked could save them. The tentacles of the dark god reached into the heart of the temple, found them and consumed them. All save the one who bore the blade, who sealed himself into the ultimate sanctuary beneath the temple and vanished behind its spell walls.

And the day of destruction came. And so was Slaanesh born. A daemon god birthed by the dark side of the eldar soul, a composite being composed of every single life-force it had devoured. He knew now why the eldar feared and hated the Lord of Pleasures so.

His eyes snapped open and he saw that Athenys and Auric were staring at him. His mind reeled from the vision he had just seen. Not for a moment did he doubt its truth.

Was this what had happened to all of the eldar, Janus wondered? Had this scene been re-enacted on their every world? Had most of an entire race really been consumed to feed the newborn deity? He did not doubt that the answer was yes. The two eldar bowed their heads as if they had been secretly reading his thoughts and were ashamed of what he had seen.

NINETEEN
THE PRIDE OF SIN

SIMON SENSED THAT something was wrong. He strode across the command deck, dropped into the Navigator's chair and began hooking himself up. He had felt a slight disturbance in the fabric of space-time, the sort that any Navigator associated with either the arrival or departure of a ship. On instinct, he barked an order to the crewmen.

'Ready for action,' he said. If this was a false alarm it might prove a little embarrassing, but what of it? He doubted that any ship appearing out of the immaterium within the Eye of Terror was going to be friendly. He would much rather look like a fool than be a corpse. The crew were surprised but they were well trained. They sped into their combat positions. At that moment, Simon realised how on edge they must have been, knowing where they were. Only after they had taken their stations and sounded the klaxons, did the helmsman ask, 'What is it, sir?'

By this time Simon had already patched himself into the command chair, and was reaching out with the sensors to scan the space all around them. He concentrated for a moment, and picked up the spoor. There! Space rippled where a discontinuity had been established. He extrapolated the inbound course from the probability wake and found his worst fears confirmed. There was no way that ship had leapt in from anywhere outside the Eye. It must be a native.

He could almost feel the tingle of the immaterium. A further heartbeat of scanning located the enemy vessel. He had not yet achieved visual contact but he did not need to. The probing fingers of his sensors told him the exact shape of the vessel right down to the last tiny gun turret.

She looked old but huge, a warship of the most ancient Imperial design. From memory he called up all the blueprints and he could see she did not quite conform. Changes had been made. Turrets had been added here and there, and weapons of a pattern with which he was not familiar. Gargoyles encrusted the hull like barnacles. A massive head grinned from the prow. It was shaped like the tip of an enormous horned phallic member bearing the scowling features of some ancient daemon. No mistaking what it was at all, it was a vessel of the slaves of darkness and it appeared to be coming for them.

Simon took another look at its wake. There was something disturbing about it, something touched by evil, and he was not sure what it was.

He was certain that whatever propelled the ship was no wholesome power. There was something about it that caused him enormous unease, that reminded him of those things he had seen in the warp. The whole thing reeked of old evil. Was it possible for a ship to be possessed, he asked himself?

Why not? If human flesh could be possessed, why not ancient steel? If the mind of a man could be devoured by daemons, why not a datacore? Who knew the limits of the powers of Chaos, particularly here in the Eye of Terror, at the very heart of darkness? He barked out more orders to the men, telling them to ready their weapons. The chanting of the tech-adepts increased as they prepared the ship's systems for action. The deck vibrated as massive bulkheads began to seal.

He continued to study the Chaos craft. His current assessment was that the *Star of Venam* might well be over-matched. The enemy ship looked to be based on a heavily modified version of the Iconoclast class of destroyer. It appeared to be much slower than normal which hinted that it was much more heavily armed and armoured than the basic version. Studying it closely, he could see that there were many odd things about it, a hint of subtle wrongness that made his flesh creep.

He knew that with Janus on the ground the command decision fell to him: stay and fight or cut and run. Staying and fighting might well result in the loss of his craft; even if they survived, the ship might well be so crippled that they would never be able to leave the Eye of Terror. On the other hand, running for it would mean abandoning the landing party to their fate. He did not relish the thought of leaving Janus Darke and the others to the tender mercies of the worshippers of the Dark Powers. Unless, of course, the Chaos raider could be drawn off in pursuit. The shuttle currently was shielded and giving off a very faint energy signature. The landing party were not even with it. Shielded by the walls of the Palace of Asuryan, they would probably not show up on any sort of divinatory scan. And any pirate would most likely to be more tempted by a trad-ing ship such as the *Star* than a small group of men on the ground.

Given the circumstances, the best bet seemed to be to make a run through normal space, hoping to lure the pirate into battle under more favourable conditions, or to draw him out and lose him in the cometary halo, return-ing to pick up Janus later. Simon quickly decided this was the best plan.

'Mister Stack, take her out of orbit at 75 per cent speed. We want to bring those Chaos bastards after us if we can. Mister Render, focus the tightest comm-beam possible on the Palace of Asuryan, and get me Captain Darke. I want no leakage – if they spot any communications we're signing the death warrant of the men on the ground. Get to it, gentlemen.'

The crew responded to their orders with well-trained discipline. Simon studied the sensor net, waiting for the next move to unfold. Let's see how the pirates respond to this, he thought.

'INTERESTING,' SAID ZARGHAN, stroking the head of his favourite pet, a naked redhead named Mara. 'It looks like their ship was crippled, judging by the speed they are making, unless it's some sort of trick.'

He took another puff on his hookah and let the drug lift his spirits as he considered his options. He had been told that he would find his prey on the surface of Belial. All of the omens pointed to it. The question was whether they had already gone down to the surface or not. If they had and they had found out what they were looking for, the ship could be preparing for a warp jump. That was not good, they might escape, and Zarghan's reputation would suffer. His secret music skirled despondently.

He looked around at his crew. They were tense and ready. The orgies were over, the pleasure feasts done. The only drugs in their systems now were combat drugs designed to increase speed, efficiency and ferocity. Zarghan kept a careful eye on them. The fact that the drugs had already driven most of their users psychotic was not entirely irrelevant. He believed he had already winnowed out the weak ones, the ones who became gibbering paralysed lunatics or who turned on their fellows in foaming madness, but you could never tell. There was always the possibility that a man might crack under stress and have to be permanently retired with a bolter shell. So far, so good, thought Zarghan. Everybody looked steady. The ground attack shuttles were prepared to go. What to do, he wondered? What to do?

If only he could be certain that the prey were down there, he would lead the ground crew down and the trader's ship could go to hell for all he cared. No, that was not strictly true, it was a working ship and armed, and seizing such a vessel would double the reduced size of his fleet at a stroke. He decided, on considered reflection and another pull at the mouthpiece, that he wanted it. The music in his head swelled in triumphant agreement.

That would mean ordering the *Pride of Sin* to pursue it, which would mean leaving somebody else on the command deck. Obviously that meant leaving no one capable of interstellar navigation on the ship.

He kept his crew loyal with the finest pleasures procurable but there were always some who were dissatisfied no matter how much you gave them or how well you led them. Given a chance, they might well take the ship and leave Zarghan and his men stranded on the surface of Belial. Being stuck on the surface of that tediously dead world, facing the prospect of an eternity of boredom, was not one that pleased the Chaos Marine. He could think of few less attractive prospects. He would only have a hundred men to toy with – and they would be depleted far too soon.

It was something of a problem, he had to admit. He had to lead the landing party himself. He was taking no chances that any of his minions would make a mistake and kill Darke.

And he understood there were a couple of eldar down there, and it had been centuries since he had broken any of them to his will. If possible he wanted at least one of them alive as well. That was a pleasure he was not prepared to forsake.

Granted it meant disobeying the spirit of the orders Shaha Gaathon had given him but he could certainly follow it to the letter. She had said kill the others, she had just not said when. Doubtless he would get round to killing the eldar soon enough once their torments bored him. That seemed fair to him. After all, he might as well gain the greatest measure of pleasure he could from this mission. He was sure it was what the Great Lord of all Pleasures would want.

This was getting him no closer to solving his problem though. He picked Hralf, one of his sergeants, a man who had on many occasions conned the ship but, as far as Zarghan knew, had no idea whatsoever about interstellar navigation. More to the point, he was as loyal as any man aboard.

At that moment, Malarys strode forward. 'Sir, we are receiving a transmission from the enemy starship. It's in a tightly focused directional beam.'

'What is the message, you old fool?'

'Janus Darke is on the planet. At the Temple of Asuryan. All we need to do is seek the shuttle craft.'

'Hralf – watch that ship, defend yourself if attacked and hold orbit over the planet. Begin a rigorous scan for any energy source, no matter how small.'

'As you desire, my lord.'

Zarghan chuckled to himself. One problem solved, he told himself. Doubtless the ship would return to pick up its commander, and when it did, he would have it too. Things were turning out rather well, he thought.

'WHAT IS THE problem, Janus Darke?' asked Athenys. Had she been reading his mind, Janus wondered, or had she just watched the way his hand cupped the earbead? He shook his head groggily. Simon's communication had woken him from a profound sleep. He checked the ambient light. It was almost dawn.

Janus spoke loudly so that his men would understand the situation as well. 'Another ship has arrived. Simon Belisarius has taken the *Star of Venam* out of orbit to try and lure it away from us, but so far he has not succeeded. Also it looks like multiple landers are being deployed from orbit and will come down close to our own. Simon has already ordered the shuttle to take off and perform evasive manoeuvres while it finds a hiding place. Perhaps it will draw them away from our landing site.'

'And perhaps not,' said Kham Bell. He did not sound hopeful. 'Is the ship an enemy?'

'It is a Chaos vessel and apparently belongs to the fleet that attacked our convoy at Conovar. At least it carries the same symbols as the survivors reported.'

'There were few enough lived through that attack,' said the sergeant. 'I do not like this at all, captain.'

'Nor I, Kham, nor I.' Janus had begun to see a pattern in these things. He did not think it was coincidence that a ship of the fleet that helped reduce him to near penury was in position overhead. There was a connection here, if he could just find it.

'What's the plan, captain?' asked Harker. The man obviously needed reassurance badly. Janus was sorry not to be in a position to give it to him. All he could do was make the best of a bad situation.

'We will proceed as before. Once we've got what we came for, Simon Belisarius will come back and take us off. With the other shuttles if need be.'

'What if he can't come back? What if the enemy ship destroys the *Star of Venam*?'

'It won't,' said Janus, wishing he was as confident as he sounded.

SIMON STUDIED THE tactical screens carefully. It looked like the Chaos commander was playing this one cautiously. The ship had not pursued. Instead it was going into a holding orbit directly over the southern city where Janus Darke had set down. It had not taken them long to find the energy pulse of the shuttle. It was almost as if they had known where to look.

Simon was uncertain what to do now. He had thought the *Star* would have made a much more tempting target than any landing party.

After all, without the starship, no one would be leaving this system anyway. It seemed the Chaos commander did not think like he did, though. Or perhaps there was something else at work here.

Perhaps there was something on the planet that they did not want us to find. Or perhaps they were looking for something specific, like the eldar. Simon knew enough about eldar culture to know that capturing a farseer would make a fantastic prize for someone.

More than that, he was disturbed by the fact that the ship belonged to the same fleet as attacked the *Valediction* off Conovar. The symbols on its side, and the configuration of the hull, were exactly the same as the men rescued from the escape pods had described. What was it doing here?

The Eye of Terror was a massive base for Chaos raiders, but getting in and out was problematic to say the least. What were the chances that the same raider would show up in both places? Very low, Simon thought. Those raiders had shown uncanny knowledge of their ships' cargoes and routes. They had always suspected there was a traitor in Darke's company feeding them information. This appeared to confirm it. Who else had known they were coming here?

Impossible, he thought. No one except Janus, the eldar and myself knew our destination until we got here and none of us are likely to be traitors. The crew did not even know where we were till a few hours ago. It was impossible for them to have got a message out, not unless there was a rogue psyker aboard.

Could the enemy ship have ridden our probability wake without me noticing? That was possible, but then why wait until we got here to attack unless they wanted us here for some reason of their own? Not a particularly reassuring thought under the circumstances.

Simon was too much in the dark, he needed to come up with a new plan. He was not going to be able to draw the enemy ship out of position. Armoured landing shuttles were already dropping from the raider to the planet's surface and their course would put them pretty much exactly at Janus's location.

The ship was going to have to be destroyed. He did not relish the prospect of a head-on attack but could not see any other way around it. It would be pointless trying to rendezvous with Janus's shuttle otherwise. The enemy ship would reduce it to so much slag as it made the sub-orbital boost, and that was not taking into account any damage the Chaos raider might do to the *Star of Venam* as it approached. Almost any plan he could think of had too many risks.

He sat back in his chair and drummed his fingers on the control panel. 'Gentlemen,' he said, 'prepare for battle.'

TWENTY
THE WAY IS OPEN

'AH, THE WORLDS of the eldar,' said Zarghan loudly, as he strode the courtyard of the Temple-Palace of Asuryan. Behind him scores of mutants, tattooed cultists and monstrous abhumans poured out onto the crystal streets of the eldar city. 'Nothing quite like them for filling you with the urge to destroy something. Makes you feel quite Khornate sometimes.'

His troops laughed loudly at his little joke. The followers of Slaanesh prided themselves on being as little like the devotees of the Lord of Blood and Skulls as it was possible to be and still remain Chaos worshippers, but they knew when to humour their leader.

Zarghan was not joking, however. There was something about this place that really did fill him with the urge to demolish things. He would have liked nothing better than to order a strike from the *Pride of Sin* on this accursed city, and he decided that as soon as the prize was taken that was exactly what he would do. He did not ask himself the reason for this extraordinary hatred; he just knew it was so.

Smashing this place to fragments, reducing it to rubble, would give him great pleasure, and that was all a follower of Slaanesh needed to know.

Apparently some of his troops felt the same way. Some of them were already testing their weapons on the statuary or blasting away at the large luminescent moths that floated against the still star-lit sky. Only a dozen or so of the hundred warriors were wasting ammunition though and he did not feel the need to make an example of any of them.

Let them have their fun, Zarghan thought; he had other things to do. It was time to locate their prey and he knew just the way to do it.

'THINGS DO NOT look good,' said Janus Darke. Kham Bell nodded his head in agreement. As soon as they had received Simon's message they had rushed to join the sentry they had set on this vantage point. From the high oval window of one of the towers above the courtyard, they had watched the shuttles arrive. They were evil-looking craft, encrusted with obscene gargoyles, forged from black steel and brass, bearing the runes of Chaos.

With mounting unease they had watched dozens of enemy troops disembark. These were the worst dregs of humanity mixed with abhumans, mutants and other things, but they looked fierce and well armed. Even as Janus watched through his night-vision magnoculars, one of them pissed on the banner he had planted earlier.

'What do you reckon?' asked the sergeant.

'I don't think we'll take them head-on,' said Janus in an attempt at humour. Both men knew how desperate things were. Both understood the implications of Simon Belisarius's tight beam message telling them he was being forced out of orbit. They knew they were trapped on the surface and desperately outnumbered.

'It's good to know that you haven't lost your keen appreciation of tactical realities,' said Kham Bell sourly. 'Think the aliens will be any help?'

Janus considered Auric's psychic powers and Athenys's deadly combat skills. He had no idea of the full extent of the farseer's abilities, but they must be considerable. They would certainly help, but he doubted that they could sway a battle against such overwhelming numbers. All it would take would be one stray bolter shell and the eldar would be dead, the same as any normal warrior. Athenys and Stiel might be put to good use though. There were certainly enough places for ambushes within the temple complex. A pity they had not brought more explosives and anti-personnel mines, he thought.

'They might be, but I would not count on it,' said Janus. 'There are just too many Chaos worshippers out there and unless I am mistaken, they are being led by a Chaos Marine from one of the Lost Chapters.'

Janus focused the magnoculars on the mighty figure leading the degenerates. He was certainly impressive. His armour was luridly coloured in bizarre patterns of purple, crimson and lime and as baroquely ornate as the shuttles that had brought him. One of his hands was a cyborg attachment of gleaming silvery metal. He held a chainsword of ancient design in one hand and a bolter in the other.

'He's one of the Emperor's Children, judging by that disgusting armour,' said Stiel, his quiet voice carrying across the empty chamber. Janus did not ask him how he knew. The assassin's mastery of a vast collection of esoteric lore had long ago ceased to surprise him. 'Let's hope there are no more of them. One will be bad enough.'

Janus scanned the darkness. 'Doesn't seem to be. Maybe a renegade of some sort.'

'They are all renegades here,' said Stiel. 'This is the Eye of Terror.'

'I am glad you told us,' sneered the sergeant. 'I would never have known otherwise.'

'What's the plan, captain?' asked Stiel.

'We find what we came for. We get out.'

'You make it all sound so simple,' said Bell sarcastically.

'All the best plans are,' said Janus, wondering why his head was starting to hurt. His sense of the darkness within himself increased. Never mind, he thought, it would be dawn soon. Even that thought did not lift his spirits.

'We've faced worse odds,' he said to the sergeant. 'Remember Crowe's World.'

Of course, there was no relief force coming from the Imperium to save them this time.

'SO THE FOLLOWERS of the Great Enemy have arrived,' said Auric. It wasn't a question. Janus nodded and squatted beside the two eldar. They sat cross-legged beside each other, looking perfectly relaxed and at ease. Janus wished he could duplicate their manner but it was impossible. He found the ancient crystalline structure deeply disturbing. There was something about it he just did not like.

'They've come in force,' said Janus. 'Far more than we can handle in a fight.'

'Then we will just have to avoid a confrontation until we are ready,' said Auric.

'That might prove easier said than done. There are a lot of them.'

'This is a large place,' said Athenys. 'And the temple-palace is a labyrinth.'

'How long do you think it will take to get what you came for?'

'It is located deep within this building. I must open the vault and activate the ancient power source,' said Auric. 'Then we shall see.'

'That might be a bit of a giveaway that we are here,' said Janus.

'There is no avoiding it, Janus Darke. We must go in.'

'Then what?'

'Then we will kill those who would desecrate this place,' said Auric.

'I wished I shared your confidence,' said Janus.

The corridor lit itself ahead of them. It was eerie, Janus thought, almost as if the building was alive and knew they were here and sensed their needs. Behind them as they marched the glow dimmed. Auric strode ahead, leading the way, pausing every now and again when they came to a junction, touching the runestones in his pouch as if communing with them over the correct direction.

'MALARYS, STEP FORWARD!' Zarghan commanded, staring around the entrance to the temple-palace. The old psyker did so. He had obviously been at the wine again. The Chaos Marine could smell it on his breath.

'As you desire, sire.'

'Find them for me. Find our prey!' Zarghan was gratified when the psyker did not ask how. It should be easy enough, after all. Aside from his own warriors, the ones they sought must be the only sentient beings on this continent.

Malarys closed his eyes and prepared to share his flesh with the daemon. He did not look too pleased, which was understandable since doing so would age him a year in a day, but he was not foolish enough to offer any protest to his master.

He began to chant, swaying from side to side, in a manner that reminded Zarghan of a serpent. His motions took on an odd sinuous quality and fire began to burn within his eye sockets. The glow was visible through the flesh of his eyelids. His body seemed to expand as the daemon filled him, but as it did so Zarghan sensed that something was wrong. The old man began to scream.

His flesh took on a ruddy tone. Lines of light played over his body, as the energy that filled him raced through his veins and lit his skin like a web of fire. An odd musky scent filled the air, at once repellent and alluring. Zarghan heard the old man's bones crack as he grew taller and watched the flesh stretch and reconfigure itself into a new and more beautiful shape. The aura of power that cloaked him was palpable. When he spoke the creature's voice was lovely, thrilling, ultimately commanding, filled with ancient evil and barely concealed malice.

'Abase yourself, Zarghan Ironfist, you stand before Shaha Gaathon, Prince of Chaos,' he said.

Such was the daemonhost's aura that, despite himself, Zarghan dropped to one knee, barely believing that he stood in the presence of one of the mightiest of the Lord of Pleasure's daemons. All around his men hurled themselves to the ground in a frenzy of adoration.

'I have come to lead this hunt myself,' said the daemon prince. 'Let us proceed.'

'As you desire,' said Zarghan, regaining his self-control.

The thing that had been Malarys sniffed the air and stretched his arms wide. 'It is good to breathe this air once more,' he said.

'SOON WE WILL arrive at the–' said Auric. Suddenly the farseer's words were cut off. He clutched at his head with his left hand. Janus looked up from where he lay propped against the wall. All around him his men sprawled, taking their rest for the fifteen minutes he had allotted them.

'What is it?' Janus asked. He glanced uneasily about. He was far too aware of the awful weight of the city that lay above them, and how deep below it they were. This tunnel seemed to go on forever.

'He has come,' said Auric. 'Far sooner than I expected. I did not foresee this at all. Gather your men, Janus Darke. We must leave this spot at once. Time is running out.'

'Who has come? What is wrong? Talk to me!'

'Shaha Gaathon is here. He has found a host and taken flesh. It would appear that he is keener than I ever imagined to take possession of your flesh, Janus Darke. Either that or he had some inkling as to why we are here.'

Fear filled Janus. He had no desire to confront the daemon prince now or ever. He leapt to his feet and began shouting orders for the men to gather their gear. There was a lot of grumbling, for the soldiers were tired, and looking forward to rest and some food. Janus cursed them into action. He knew somehow that their enemy would be closing fast. For one thing, they did not have to wait to have all of those huge warded gates opened. Auric had already done that for them.

'Move, damn you! Or I'll make you wish your sorry mothers never bore you!'

He already wished his mother had never borne him.

THE CHAMBER WAS huge. Bizarre engines lined the walls. At least Auric had assured him they were engines but Janus was not so sure. They might have been statues or plants or some strange form of abstract art. They were towering shapes: sleek, smooth concave pillars. They looked as if they had been moulded from many-coloured glass and twisted in ways that caught the eye and tricked it. Trying to follow their lines for too long gave you a headache. They seemed to fold in on themselves and disappear. Janus could sense the power in them.

'Unshielded spirit engines,' said Auric, in a voice that Janus now knew was not a voice, but within his head. It held a note of horror and awe that was quite chilling. 'They draw psychic power from the very fabric of the immaterium, and yet they have no safeguards. For all their great knowledge, my ancestors were fools, playing with fire in a house made of wood and lacquered paper. And yet, how could they have known the dangers? By the time they understood them it was too late.'

'Very good,' said Janus. 'But what does it mean?'

'It means that in order to open the vaults, we must activate these engines, and that will be very dangerous. It will be like lighting a beacon for the one who follows us. It will know where we are and what we do.'

'Excellent, that is all we need,' said Janus. 'Could it get any worse?'

'Indeed it could, Janus Darke. It will get much worse before we are done.'

'Can't you recognise a rhetorical question when you hear one?'

'Hush, human. I must work the rituals that will revive the engines. They must be recalled to life.'

'Be my guest,' said Janus.

The eldar did not need to be told twice. He strode between the massive, intricate columns and confronted the huge rune-encrusted door of the vault before them. He spread his arms wide and began to chant. As the eldar did so, the hairs on Janus's head began to lift. His men fell back towards the exit. Janus could feel their fear even through the shielding of the dreamstone. It was not a good sign.

A ball of fire appeared between the farseer's outstretched fingers. It hovered there for a moment and then began to spin. As it did so, tentacles of lightning flickered out to strike the pillars. The smell of ozone filled the air. Janus could see a number of runestones orbiting the farseer now. They glowed with their own internal light. He looked away, not wanting to be sucked into contact with Auric again, and yet feeling their irresistible tug.

The monstrous pillars on either side sprang to life. Fire burned within them, dim at first, but growing in intensity with every passing heartbeat. Janus saw a look of wonder appear on Athenys's face. Despite himself, he felt the triumph that filled Auric over the link that they shared. The farseer's cloak writhed around him now as if shifted by a strong breeze, although there was no wind. The runestones swung in ever wider orbits around him, leaving trails of fire that burned into Janus's field of vision.

It was like witnessing the waking of a sleeping giant. A sense of awful potency grew around them. He knew that energies lurked within those pillars that were capable of levelling this city or sinking the continent. The great doorway dilated. A smell of death filled the chamber, as air that had been held within for ten thousand years was released.

Janus looked down a long corridor where more and more of the spirit engines came on-line. It was massive and receded down into the distance, to a place far below the world. Auric stood limned by an aura of power, floating just above the floor, his gems spiralling around him so fast that their contrails blurred into a cage of light.

'The way is open,' he said in a voice like thunder. 'We go down.'

TWENTY-ONE
THE DEATH GOD SPEAKS

ZARGHAN STRODE THROUGH the corridors of the temple-palace. In his mind, he could hear distant music playing loudly. He felt the words of his men, saw some of the sounds they made. He smiled. Kinaesthesia was always interesting and it had been decades since he last experienced it. It seemed to be getting stronger in the presence of the daemon prince.

A glowing aura surrounded the thing that had been Malarys. It shimmered through all the hues of the rainbow and several more besides. With an effort of will Zarghan forced himself to think of the daemon prince as 'he'. While he occupied Malarys it seemed only sensible. The old psyker's body was growing gaunter as the essence of the daemon within consumed his vitality. As his flesh withered it gave off a strong but not unpleasant musky odour that caused distortion in the music the Chaos Marine was hearing. Zarghan considered whether this manifestation of the daemon prince meant anything. Did he not trust Zarghan to carry out his mission?

It was almost an insult. Awesome though Shaha Gaathon's powers might be, Zarghan was not daunted, or at least not much. He had basked in the radiant presence of the Primarch Fulgrim, and strode side by side with the Emperor at the dawn of the Imperium. It took a lot to impress him.

And yet there was something about the daemon that did impress. The stooped, ancient-looking form of Malarys stood taller, and moved with a pride and dignity that the former priest had never possessed. His eyes looked out on the world with a great lust, as if their owner wished to drink in everything it saw and possess it utterly.

He knew that Malarys contained only a fraction of the daemon prince's true power. He had seen what such beings were capable of on the inner worlds of the Eye of Terror, where they had sculpted entire planets in their own image. Out here towards the edge, they did not have quite that power.

Zarghan knew that there was some overlap between what was considered the Eye of Terror and what was not. Here at the edge things were almost as stable as within the accursed Imperium itself. Slowly that was changing, as the Eye grew and the influence of Chaos with it. Perhaps in another ten thousand years this world would be like the daemon worlds. Perhaps he would come back then and take a look.

His attention returned to the thing that had been Malarys. He doubted that he would ever see the old man again after tonight; Shaha Gaathon was consuming him too quickly. He would need to find someone else to make the sacrifice when the *Pride of Sin* departed. So it goes, he told himself.

'I am talking to you, Zarghan,' said Shaha Gaathon. The Chaos Marine gave his attention back to the daemon host. He wondered how long the daemon prince had been talking to him. The penalty for not knowing might prove severe.

'Yes, great prince.'

'I said we will proceed deeper into the temple. I sense the presence of the tricky eldar and my prize.'

'May I ask a question, great prince?'

'Whatever you desire, Zarghan.'

'Why are you with us? I am perfectly capable of doing what needs to be done here.'

'Ah, is this the fabled arrogance of the legendary Space Marines, Zarghan?' The daemon's voice was beautiful. It sounded like it was singing the lyrics to the song of the music that played within Zarghan's head. He realised that the daemon prince had brought his full attention to bear, and that he was in danger of becoming enthralled. With an effort of will he threw off the spell.

'Perhaps, great prince.'

'Who is not to say that the whole purpose of your mission, or perhaps your life, was to be here at this moment, to bring this festering ancient husk of a body to this place, so that I might manifest myself and seize the instrument of my destiny?'

'With all respect, great prince, I suspect that the purpose of my life was something else. I was created to be a warrior, to fight in the greatest battles. I was chosen, first by the Emperor, and then by the Lord of all Pleasures for this role. I very much doubt that my destiny was to be a delivery boy.'

'You are indeed most arrogant,' said Shaha Gaathon. The caressing tone held an undertone of menace now. 'However, you are also correct. It is your destiny to fight in great battles, Zarghan, and the greatest of them will begin once we have achieved what I intend here.'

This piqued the Chaos Marine's interest. War was his greatest pleasure, more than drugs, more than music, more than any of the manifold pleasures of the flesh. His brain had been rewired by an ancient techno-sorcerer, so that the smell of blood stimulated his pleasure centres like fine food, and the roar of battle was sweeter than the finest music. He had been made into a connoisseur of carnage. There was a promise in Shaha Gaathon's words to which he could not help but respond.

'What do you mean, great prince?'

'Soon I will bring war to the galaxy on a scale not witnessed since the time of Horus.'

'That would be a great thing,' said Zarghan sincerely. The Warmaster had almost torn apart the Imperium in his rebellion against the Emperor. 'Those were fine days.'

'They will return, my friend, I promise you.'

Zarghan knew he was being courted, that the daemon prince sought to win his loyalty by promising what he wanted most. Such was the way of daemons, so had it always been.

Still, if he could make good on that promise, Zarghan knew he would do what was asked of him. War on a galactic scale would be like a return to the days of his youth, and those had been glorious indeed.

'The eldar seeks something of great value, something that belongs to me. I want him stopped. Now he has activated the ancient spirit engines. Powers are awakening here that might prove too much for even you without my direct aid. I have come to help you, my friend.'

Zarghan felt sure Shaha Gaathon was lying, which was only to be expected since he was a daemon prince. Helping Zarghan Ironfist was not something that would ever appear on his list of priorities. There was something going on here that had even the mighty daemon prince worried, and the Chaos warrior intended to find out what it was. If there was something here powerful enough to disturb the plans of a being as potent as Shaha Gaathon then it was something that would surely be worthwhile for Zarghan to get his hands on.

'Follow me,' said Shaha Gaathon.

'As you desire, great prince,' he said.

'First, let us find Janus Darke. This form grows weary, and I would wear new flesh by dawn.'

'So shall it be.'

The daemon gestured and summoned his power. Suddenly the walls of the palace blurred past.

* * *

JANUS STOOD IN the centre of a massive mandala. Intricate patterns swirled away from his feet, reminding him in some esoteric way of the things he had seen when Auric cast his runestones. Looking back he could see the long avenues of the spirit engines. Power crackled between them now, the air vibrated with it.

'Hurry,' said Athenys. 'We must be away.'

The men stood nervously at the edge of the great circle. Evidently they too could sense the power flowing through it and were not anxious to step forward.

'Do as she says,' said Janus coldly, 'or our foes will over-whelm us in this indefensible place.'

Janus did not know what was going to happen, but he knew that they were trapped. The corridor had ended in this enormous circular pattern, and there seemed to be no way out but up. Far, far overhead, he was sure he could see the cold glitter of the stars. He was looking up an enor-mous crystalline chimney, towards some sort of massive dome. He tried to remember the layout of the city as he had seen it from the air, and place any such dome in the map of the place he carried in his mind's eye, but he could not.

He noticed also that the air was getting colder and the stale smell of death stronger. The walls depicted some sort of mighty bird, its wings dripping flame, pursuing tiny men. A phoenix, he thought, the bird of fire. Was this some sort of sacred symbol for the eldar?

The men edged onto the disc. Auric made another invo-cation and power swirled out from him to touch the mandala. Lines of fire illumined the face of the disc, and it seemed to shift and whirl dizzyingly. The walls were rising now, Janus saw, as the phoenix rose above him, and was replaced by the depiction of some ancient god-king. It took him a few moments to realise that it was not the walls that were moving but themselves. They were dropping down the great shaft into the gloom deep below the world's surface. There was no sense of motion, no dis-turbed air. Nothing to give any sign that it was the disk and not the walls that were moving. Only common sense told him that the first option was the more likely of the two.

Some of the men whooped. Some stood in uneasy silence. All of them were aware of the lines of fire swirling around the crystalline mosaic beneath their feet. They dropped a long, long way. The sheer scale of the excavation beneath the temple impressed Janus. He also wondered how their enemy could ever expect to find them now.

He was sure, somehow, that they would find a way.

IN THE DARK depths beneath the temple-palace, the mandala drifted down into a massive chamber. It floated down through a hole in the massively domed ceiling and came to rest atop an enormous plinth. Huge masks covered the walls, each perhaps ten times as tall as a man and sculpted from living crystal. They seemed to watch the descent of the disc with sad eyes full of infinite wisdom. It took an effort of will for Janus to believe that they were not alive. Around the edge of the chamber ran various lesser daises and the stairways needed to reach them. Each raised dais faced a major mask.

Janus noticed that the space between the huge faces was filled with smaller disks all with their own roughly humanoid faces. Every centimetre of space on the curving wall was covered in a sea of faces to a height of nearly thirty metres.

'This was where my forebears spoke to their many gods,' said Auric. 'All the deities of the eldar are represented here.'

'Except Slaanesh,' said Janus sourly. He half-expected a protest from the xenogen, but all he got was a nod of agreement.

'Speak not that name here, Janus Darke,' said Athenys. 'It is a blasphemy.'

'As you wish,' said Janus, wondering what was going to happen next. The sad-faced immortals continued to survey him.

'All but a few are gone now,' he heard Auric mutter. 'All swept away like petals blown by a whirlwind.'

Janus was not sure whether he meant the gods, the occupants of the city, the eldar's past greatness or all three. At the moment, he did not care too much. He did care that the place looked indefensible. By the Emperor, they could be wiped out by someone simply dropping warheads from above. He pointed this out to Auric.

'No need to worry, Janus Darke. We are where we need to be. Now all we have to do is open the final doorway and we shall have what we came for.'

'What then?' asked Janus.

'Then we make ready to face the daemon who pursues us.'

'I can hardly wait.'

THE FARSEER BEGAN to chant once more and to Janus's surprise the monstrous faces on the wall responded. At first he thought what he was hearing were merely echoes, but then he realised that words were coming from those massive mouths and light glowed in those huge sad eyes.

'I thought these gods were dead,' he murmured to Athenys.

'They are,' she said softly. 'He draws them forth from within himself, from the memories of what he has been taught. He animates them with projections of his own power. For a heartbeat they live again and then pass into the great void.'

Light from the farseer's aura flashed over the features of the ancient deities now and gave them some semblance of animation. For a moment, he thought he saw tears glisten in the eyes of the face of a monstrous woman. He thought a smile twisted the lips of the sinister mask of some harlequin god. He thought flames burned within the nostrils of a face that was half-eldar, half-dragon.

The words of the farseer echoed around the chamber, gaining strength, becoming louder until they were almost deafening. Some trick of the acoustics, or perhaps of magic, made them sound in a hundred different tones, in a thousand different voices. The music of it echoed through his head, burned in his blood, and he found himself speaking the words in time to the rhythm of the farseer's speech that was also attuned to the drumbeat of his heart.

As Auric sang, he began to move, whirling to face each of the massive masks in turn. As his call reached a crescendo and fell silent, he collapsed facing an enormous dark face set low in the south wall. It seemed a mask of metal that resembled more a daemon than an eldar, and within its eyes burned fire.

'Speak, Khaila Mensha Khaine,' said Auric. The massive mouth of the mask swung open, revealing the darkness within.

TWENTY-TWO
BATTLE BEGINS

THEY ENTERED THE crypt. It was much smaller than Janus had been expecting. The glassy crystalline walls were etched with strange labyrinthine patterns that seemed to be trying to burn themselves into his brain. Trying to follow their contours disturbed the eye and the mind. In the centre of the chamber was an altar on which lay an armoured eldar. On his breast, clutched in gauntleted hands was a sword.

'For ten millennia he has lain here,' said Athenys. 'Without a waystone. He has been alone in death.'

'The runes on this chamber would have saved his soul from being consumed,' said Auric.

'But we have opened this place now. The seal is broken.'

The farseer ignored her, seemingly lost in his own thoughts.

'He came here to die,' said Auric. 'To this sanctuary. He must have lain down here, the last of his order, and meditated until death came for him.'

Janus did not want to consider what had happened here but the thought forced itself into his imagination. What must it have been like, he wondered, to entomb oneself, to wait for death to come? Did the eldar starve, die of thirst or lack of oxygen?

'This is what you came for?' he said, gesturing to the sword. It was a very long narrow blade, seemingly shaped from some form of crystal, etched with complex runes, with three glowing gems set down its length. Another was set in the hilt. He knew he had seen it before, in the dream that had showed him the coming of Slaanesh.

Auric nodded. 'It is the deathsword, an echo of Khaine's mighty blade, set in crystal, made to be the bane of daemons. It failed in its original purpose, but I hope it will serve ours.'

'Then let us take it and leave this place.' Janus did not know what possessed him to do so, but a compulsion stole over him and he reached out to grasp the blade. Athenys gasped, then Janus felt a hand upon his shoulder, restraining him. It stayed there as Auric reached down to pick up the weapon. Only once the weapon was in his hand did the farseer let Janus go.

Auric held the deathsword reverentially, but also gingerly, as a man might hold a venomous serpent. He held it up to the light and Janus could see how although the blade glittered, it gave out a strange dark glow, as if some poisonous energy were seeping out now that it had found a wielder. Even from where he stood, Janus could sense its deadly power.

Athenys reached forward and took the scabbard from the corpse. 'Isha's tears,' she said. 'Sheath that thing until you are ready to use it.'

Like a man emerging from a trance Auric nodded and rammed the weapon home into its scabbard. He let out a long breath and shook his head. 'It is a thing of awesome deadliness. It will serve.'

'Such a weapon should never have been made,' said Athenys. Auric laughed.

'Many things should not have been made. Many deeds were done that should not have been. But they were. Who can foresee all the ways the web of the future is warped by the works of the past? Not I, not even Eldrad Ulthran. We may yet have cause to be grateful to those ancient priests for what they did here.'

'Why does the blade frighten you so?' asked Janus. Hoping to provoke an answer, he added, 'It's just a sword.'

Athenys's smile held no humour. She seemed shaken out of her usual composure. 'It is not just a sword. It is *the* sword, or an echo of it. It is an image of the sword of Khaela Mensha Khaine, the death god, trapped in crystal, which is to say it is death made manifest in the form of a weapon.'

'Athenys exaggerates, but only slightly,' said Auric. Janus noticed a change had come over him since they had found the weapon. He seemed tenser, and yet at the same time a fatalistic note had entered his speech. He was like a man who had finally come to terms with something he had long foreseen but had hoped to avoid. Janus had known a man once who had long put off visiting a physician although he had all the symptoms of a fatal illness. The man had sounded just like Auric the day after he visited the physician.

Janus was not reassured. He remembered the farseer's words: *While you live, I live. While I live, you live. If one of us dies, so does the other. Our fates are intertwined*. If the eldar was preparing to die, it was not a good thing for him. After all, he had no waystone. 'The blade is merely a representation of that fatal weapon. It does not share its full power – no mortal weapon could. And this one is not as powerful as it once was, when it had the spirit engines of an entire world to draw upon.'

Athenys looked away. She looked as if she wanted to say something but was deliberately restraining herself. It was as passionate as he had ever seen the two eldar. Normally their control was so perfect. Still, he could understand that. There was something deeply disturbing about the sword. Even the soldiers sensed it. They held themselves away from the altar, trying to get as far away from the eldar as they possibly could. Janus did not blame them. There was something about the weapon that made his flesh crawl.

'You hope to use it on those who hunt us?'

Auric shook his head.

'I hope to use this on the daemon that hunts us. Even then it may prove insufficient. Shaha Gaathon is a daemon prince and a power.'

'I thought you had seen the future? I thought that was why you brought us here.'

'There are many futures, Janus Darke. Sometimes not one of them is bright.'

'THEY ARE DOWN there,' said Shaha Gaathon, pointing into the mighty pit. The vortex of energy enshrouding them had dissipated in a perfumed cloud. Zarghan looked around and noticed that not all of his men were present. Nearly half had vanished. Had they simply been left behind or had something else happened to them? Daemons had been known to suck the energy from mortals to power their spells, after all. He shrugged. At this moment, he did not care.

Zarghan did not ask him how Shaha Gaathon knew what he sought was below. The daemon's voice was filled with utter certainty. 'They have opened the vault and found what they were looking for. Much good may it do them.'

The daemon prince's laughter was not a pleasant thing to hear. It echoed through Zarghan's bones and caused bright colours to flood across his field of vision. For a moment, all he could see was the outline of the thing that had once been Malarys. It looked ten years older. The skin was wrinkled, the hair bleached white. Baleful fires burned in his eye-sockets. The musky perfume of flesh that consumed itself was stronger than ever. The men at their back were restless. They wanted something to kill.

'What is it they are looking for?' Zarghan asked.

'A weapon. A sword created by fools who thought they

could stave off the inevitable. They sought to use it to prevent the coming of our master. Fools. It was like using a needle to try and stave off the attack of a mastodon.'

'You have no fear of it then?'

Shaha Gaathon shook his head. 'Once I am in possession of what I seek I will have new flesh and the weapon too. Then I will give the eldar cause to weep.'

'All very well, but how do you propose to get us to the bottom of this pit?'

'With no great difficulty. Behold!'

The daemonhost stretched out his arms and a wind from nowhere sprang up. His long white hair flowed in the breeze. His eyes glowed bright as two burning coals. A huge perfumed cloud billowed out from the space between his arms. It formed a swirling vortex in the air before them and hovered in a way that could not remotely be described as natural. The perfume it emitted made Zarghan's senses sing. Behind him his men stirred. He looked around to see a few of them rush lemming-like to the lip of the pit. Crazed by the infernal scent they threw themselves out into space and sank into the cloud. Zarghan expected to hear their screams as they plummeted to their doom, but instead he heard only their joyous cries from within the cloud itself.

Overwhelmed by the daemon's magic, and in haste to experience the new pleasures the cloud promised, more and more men hurled themselves into space, vanishing within the swirling cloud until only Zarghan and Shaha Gaathon were left on the edge of the mighty drop. Zarghan was proud of his self-control. He had been very tempted to join his warriors, but he had resisted. A cynical smile quirked the lips of the daemon host, almost as if it could read his thoughts. Shaha Gaathon gestured politely, indicating that Zarghan should proceed.

The Chaos Marine was not lacking in courage but he wondered if this might not be some dreadful jest on the daemon's part. The daemon princes of Slaanesh were not known for their bizarre sense of humour. Perhaps once he had joined his men, Shaha Gaathon would release his spell and send them all to their deaths. Stranger things had happened in the past.

On the other hand, he could not see what the daemon had to gain from such behaviour, and he had to admit the ecstatic cries from within the cloud made the prospect of entering it very enticing. He shrugged and calmly stepped off the edge.

His stomach lurched momentarily as he anticipated falling to his doom. But somehow the scented billowing mist managed to partially support his weight and he felt himself sinking into it slowly, and as he did so a delicious languor stole over him, relaxing him utterly. Waves of pleasure pulsed through him. He cast a glance back just before his head sank beneath the top of the cloud and saw Shaha Gaathon stride forward to join them. Moments later there was a sense of motion. All around him bodies writhed as they dropped, their senses temporarily overcome by the spell of the violet cloud.

'COME AND SEE this,' said Kham Bell. Janus strode out through the entrance of the tomb and looked up in the direction indicated by the sergeant's outstretched arm. He saw a strange cloud descending towards them. Small lightning flashes danced on its underside and with every flash it pulsed and swirled and changed colour, becoming first lilac, then lime green and then a shocking pink. The effect was ghastly. From within he could hear howls and screams as if a horde of lost souls was being tormented by daemons. A faint, strange scent filled the air and made his skin tingle. An odd tang filled his mouth. It reminded him of some sickeningly sweet lozenges he had once eaten as a child.

He barked orders to his men to come out of the crypt and open fire. They did not need to be told twice. A hail of bolter shells and las-rifle pulses rose to greet the descending cloud. For a moment, the screams intensified and yet there was still a hideous note of pleasure in them. It seemed that whatever combat drugs the Slaanesh worshippers gave their followers were extremely effective. Then from inside the cloud came the sound of chanting. An odd flesh-coloured glow suffused the cloud and the screaming sound died away, as if some barrier were cutting off the sound.

'It appears our foe has arrived,' said Auric from behind him. 'Let us greet him properly.'

The cloud came to rest atop the massive dais that was the mandala. From this angle it was impossible to get a good shot at the centre of it. Not that it mattered. Janus yelled at his sergeant, 'Heavy weapons! I want krak grenades into the cloud. Now!'

The roar of explosions told him his command had been answered. He hoped his men would make the most of this opportunity. Something told him it was the last advantage they were going to get. He raced forward, heading for one of the smaller daises around the edge of the Chamber of Faces, hoping to get to a position of vantage where he could observe the action.

By the time he got there, the cloud had begun to evaporate. As Janus watched, figures appeared to take shape out of the solid mist, slowly resolving themselves into a mass of mutants, men and abhumans. They had taken far fewer casualties than he would have expected, and Janus guessed that the glowing dome that surrounded them was the reason. It looked like a pinkish semi-translucent bubble whose surface rippled like a jelly every time a grenade connected. It rippled but it held. A potent spell was at work here, he knew, and it was most likely being cast by that white haired ancient in the middle of the enemy formation.

For some reason, the old man looked even more threatening than the hulking Chaos Marine in the bizarre multi-coloured armour beside him, although there was no sign of any daemon, for which Janus was profoundly thankful. It seemed that the farseer's visions might have been wrong after all.

'Auric, can you destroy that dome?' Janus shouted. 'It will give the heavy weapons a chance to work!'

The farseer gestured with the sword and a bolt of blazing energy brighter than the sun slashed out towards the dome. For a moment the dome quivered and began to fold inward, but only for a moment, and then it sprang back into shape. So much for the mighty weapon of the ancients, thought Janus. It looks like we are going to have to do this the hard way.

Already his mind had fallen back into its old patterns. He studied the enemy forces, calculating probabilities, trying to work out the best line of attack. The enemy were a motley assortment of drug-crazed lunatics, but they outnumbered his own men by nearly three to one. Just from their wild appearance he suspected that they would be no match for his own men when it came to exchanging disciplined volleys of fire. On the other hand, if things came hot and heavy and they had to fight hand-to-hand, the balance of power would shift enormously.

Those beastmen were enormous and the massive weapons they carried would doubtless smash through armour with ease. Some of the humanoid mutants looked deadly too. He could make out one huge man with tentacles instead of arms. His limbs looked strong as a constricting serpent. He saw another muscled and horned like a bull. He could see another giant with two heads protruding from his burly chest, and a furred creature with three limbs each carrying a chainsword. The appearance of the mutants was enough to strike terror into even the bravest human warrior.

For all the ferocity of the mutants, it was the sorcerer and the Chaos Marine who worried him most. It looked like the wizened ancient was at least a match for the farseer in power. The Chaos Marine, despite his blotched armour and unkempt appearance, could prove to be a terrifying foe. In his time, Janus had fought alongside many an Imperial Space Marine and knew how tough they were. He expected the Emperor's Child to be, if anything, even tougher.

Then the sorcerer turned and stared in his direction, and a thrill of pure terror passed through Janus as he looked into its glowing eyes. He knew then that what he gazed on was not even remotely human. He sensed an intelligence alien, wicked and totally without mercy. When it spoke, he recognised the voice as belonging to the being that had talked to him during the ritual of the runestones. It was not quite as beautiful, but then you had to make allowances for the fact that it was speaking through an ancient human throat.

'Surrender the human Janus Darke and I will let you all live,' it said, almost conversationally. 'Oppose my will in this, even for an instant, and your lives and souls are forfeit.'

Janus was shocked. This was the last thing he had expected. He had thought it would all come down to a furious battle no matter how one-sided. He had not believed for an instant the Chaos worshippers would be prepared to negotiate. It was just not their way. A faint sweet, hypnotic smell of musk filled the air now and Janus glanced at his men to see what they would do.

Under the influence of that narcotic scent, facing that seemingly overwhelming force, listening to that pleasantly persuasive voice, it seemed utterly plausible that his men would hand him over. In fact, he thought, it might be for the best. Much senseless bloodshed could be avoided. Indeed, as a leader, it was his duty to spare as many of his men as he could from death. If giving himself up would achieve that aim, it seemed only noble and right that he should do so. Not only that, he could get closer to the source of that fascinating perfume.

He almost got to his feet. The urge to do so and raise his hands in the air was near overwhelming. Part of him knew that it would be wrong, suicidal in fact, but it did not make the course of action any less appealing. It was the scent, he knew, it carried some strange magic that overcame reason and made you do whatever its possessor desired. He had to force himself to stay low, to keep only his head above the level of the dais, to shield the rest of himself with the stairway. He bit the inside of his cheek, hoping that the pain would distract him from the overwhelming compulsion, but it only provided him with mild stimulation. If pain could be so entrancing under the influence of that intoxicating smell, part of him thought, what might pleasure be like?

He forced his hand to move, to place his rebreather over his mouth, but it made no difference. Either the perfume had already taken effect or quite possibly its magic was too subtle for any sort of chemical filter. He still felt the blind compulsion to obey. Once more it was all he could do to stay in place.

As if aware of the effect the scent was having, the sorcerer gestured and his followers began to rush down the stairs at the edge of the great mandala. Suddenly Auric shook his head and gestured. At once a great wind sprang up, roaring through the tunnels, sucking the perfume upwards and away in a whirlwind vortex of mystical origin. For a moment, Janus felt like weeping as the drugging effect of the perfume receded, then sanity took hold and he snapped off a shot at the enemy, shouting for his men to do the same.

A hail of fire swept across the dais. Krak grenades tore mutants limb from limb. The enemy, despite being in the open, responded with fire of their own. Bolter shells chipped the dais close to Janus's face, and he dropped down the stair and out of the direct line of fire.

The battle had well and truly begun.

TWENTY-THREE
DEATH IN THE VAULTS

ZARGHAN LISTENED WITH glee to the roar of battle. It echoed through his bones and brought a delightful tinge of distortion to the music in his head. The intoxication caused by the perfumed cloud of Shaha Gaathon did nothing to reduce his happiness. He strode forward through the hail of bolter shells, looking for something to kill. A few dozen deaths, he knew, and his happiness would be complete.

'Over there,' said Shaha Gaathon, his beautiful melodious voice carrying easily above the thunder of weapons and the screams of the dying. 'There is Janus Darke. Do not kill him.'

Zarghan nodded. He might or he might not obey depending on how he felt in the next few minutes. He strode across the mandala, bellowing instructions to the abhumans to follow him, and snapped off a shot at the blurry mix of figures crouched in the entrance to what appeared to be a tomb. He howled with triumph as one of the figures fell. His shooting was as good as it always had been.

The colours of the faces on the walls changed from purple to gold as if in agreement. It was an interesting effect. The mandala appeared to pulse and swirl beneath him. Most people would have found it dizzying, but for Zarghan it simply added to the exhilaration of the moment. The howls and bellows of his mutant followers throbbed inside his brain. The colours flickered with every change of pitch and tone. Interesting, he thought, the narcotic quality of Shaha Gaathon's sorcery appears to have enhanced my perceptions of reality.

A bolter shell clanged off his armour. The force of the impact was enormous. A yellow wave of pain pulsed across his shoulder. His armour changed colour around the affected area in sympathy. Zarghan felt himself being spun around by the impact. He kept to his feet with an effort of will and the use of his perfect coordination, and stormed on, coming ever closer to where the humans waited. Unless he was much mistaken, there were some eldar with them.

Excellent. It had been a while since he had had any of them to play with.

JANUS POPPED HIS head and shoulders over the edge of the dais and aimed an enfilading shot into the mass of Chaos worshippers racing towards the crypt's entrance. He saw one man scream and go down, and he fired again. The enemy was packed too closely to miss.

He watched their leader, appalled. The Chaos Marine was huge and seemed to know no fear. He staggered forward like a drunk man, ignoring the hail of death all around him. His bizarre multi-coloured armour changed colour at the spot it was hit, every time it was hit. On every impact the gargoyle heads set in the shoulder pads shrieked and screamed in a terrifying manner. He occasionally paused to raise his bolter and snap off a shot seemingly at random.

The bolter's muzzle changed colour every time he pulled the trigger. What was the point of that, Janus wondered?

Was there some dark sorcery involved? If so, it was incomprehensible to him.

It seemed obvious that the Chaos Marine and his followers were going to get to grips with his own men and the eldar though. There were just too many of them, and they kept on coming, despite their enormous casualties. Perhaps they were simply too drug crazed to care about the deaths of their comrades. Perhaps they felt no pain or fear. They came on in an irresistible wave, like crazed orks storming towards a barricade.

He glanced up and saw that more and more of them were shambling down from the great dais. Showing some hint of intelligence, they were circling the outskirts of the chamber, under the gazes of those crystal faces, in a pincer movement that would take them to the entrance of the crypt, all the while keeping them out of the line of fire. Janus was not sure whether they were doing so simply by instinct or whether there was some greater intelligence at work.

A flash of energy emerged from the mouth of the tomb and blasted the old man who now hovered over the dais, his hair streaming in the wind, his robes fluttering, his eyes glowing balefully. With a contemptuous gesture the Chaos sorcerer negated the blast and as he did so Janus noticed that his skin grew more wrinkled, his posture more stooped. With every use of power he appeared to be aging, consumed by some internal rot. At least, thought Janus, Auric was keeping him pinned down.

Or perhaps not. The old man gestured and a gap appeared in the air below him. Through it, bolts of energy emerged to touch the three nearest Chaos worshippers. The men screamed in ecstasy as their forms writhed and changed. Their skins split like cocoons from which a butterfly was emerging, and three eldritch figures stepped out. They looked like beautiful shaven headed women, but they had arms that ended in pincer claws. They clicked them like castanets in time to the beat of a music only they could hear. This was looking bad – those things looked

like daemons of some sort. How many more such rein-
forcements was the aging sorcerer going to be able to
summon? Doubtless enough to swamp the hard-pressed
defenders.

Things went from bad to worse when the sorcerer gestured in his direction. The daemonettes nodded and
bounded towards Janus. Great, he thought, just what I
need, an attack from two sides, she-daemons from hell
coming from the centre of the chamber, and the right hand
pincer of the Chaos force circling the wall on the other side.
No line of retreat visible. Surrender was not an option.

He prepared to defend himself to the death.

ZARGHAN BELLOWED WITH laughter as he cleaved down a
human soldier. His chainsword blade passed right through
the corpse and buried itself in the body of one of his own
men. Served the fool right for getting in his way. The delicious shiver of impact, the vibration of blade on bone,
made his gauntlets and vambraces flicker black-red-grey-
lime-puce-lilac in eye-blurring succession. Ah, he thought,
nothing like the sensations of battle for clearing the head
and driving away ennui. This was what he lived for.

Ahead of him, he could see the farseer. He stood calmly
in the midst of battle and sang spells aimed at Shaha
Gaathon. Zarghan could almost see the words forming
around his head; to his mixed senses they formed a dancing halo of runes that orbited the eldar before streaming
off to attack their intended target. An impressive, indeed
fascinating, pyrotechnic display he thought, pausing to
watch for a second, his attention held rapt by the stream of
colours and sounds and crossed sensations.

A blow on his helmet brought his attention rudely back
to the combat. His head shivered from the impact of a las-
rifle butt. How rude, he thought, smashing the man's skull
with a downward sweep of his bolter muzzle and then
pumping some shells into the spasming corpse to drive the
lesson home. Oh well, he had work to do anyway. It was
time to capture the mage.

He strode forward, batting aside friend and foe indiscriminately, determined to take the farseer prisoner. *How well will he sing when he's tied to the autorack?* The thought amused him. He smashed another man down and found himself in striking distance of the mage. At that moment, an eldar woman stepped out of the crowd to confront him.

She was a blurred figure of black and white, but he guessed her hair was long, and she was armed with a pistol and some sort of blade. She was tall and willowy, like all eldar women.

'Surrender at once. I will put you on a silver leash and train you to be my pet,' he informed her pleasantly. 'You shall be fed tidbits from my own hand, and learn to please me in the manner your ancestors did.'

It seemed a perfectly reasonable offer to Zarghan, and infinitely preferable to the boredom of death but she apparently was having none of it. She smiled nastily at him.

'Perhaps I shall make you the same offer,' she said. 'Then again, perhaps not.'

The blade swept toward Zarghan and he parried it easily, too late realising that it had been a feint. Her armoured boot smashed into his helmet, sending him reeling backwards, his armour flaring a bruised purple.

'I like a woman with a sense of humour,' he said and advanced to the attack once more.

JANUS UNCLIPPED a grenade from his belt, and lobbed it at the onrushing mutants. It landed in their midst and detonated. A tidal wave of blood and broken bone flew everywhere. The Chaos worshippers did not stop, but came racing on. Most continued towards their original objective but a few of them detoured to attack him. Judging by their expressions, they had forgotten any orders they might have had to take him alive.

Janus snatched up his bolter and pumped a stream of shells into his attackers. A head exploded, a second human went down clutching at a huge hole that had suddenly appeared in his stomach. Three more came up the stairs and he met them with his blade.

The leading man chopped at him with an enormous cleaver, and he ducked. The second stabbed upwards with a power-axe that Janus barely managed to parry. The third waited behind his compatriots, unable to find a gap to attack through, for which Janus was profoundly grateful.

He pushed forward with his sword, hearing its blade grind against the swiftly rotating teeth of the axe, and then punched forward with barrel of his bolter. The man's nose broke and he fell backwards into the man behind him, both tumbling headlong down the stairs. Blood spurted where the out of control axe bit flesh. Janus smiled triumphantly.

The last man took advantage of the moment to aim another blow at the rogue trader. Janus leapt back up the stairs, his heel catching on the lip of the topmost step. It saved him by sending him tumbling backwards to land sprawled on the dais. The man's cleaver passed clean over him. Janus stabbed upwards, catching him in the crotch with his blade. The man gave an eerie high-pitched wail; its tone rising as Janus viciously twisted the blade.

The castanet clicking of claws behind him warned him that the daemonettes had arrived on the dais. He tried to roll to his feet but a claw bit into the flesh of his shoulder. At first the pain almost immobilised him, but he realised the claw must contain some form of narcotic venom, for the pain swiftly vanished, replaced by a wave of pleasure that left him utterly relaxed and just as incapable of movement.

With a strength that belied her slight form, the daemonette hauled him to his feet, like a man lifting a puppy by the scruff of its neck. He wanted to resist but the drug left him immobile. He gazed into the smiling faces of his captors and responded in kind as they licked their lips lasciviously. The smell of their musk was almost overpowering, and threatened to sweep away all his self-control.

At this range he could study them closer. They were tall and well made with one bared breast. They were garbed in shiny black leather but looking closer, he could see that at least one of them was wearing what appeared to be garments made from tattooed human flesh. He had seen similar tattoos with the names of sweethearts and children on the arms of sailors, and he did not want to speculate on where these had come from. One patch of skin showed an anchor and the word 'Sengha'. A name or perhaps a brand of beer, he wondered dully?

Steps sounded on the stairs behind him as more of the mutants had come into view. He recognised the man whose nose he had broken. His head was shaved and tattooed and small horns emerged from his forehead. Blood streamed down his nose.

'Datz da basturd,' he said, pain blurring his words. 'Hold 'im while I gut him.'

The daemonette smiled and shook her head, but the man advanced anyway, the blade of his axe sending out an eerie high-pitched whine. A look of brutal cruelty passed over his features. The daemonette did not warn him a second time. Instead, a claw flickered out almost too fast for the eye to follow and snipped closed around the man's neck. Blood fountained and the severed head rolled down the stairs. The bright, pleasant expression on the she-daemon's face never changed although now both she and Janus were splattered with droplets of blood.

In a moment, her long serpent-like tongue flickered out to lick her lips and cheeks clean. Janus shuddered. There had been nothing even remotely human in that gesture.

He let himself go limp in her grip, and brought his heel down very hard on the instep of her foot. Had he done this to a human, there would have been a crunch of breaking bone. The daemonette merely shook him a little, and short spasms of agony from the movement fought against the anaesthetic effect of the poisoned claw.

It came to him that he had more effective weapons. He turned the bolt pistol around, slid it through the gap under his armpit and pulled the trigger. The blast of muzzle flare seared his flesh, for his body armour did not cover that area completely. He felt flesh tear and blood begin to flow as the force of impact blew the daemonette backwards, sending her sprawling obscenely back against the dais.

Her two sisters shrieked their displeasure and clicking their claws advanced towards him. The creature he had shot pulled herself to her feet and began to advance again too. It appeared her sorcerously-tainted flesh was immune to his weapons.

At that moment, Janus found himself wishing that he could tap into the psychic powers that had so threatened his sanity, but it appeared that the eldar gem still prevented it. He shook his head, wondering whether the thought of using his powers had even been his own. Surely in the presence of the daemons and an experienced Chaos sorcerer they would be much more likely to work to his undoing than his advantage.

Not that it would make much difference if he did not staunch the flow of blood from his open shoulder. So far the daemon venom had dulled the pain, but he could see, even at a cursory inspection, that his armour had shattered and shards had been driven bone deep into his flesh. Such things could go very bad very quickly, he knew, back peddling towards the stairs, all the while keeping his eyes upon the advancing she-fiends.

One of them paused and made enticing motions with her hips, gesturing for him to come back. With the cloying influence of the musk still in his nostrils, part of him wanted to obey. He fought for control and they sprang, covering the distance in one easy fluid motion. This time two sets of claws bit into his flesh immobilising him. The one he had shot caressed his face with the edge of her claw. It was a motion that promised an eternity of hideous pain.

Then as one they turned and bore him back to the great mandala atop which the floating sorcerer waited.

* * *

'THEY HAVE JANUS Darke!' Zarghan heard the eldar woman shout. Her words had a reddish tinge, he noticed, as she chopped into his shoulder with her blade.

'I know,' the eldar psyker replied. 'Now comes the moment of maximum peril.'

Zarghan considered the farseer's words. It sounded like he had anticipated this happening and had some sort of plan. Zarghan supposed that it was only to be expected. The eldar seers were supposed to be spectacularly gifted prophets, although it had not saved them when the Great Lord of all Pleasures came for them.

The woman moved into a strange whirling dance, her blade swirled around her, driving Zarghan back among his men. Almost incidentally the whirling storm of death cut down two beastmen. It was all Zarghan could do to prevent her from cutting him down. In truth, he had to admit she was extraordinarily skilled.

As Athenys moved the farseer fell into step behind her, drawing a foul-looking black crystal blade around which trapped lightning flickered and danced. The sight of it filled Zarghan with sudden fear. He knew that whatever that weapon cut would suffer a fate worse than death. The sword sang to him, the flickering along its length being transformed into wild music by his crossed senses.

The humans rallied behind her and in a wedge began to cross the chamber. Under normal circumstances their bravery would have been suicidal, for the rest of the Chaos force was just arriving to take them in both flanks, but these were not normal circumstances. The farseer's blade flickered out to touch the foremost mutant. The man's skin split and blackened. At the point of impact the flesh seemed to curdle and lose all moisture and then flake away to reveal the bone beneath. The man barely had time to scream before his entire body was mummified, drained of all life. Zarghan wondered briefly if even his sorcerously reinforced armour could protect him from such a weapon and decided that on the whole he would rather not find out just yet.

'To me!' he bellowed, seeing how his men wavered when they saw the fate of their comrade. The eldar struck out again and two more men were gone in as many instants. Mortal armour appeared to provide no protection against the ravening power of that evil eldar weapon.

I wonder if I could get someone to make one of those for me, Zarghan pondered? It would certainly prove useful the next time I meet Khârn the Betrayer. Then he had no more time for such thoughts as the eldar woman pressed home her attack and he had to give all his attention to keeping himself alive.

TWENTY-FOUR
FARSEER'S DOOM

JANUS FOUND HIMSELF being hauled across the Chamber of
Faces and onto the great mandala. The daemonettes were
very strong and they were not gentle. Not even the narcotic
effect of the venom in their claws could drown out all of
the pain, although it did mingle a bizarre euphoria with
his sense of hopelessness and defeat.

He knew that the only thing keeping him alive as they
moved was the presence of the she-daemons. The mutants
glared at him with death in their eyes. They would strike
him down in an instant if given the chance. Despite this,
he writhed in the grasp of his captors knowing that a clean
death at the hands of the raiders would be preferable to
what waited him when he reached the sorcerer.

It seemed that Auric had been wrong, all of this time.
His vision of the future was flawed. Janus was certainly
going to be taken now and it looked as if the eldar himself would be swiftly overwhelmed. Janus risked a glance
back to see how things were progressing. He was surprised. Following the two eldar his own men had broken

out of the vault, and were smashing a path through their foes.

Even as he watched, Athenys broke through the guard of the Chaos Space Marine who led the beastmen and knocked him to the ground. Auric stood in the forefront of battle and killed anything that got within the reach of his blade. He did not need to inflict a wound: the merest touch of that crystal sword was enough to destroy anything it came into contact with.

In a swift burst of speed, the farseer covered the ground that separated him from the daemonettes. Two of the she-daemons broke off to oppose him. They moved with eye-blurring swiftness, moving to flank the eldar, one approaching from each side, so that whichever way he turned, the other would get a clear attack at him.

Auric did not wait for this to happen. He leapt forward swinging the deathsword two-handed in a great figure of eight. It struck the right hand daemonette full on the breast, but something protected her from the full fury of the weapon. Perhaps it was some mystical force, perhaps it was the unearthly composition of her own flesh, but where a man or mutant would simply have collapsed into a swift-shrivelling pile of dust and bone and ashes, the Chaos daemon came on.

Her claw clicked closed where the farseer's head had been mere moments ago. Only a swift last second duck saved him from decapitation. The other daemonette made a grab for him, but Auric blocked the blow with the deathsword. Somehow it became lodged in the daemonette's claw, and for a moment it looked like she might wrest it from him, but then the flares of chain lighting dancing along the blade increased, and she let out an unearthly scream that froze everyone within hearing.

It was worse than the wail of a soul in torment. It was the death cry of a being that had lived since the dawn of time and who knew the moment of its end had now come. It was the call of someone who was dying in the utmost pain and terror.

Everyone, Chaos worshipper and human mercenary alike, halted when they heard that terrible cry. Even as Janus watched the daemonette's claw turned red and cracked revealing the pale but swiftly putrefying flesh within. The darkness passed on up her arm, which became black, puffy and swollen and burst with a shower of horrid, sweet-smelling pus.

Janus saw that a similar thing had happened to the second daemonette. Where the blade had touched her breast earlier her skin was blighted, cracked and broken, and was weeping black tears. It seemed that whatever protective enchantment surrounded them, it only slowed the sword's effect. The second daemonette let out an unearthly shriek and sprang forward, as if determined to slay the thing that had caused her such torment. Her attack was so furious that for a few moments it looked like she might overwhelm Auric, but the farseer fell back, parrying the hail of blows with the black sword, and was rewarded by wails of purest terror whenever the blade made contact.

Within a few heartbeats it was over, the two daemonettes had already started to decompose into pools of oddly smelling slime. It was like watching the decomposition of a corpse, only thousands of times faster, and it left Janus both appalled and encouraged by the sheer power of the eldar weapon.

The surviving daemonette continued to drag Janus forward towards the stairs leading up to the great mandala. He slumped down, ignoring his pain, and doing his best to become a dead weight, hoping to give the eldar time to reach him, praying to the Emperor that the strange sorcerer above would not come down to meet them.

More of the Chaos worshippers threw themselves forward between the daemonette and the farseer. He had to say this for them, whatever else they might lack, they did not want for courage. Janus doubted that he would have gone forward against Auric with quite such ferocity, having witnessed what that terrible blade could do. On the other hand, he thought, he was not under the influence of noxious combat drugs and the strange intoxicating musk of the daemonettes.

They moved forward to protect her with the determination of men fighting to protect a wife or a child. If he had not known better he would have said that they loved this sinister thing. He supposed that maybe they did. Who could tell what such depraved cultists were truly like, and what sort of spell the evil creature had worked on them? Janus was glad that she had not had time to do something similar to his own men. Either that, or the sorcery of the eldar was protecting them.

The mutants and beastmen hurled themselves forward in a vast wave. They were met by Auric, Athenys, Kham Bell and the few surviving warriors of Darke's Company in a struggle that was bestial in its ferocity. Darke's comrades were every bit as savage and determined as their assailants, and the sheer desperation of being so badly outnumbered just added to their fury. There was no sign now of any prejudice against the eldar. They were all fighting on the same side against a common foe and it seemed like nothing was going to get in their way.

Even as Janus watched, Athenys dispatched a huge bull-headed man with her blade, while at the same time blasting with a shuriken catapult into the nearest mutant. Beside her Auric strode confidently forward, reaching out to kill with the lightest touch of his glowing black blade. Kham Bell fought alongside them, smashing at the mutants with the butt of his rifle, stamping on the necks of the fallen, bellowing encouragement to the surviving soldiers.

The daemonette pulled him onwards. The crystal steps bruised his back and legs. He tried throwing himself forward and down the stairs, thinking that perhaps the blood slicking her claw would loosen the daemonette's grip, but it was not to be. The jagged edged claw was buried too deep, had perhaps even lodged itself in his collar bone. As he moved Janus felt the grinding of bones. Sparks danced before his vision and pain lanced through him, suddenly, sickeningly, shockingly.

A moment later he looked up at the glowing figure of the Chaos sorcerer. An amused grin spread across its rapidly aging face. Recognition glittered in its glowing eyes. It gestured and the daemon let him go. A wave of pure euphoric energy followed its gesture, and Janus watched his wound close, the flesh slurping together and knitting as if it had never been open.

'At last,' said Shaha Gaathon. 'A vessel worthy of my power. Now, let the eldar attack us with his puny toy sword.'

Janus did not like the sound of this at all.

ZARGHAN LOOKED UP from where he lay, and saw the figure of Janus Darke rise into the air and hover in front of Shaha Gaathon. Sparks of purple lightning flickered between them, and the human opened his mouth and let out a howl that was in its way no less frightening than the death cries of the daemonettes. Zarghan guessed that it could not be too pleasant to have your soul sucked right out of your body and used as food for daemons. The sound echoed within his bones and caused flickering yellow waves to ripple across his field of vision.

He had his own problems. That eldar witch had done him some damage. It felt like ribs were broken within his armour. It was not just his body that was hurt. It was his pride. She should not have been able to do that. It was impossible, in fact. Over the millennia, Zarghan had fought against the eldar and dark eldar many times, and no mere trooper had ever been able to harm him. There was no way a lightly armoured female should have been able to, not unless she was much more than she seemed.

He would have his revenge shortly though. As soon as he got himself back on his feet, he would make her pay. Somehow, his body just did not seem to want to obey him.

JANUS SCREAMED. THE flow of power from the Chaos sorcerer was almost overwhelming. He felt his mind being eroded by the wash of energy, his soul being whittled away by the corrosive evil of the daemon that lurked within the old man's rapidly aging form.

The worst part was that it was not entirely unpleasant. There was even a certain pleasure along with the agony: at moments the two were so intense that he had some trouble deciding which was which.

The gem on his forehead glowed like a red-hot coal. He could feel and smell his own flesh burning around it, and he knew that the stone's powers were all that allowed him to resist Shaha Gaathon's might. As an untrained psyker he had no chance whatsoever of withstanding the daemon's ages-old malevolence. The daemonic entity knew it too. It smiled at him.

'Give in,' it said. 'You will enjoy millennia of ecstasy as part of my consciousness before you are finally absorbed. What is your mortal life but an eyeblink of time anyway, before your soul is reabsorbed by the warp? This way you gain tens of thousands of years, and they will be years of utter pleasure.'

'Go to hell,' Janus told it.

'Did you not know? Most of me is still there, at least according to the bizarre doctrines of your pathetic church. This pitiful human host is barely capable of holding a tenth of what I am. You on the other hand are capable of so much more. As I will shortly demonstrate.'

A lance of pure agony passed through Janus's forehead. The gem there felt as if it were on the verge of cracking. He forced himself to resist but knew he could not hold on much longer.

Resist, Janus Darke, hold out! You are doing much better than the daemon wants you to believe, said another voice, which sounded like Auric's but might just have been a product of his own pain-twisted mind. Janus was not encouraged. What was the point of resisting, he was only prolonging the agony?

Just a little longer, the voice whispered. *Then I will be in a position to help you.*

Janus exerted his will. He did not think it was going to be enough.

ZARGHAN WATCHED THE eldar and his cohorts storm the stairwell. By Slaanesh, they could fight, he had to give them that. Of course, that terrible sword made a huge difference but even so, it was impressive. Normally, he would not have expected them to cover twenty strides, but they had gone all the way to the foot of the stairs and were making their way up it.

Half a dozen humans even managed to survive, although there was a daemonette waiting for them at the top of the stairs.

Zarghan tried to force himself to move, desperate now to get into combat, before the battle ended, but his body refused to obey.

JANUS FELT AS if he was caught in a massive vice. He had reached the end of his strength; he could not go on any longer. He was about to let his mental defences crumble and the daemon flow in when he heard a real voice speaking behind him.

'Your day is done, daemon,' said Auric. A whirlwind of magical energy surged around Janus. The pressure on his mind relaxed. He felt capable of movement once more, but when he tried to do so, he found that all he could do was stumble a few steps and then collapse onto the ground.

He noticed the glow of eldar sorcery still surrounded him, cocooning him against the daemon's evil energies. Looking up, he could see that Auric had cut down the last daemonette and had emerged onto the top of the great mandala. Behind him stood Athenys, Kham Bell and a few of the surviving warriors.

'What an amusing concept,' replied Shaha Gaathon. 'You think to pit your pitiful spell-singing against the power of a daemon prince. You must be more drunk on the life energy of those you killed than I thought possible.'

Somehow, over whatever tenuous psychic link they now shared, Janus sensed the eldar's shock. It seemed the daemon did too.

'Do you think I do not know what that weapon does?' asked Shaha Gaathon. 'My, my – how will you explain this to your precious council? How will you manage to preserve your fabled purity having drunk their tainted life force?'

The daemon's voice was at once conversational and malevolent. Janus could sense that it was summoning more and more energy from somewhere, plotting a killing stroke. The body it wore was now truly ancient, withered and stooped; it looked as if it were a hundred years old. Janus could smell the burning flesh and noticed that its perfumed sweat glistened the colour of blood. The eyes were now pure raging furnaces of hate, windows into the deepest, darkest levels of the most forbidden hells.

'Kill him, kill him now!' Janus gasped, trying to warn the eldar before it was too late.

The daemon's laughter roared across the room like thunder in a storm. 'Not even with that sword could he do so,' said Shaha Gaathon. 'All he could do is kill this host form. I would survive.'

'Not if the deathblade feeds on your soul,' said Auric.

'Not even then,' said Shaha Gaathon, 'for only a part of my essence is present here. Your little toy might prove painful temporarily, but it would not slay me. Now I am too great.'

'We shall see!' said Auric, springing forward and lashing out with incredible speed. The daemon leapt back to the centre of the mandala. Janus slumped to the ground. The constant attack on his mind had suddenly let up, as the daemon concentrated on his main opponent. The shield of energy slipped away from around him as the eldar focused on Shaha Gaathon. The daemon prince gestured and a sword of coruscating energy appeared in his fist, flickering like a dark flame. For all of the decrepit appearance of the body he wore, he moved with eye-blurring speed.

Watching the two of them fight was like watching a swift intricate dance. Their movements were amazingly quick and supple, and utterly fluid. Their actions appeared intertwined and almost ritualistic. When Auric advanced a step, the daemon gave ground. When the daemon won back two steps, Auric matched him pace for pace in time to the rhythm of his movements. Their blades flickered faster than the eye could follow, leaving lines of solid-seeming light burned on the observer's retina. Nobody, not even Athenys, moved to intervene. Everyone there sensed that they were in the presence of powers far greater than they, witnesses to a struggle the outcome of which it was far beyond their feeble powers to affect.

At first Auric had the upper hand. Slowly, making progress painfully, advancing two steps for every one he was pushed back, he drove Shaha Gaathon back to the centre of the mandala. With every parry, the daemon's blade grew a little dimmer, as if its energies were being consumed bit by bit when they came into contact with the lightning entwined crystal of the eldar artefact.

The eyes on the Wall of Faces seemed to flicker and grow brighter. The effect was eerie, making some of the ancient deities appear to twist, giving them a semblance of a smile. Janus began to feel a little hope.

Perhaps, armed with the deathblade, Auric might triumph. Perhaps his own life need not be forfeit. Perhaps he would live to learn what the eldar could teach him, and avoid having his own soul and body consumed, in the way the ancient form Shaha Gaathon inhabited was being devoured.

Auric advanced in a whirlwind of blows. His movements were graceful and utterly controlled. The daemon's form seemed to be flying apart. Multi-coloured light leaked from cracks in the disintegrating skin. Bones were becoming visible through the parchment thin flesh. His eyes glowed ever brighter.

Then, just as it seemed the deathblow might fall, Shaha Gaathon's blade flared brighter than Auric's and he parried.

The two figures stood locked in position, their power apparently equally balanced.

'Enough,' said Shaha Gaathon. 'This farce has gone on long enough. Did you think you might actually win here, eldar? Do you not realise that I have been toying with you? Do you think that your puny powers might actually be a match for those of a daemon prince? I have grown stronger since this weapon was forged, and it is grown weaker. Watch and learn wisdom in the few moments remaining to you.'

He moved his arm suddenly and the blade was sent flying from Auric's hand to land at Janus's feet, then the daemon lashed out with the fiery blade and drove it directly through the breast of the farseer's armour, pinning him to the floor of the mandala. The farseer's whole body spasmed and an eerie cry was torn from his lips. His body flexed and went still.

'Death has come for you, Auric Farseer,' Shaha Gaathon said. 'Just as it will come for your world.'

The daemon prince reached forward to pluck the waystone from within Auric's armour. He held it up to the light, an amused smile playing on his decaying lips.

'And your soul will find no haven,' he said and thrust the gleaming waystone into his blazing mouth.

TWENTY-FIVE
THE FINAL BETRAYAL

THE DAEMON PRINCE stood there roaring with laughter. An aura of blazing power played around his head. His smile was broad and triumphant. At that moment he was the very picture of invincibility. Athenys and the others looked appalled. Janus, who had believed in Auric's prophecies insofar as they concerned him stood there, awaiting death. He was sure that it would not be long in coming. After all, the eldar was gone; not even his soul would remain once it was sucked from the waystone and consumed by the daemon.

Shaha Gaathon would take Janus too, and eat his soul, and he would become a vessel of wrath, as the daemon prince worked his wickedness on the eldar and upon humanity. He considered how he might avoid this fate and could see only one way. The deathblade was close at hand. Lightning still flickered around it, discharging itself into the mandala. The air smelled of ozone. The heat of the gemstone embedded in his brow was almost unbearable, and if anything seemed to be increasing.

He decided that he could throw himself upon the
weapon and kill himself, thus denying Shaha Gaathon
what he most desired. It was pathetic, he thought, that his
whole life should be reduced to this, but he could see no
other way out. His fingers closed around the hilt of the
ancient eldar weapon. Instantly strength flowed into him.
He felt his despair lift, and he recognised it for what it was
– the product of the daemon prince's magic and the corruption from the daemonette's venom that still flowed in
his veins.

The power surging into him increased. As it did so, he
heard a myriad of voices babbling in his head. Chaos
cultists, daemonettes, even faint eerie echoes of the voice of
Shaha Gaathon himself, as stolen vitality poured in and
made him stronger. He raised himself to his feet, filled with
a renewed confidence. Careful, he told himself. Such confidence might be a trap. If he was going to use the weapon
on himself, he should do so now, while Shaha Gaathon
was occupied with digesting the soul of the farseer.

Even as the thought occurred to him, he knew he was
not going to do it. He was not going to kill himself, not
when he had a weapon of such power in his hand, and a
foe before him. Now, for the first time, he noticed how
weak the daemon's body seemed. It looked on the verge of
coming apart. Perhaps because it was just about used up,
burned through like a log in a fire. Perhaps because of the
wounds Auric had inflicted. Perhaps due to some combi-
nation of both. It did not really matter. All he wanted was
the chance to kill it.

Bright anger burned in him. This creature had hounded
him right across this sector of the galaxy. It had tortured
him, tormented him and driven him to the edge of despair
and madness. It wanted to kill him and eat his soul, just as
it had already done to the one man who had tried to help
him in his extremity.

No more, he thought. I have come far enough. I will be
hunted no further. I will make you pay for what you have
done to me.

He strode forward, filled with the evil energy of the blade. Shaha Gaathon stood there frozen for a moment. Perhaps he was having more difficulty than he had expected consuming the eldar's soul.

'Curse you, eldar,' the daemon shouted. 'What have you done? How have you eluded me?'

Janus did not know what Shaha Gaathon was raving about but the anger and frustration were evident even in the daemon's beautiful voice. He bent down over the eldar's corpse to inspect the body, as if he suspected that Auric was not quite dead yet, and that perhaps he had devoured the waystone prematurely. Even as these thoughts flashed through Janus's mind, he felt the gem-stone on his own forehead grow warmer still.

He raised the sword to strike and as he did so, Shaha Gaathon turned to face him. The daemon's anger sub-sided. The rage vanished from his face.

'You at least will not escape,' he said, and raised his burn-ing sword.

Janus lashed out with a mighty blow. The ebony blade felt light as a willow-wand in his hand. The daemon blocked it and parried. Shaha Gaathon's response was so fast it should have been impossible to stop, but somehow the deathblade was there, turning in his hand to block the daemon's stroke. Janus felt a surge of pain flash up his arm from the point of contact, a burning stinging sensation. It was as if the deathsword had become an extension of his own flesh and his own nervous system. What it felt, he felt. It was not a reassuring idea.

Even as the thought crossed his mind, he realised that battle was being joined on another level. A wave of psychic power surged outward from the daemon's host form and threatened to overwhelm him. Perhaps it was because of the sword, but he sensed more of the mind behind the attack, its unquenchable hunger, and its desire to possess him utterly and devour his immortal soul. He caught a glimpse of bottomless hells in which evil immortals writhed in what might have been ecstasy or might have been torment, over which presided Shaha Gaathon, a luminous being of tremendous will, and over which loomed the titanic presence that was the immortal entity Slaanesh. He found the image being forced into his mind along with promises of eternities of pleasure if he surrendered, eternities of pain if he resisted.

Frantically he closed his mind to the daemon's whispered promises and tried to block out the hot waves of pleasurable pain that gripped his body. The sword lent him strength. In the depths of his mind, he tapped into his own rage and pain, as he had done what seemed a lifetime ago, in the meat processing plant. He forged his emotions into a thunderbolt and cast it at the daemon and at the exact same moment lashed out with the deathblade.

It was a feeble, clumsy effort and Shaha Gaathon blocked it easily. He knew that even if his sword-augmented powers matched those the daemon prince had vested in his host-body, he simply did not have the skill to match the daemon's. He was like an inexperienced boy facing a grand master at pharaoh, or a novice warrior going blade to blade in close combat with a Space Marine. He did not have a chance.

At least he would go out fighting. The daemon countered both his strokes and his riposte was fierce. The burning blade seared flesh; the awesome psychic pressure scarred his soul. It was all Janus could do to retain consciousness. Red darkness threatened to drown him, but from somewhere came knowledge that told him not to try and resist the pain, but to bend before it like long grass in the wind, which endures the hurricane that a mighty oak cannot. He obeyed and rode out the waves of pain, like a sailing vessel at anchor riding the waves of a giant storm. The gem on his brow burned brighter, but now it caused him no pain, instead it seemed to be feeding him the knowledge he required to match his power, and the power and the sword.

And now he noticed something more. The runestones that had once hovered over Auric's body, and now lay atop the eldar's corpse, were starting to rise into the air. One by one, they flashed towards him and began to rotate around him as they had once done around the farseer. As they did so, greater and greater confidence filled him, as they added to his strength.

'I see your plan now,' said Shaha Gaathon. 'You desire this one for yourself.'

Janus wondered what the daemon prince was talking about. Without quite knowing how he did it, he fashioned a mighty psychic bolt, drawing all of his power together then sending it scything outwards. As the daemon prince parried the bolt, it split into two. Part of its force slid around Shaha Gaathon's psychic defences, and split again and again. Janus sensed the daemon's desperation as it attempted to block all of the incoming attacks and failed. Two parts of the bolt struck home, causing the crumbling flesh to disintegrate still further.

Perhaps, Janus thought, he might actually be able to win this. The earlier battle with Auric had weakened the daemon. Janus sensed too that drawing on all that power had weakened the host body to the point where it could barely contain the power Shaha Gaathon was sending it. Briefly, he wondered where the knowledge was coming from then decided he did not care. The important thing was to win the battle, then he would have time to ponder mysteries.

'If I cannot have this vessel,' Shaha Gaathon stated in the voice of an angry god, 'no one will.'

Apparently Shaha Gaathon had come to a similar conclusion. Janus felt a change in the aura of magic swirling around him. A shield of pure dark energy sprang into being around the smouldering corpse inhabited by the daemon's essence. It resisted all of Janus's attacks, while within it, he could see an enormous firestorm of force being assembled. He knew that if he did not smash through the daemon's defences now, he would be unable to survive the counter-stroke when it came.

It seemed the daemon prince wanted him dead. Why? He appeared to think that Janus's body and soul were now beyond his reach, so he might as well destroy them. Does he really fear me so much, Janus wondered as renewed despair filled him?

Even as the thought crossed his mind, he decided that the thought was not his own, that it had been shaped somehow by some malevolent power that wished him ill. Perhaps the daemon was attacking on a subtler plane than he could understand. He cursed, knowing that he just did not know enough, that he was still an arrant amateur when it came to this sort of warfare.

You are being attacked subtly, Janus Darke, whispered a voice in his head. *Shaha Gaathon seeks to undermine your confidence, your will to win. It is will that enables you to wield these vast powers. If your confidence breaks, so will all of your defences, and you will yet know ultimate defeat and an eternity of bondage.*

Janus recognised the voice. It belonged to Auric. It seemed that somehow the eldar had survived, that his spirit had been swallowed by neither the daemon, nor the warp. Janus was not sure how the farseer had accomplished this, but he was grateful.

Even as these thoughts flowed across his conscious mind more knowledge poured in along with it. He saw that there were many and various frequencies on the psychic plane just as there were in the sensory one. Just as there were sounds too high-pitched for the human ear to hear, or colours too subtle for the human eye to perceive, so there were wavebands of psychic energy that it was all but impossible for a master to perceive and manipulate. The vast sweeping flows of destructive energy that Shaha Gaathon had used were visible even to the naked eye, but the waves of despair were subtle tendrils infiltrating Janus's psyche, almost invisible against the backwash of mightier energies. He swiftly realised that they could be nonetheless deadly for all that.

He saw also that some of the tendrils had fastened themselves leech-like to his aura and were draining off his strength and will.

Swiftly, he swept the blade around in a mad dervish dance, breaking the psychic links. The runestones swirled through the air around him avoiding the passing blade, moving into new patterns and conjunctions which he was certain, that if only he could read them, would tell him all about the flow of powers around him. He cursed. Perhaps Auric could have read them and used that information to his advantage, but he could not.

Instead, he strode forward, striking with the mighty blade at the sphere of energy that surrounded the daemon prince. The blade impacted and recoiled like a sword struck against a stone pillar. He could feel the resonance of the stroke passing up the blade. Cold fury filled him now. He wanted nothing more than to get at his foe and smite him, even if it cost him his own life. He drew back his arm for another blow.

Do this! said the voice of Auric from within his head. Instantly a complex pattern of energies was diagrammed within his mind. He saw how to tap into his own power and the power of the sword, and intermesh the forces in such a way that they became vastly amplified. Almost without thinking, he duplicated the web he had been shown. The flow of lightning enwrapping the blade increased to eye-dazzling brightness. This time when it struck, the shield of energy around the daemon prince cracked. Fault lines appeared in its surface.

Once more! Janus fed more power into the pattern and struck again, smashing the daemon prince's defensive orb into fast dissolving shards of energy. Janus saw what lay behind it. His psychically attuned senses perceived a huge snaky mass of interlocking black and red thunderbolts. Their energy was greater even than that which lay within the blade.

All at once they lashed out, a great multi-headed hydra of energy he could not hope to completely block. Once more despair filled him. This time he knew it came not from outside but from within. Despite of all his efforts, and all the efforts of Auric, he was going to be beaten. At least, he thought, with bleak satisfaction, he would have denied the use of his body and his powers to Shaha Gaathon. It was not much of a victory but it was all he was going to get.

No, human, do not give up! Not now! We are so close to victory!

What can I do, Janus fired back in response?

Give me control!

How?

Relax! Do as I show you! Do not fight it! We have but instants left to act!

Immediately knowledge of what to do flowed into his mind. He sensed the presence of Auric, closer than he had ever been before, and yet somehow infinitely distant.

And then, he knew how the farseer had survived, and the nature of the connection that had been made between them, and why he had become so sensitised to the actions of the eldar psyker on the trip to Belial. The gem on his forehead was more than a mere protective device. It was a waystone linked to the one that Auric himself had worn. He saw that in the last seconds before being consumed the eldar's spirit had flowed down the link and now dwelled within the glowing gem on his own forehead. Thinking back on what the daemon prince had said, he realised that Shaha Gaathon knew this too.

Even as the thoughts flashed across his mind, he became aware that he was willingly ceding more and more control to the eldar psyker, who was using his life force and his power, preparing to counter the daemon's stroke. As this happened, he caught glimpses of what was going on within the eldar's multi-compartmented mind. It was like running down the corridors of a vast gallery, catching sight just for a moment of innumerable painted scenes.

He saw the eldar as a child greeting a tall farseer. He caught glimpses of thousands of futures, and the way Auric had striven to see some born and some unborn. He saw the beginnings of the eldar's training and the perhaps too swift progression through ranks of warlocks to the robe of farseer. He saw battles fought on a hundred worlds against men and daemons and orks. He saw psychic powers unleashed of a magnitude he would not have guessed existed.

Each image came bathed in emotions, not the pallid emotions of mortal men, but the titanic, insanely strong feelings of the eldar, feelings that must be kept in check by rigid mental discipline and the application of pure strength of will. He caught something of Auric's towering loneliness, not just because he was an eldar but because he was a seer, and had always been one even from childhood, destined to stand apart even from those he shepherded. He saw also how early Auric had foreseen the coming of Shaha Gaathon and the path that would take him to Belial, and how he had decided to follow it to the bitter end. He saw that the other seers had opposed it, as an abomination, and why Auric had been forced to set off in secret with only the enigmatic Athenys as a companion. And at that moment, much too late and much to his own horror, he saw where the eventual end of that path led. He saw how truly honest, and how utterly dishonest, the farseer had been with him.

While you live, I live. While I live, you live. It was true, but it was true in a way that no man would ever have dreamed or wanted. He saw now the mistake he had made surrendering his will and his power to the eldar's control, and how subtly he had been led to it. In the last few heartbeats before the climactic clash with Shaha Gaathon he understood what was going to happen.

Briefly he considered fighting against it, unleashing his pent-up rage and frustration against the eldar sorcerer, but he knew that he would not do so. All that would result in would be a weakening of the farseer's psychic defences and inevitable death for them both. And most frustrating of all was the knowledge that Auric had foreseen this and was counting on it. Almost in blind mad rage, he considered doing it anyway, just to frustrate this cruel alien creature who would steal his flesh and his power. And yet he did not do so, for he knew too that the eldar would provide a haven for him against far worse things, such as the destruction of his soul.

So he did not resist as his mind and his spirit were sucked inexorably into the waystone and Auric took possession of his body. Instead he watched, knowing that some day he would get the opportunity to reverse the situation, and that he would take it.

Simultaneously, the farseer and the daemon prince unleashed their psychic bolts. Evil energies drawn from the daemon worlds clashed with the unleashed power of the deathblade. A million sub-bolts thrust and parried against each other. Like armies of warring serpents they intertwined, writhing against each other. The air stank of ozone and musk. A colossal lightning flash illuminated the Hall of Faces and suddenly silence fell.

SIMON BELISARIUS LEANED forward in the command throne. 'Damage reports!' he shouted into the comm-net.

From where he sat things looked bad, but not too bad. The fires blazing around the command deck were being put out. Tech-adepts were already moving to replace the overloaded circuits that had sparked the blaze. Things could be worse, he told himself. Things could certainly be worse.

Slowly, reports filtered in from the ship's various stations and he made a calm assessment of the damage. Number two turret was gone. The entire reserve drive section was destroyed. Over a hundred crewmen were dead. The hull had been breached in a dozen places but so far nothing appeared critical.

They had been lucky, all things considered. A competent enemy captain might have been able to outfight them: the Chaos ship had fought with ferocity but a strange lack of skill. It had allowed Simon to stay at long distance where he could pound it at his leisure, and only at the last had it managed a desperate rush to close range where its superior armament might earlier have made a difference. By then it was too late, the damage had been done.

Simon was not complaining. Now they could pick off the Chaos shuttles almost at will. He offered up a prayer of gratitude to the Emperor and then spoke once more to the tech-adepts.

'Open hailing frequencies,' he said. 'See if you can get me Commander Darke.'

AURIC MOVED SLOWLY. He felt different. This borrowed body was too clumsy, its balance was all wrong. The senses were so dull, the reflexes so slow. Worse, it was already starting to affect his thinking. He felt stupider, less sharp by far than once he had. The strange chemicals in the glands were affecting his mood.

A sluggish sense of triumph filled him. So far things had gone as he had foreseen. So far his plan was working out. He had acquired the sword, and prevented Shaha Gaathon from taking Janus Darke to be his host, hopefully for all time. All that was now left of the daemon prince's former host was a shrivelled corpse that even as he watched disintegrated into dust.

The mutants and Chaos worshippers were all dead. As a last stroke he had collapsed part of the wall on the survivors using psychokinetic force. Overhead, he knew Simon Belisarius had mounted his surprise attack on the *Pride of Sin*, the Chaos commander no match for him in spatial combat. Soon a call would come through on the comm-net and he would have to respond. It was time to head back to the surface and depart.

He saw that the surviving humans looked at him with a mixture of awe and fear. He had saved them and yet they hated him. It was only to be expected. They feared psykers like his own people feared the Nameless One, and with good reason. He did not think they would attack him. They still thought he was their leader after all, which would prove useful in the future. Even as he watched, the one called Stiel emerged from the crypt, carrying the heavy rifle with which he had sniped through the fighting. There was one to watch, Auric thought.

'Where to now?' asked Athenys. She knew what had happened, he was certain. She could tell simply by observing the way he stood. It was part of the peculiar training she had received to be able to do such things. A good question, Auric thought, knowing that things were far from over. He had won merely the first round of his battle against Shaha Gaathon. Somewhere out there the greater part of the daemon prince survived and schemed revenge. And behind him stood something worse. Before he faced that though, there were other things to do, other enemies to confront.

'Ulthwé,' he said out loud, his own croaking voice harsh in his clogged ears. 'We have unfinished business there.'

He let out a long breath and looked down at the sword in his hands. It was an obscene thing, he thought, feeling the deadly power that thrummed through it, but there was work for it yet. Before he was finished many more would feel its power.

Inside the gem on his forehead he felt the presence of Janus Darke. I am sorry for this, my friend, but the need was great, and will be greater yet. Guilt settled on him as he felt the power of the man's protests. He knew that great though it was, it was still far less than he would feel once he had finished what he set out to do.

'Come,' he said to the survivors. 'We must go to the surface. Our ship awaits us.'

Slowly the great mandala began to rise. Beneath them, Auric heard another part of the wall of faces collapse.

ZARGHAN ROSE FROM the rubble of the Hall of Faces and checked the bodies of his followers. They were all dead, which did not surprise him. Most had been killed in the battle, a few like himself had been buried when half of the carved faces had collapsed at the peak of the duel between Shaha Gaathon and the possessed human. Only Zarghan's armour had kept him alive, and he shuddered to think how long it had taken him to dig his way out from under the wreckage. Still, he was an immortal; he had all the time in the world.

Of course, he would need it. He guessed he would have a very long wait until another ship came this way, and this world was so insufferably dull. The music in his head played a despondent chorus and then fell silent.

ABOUT THE AUTHOR

William King was born in Stranraer, Scotland, in 1959. His short stories have appeared in *The Year's Best SF, Zenith, White Dwarf* and *Interzone*. He is also the author of six Gotrek & Felix novels: *Trollslayer, Skavenslayer, Daemonslayer, Dragonslayer, Beastslayer* and *Vampireslayer*, and three volumes chronicling the adventures of a Space Marine warrior, Ragnar: *Space Wolf, Ragnar's Claw* and *Grey Hunter*. He has travelled extensively throughout Europe and Asia, but he currently lives in Prague.